BURNER

BOOK ONE OF THE AFFINITY SERIES

J. S. LENORE

BURNER

April 2017

Published by Paranoid Shark Productions, LLC
Indianapolis, Indiana

This is a work of fiction. Names, characters, places, and incidents
are the product of the author's imagination or are used fictitiously.
Any resemblance to actual persons, living or dead, events, or
locales is entirely coincidental.

ISBN-13: 978-0-9987560-0-4

affinityseries.net

To my husband.

CONTENTS

CHAPTER ONE

I fall to the ground, hard. My breath frosts in the air, and the palms of my hands scrape and tear as they slide across the broken concrete of the warehouse floor. The pain fades to a dull throb, blood slowly beading against my skin. I cough out a breath and push myself up, laboring to my feet. A table on the far end of the room wobbles and starts to rise into the air.

"Look," I say, holding out a dirt-stained hand while trying to catch my breath. "You're kind of overreacting here."

The table hovers for a moment before lurching toward me. I quickly dodge to the side, the breeze whipping my blond hair into my eyes.

"I just want to talk," I say, tone calm as I try to assess the situation. Light from surrounding buildings seeps into the warehouse, slightly illuminating parts of the interior, but it's pitch black where I am standing. I can't see the table anymore but can still sense the lingering touch of the ghost who threw it.

"I know you're mad. That's understandable. No one *likes* being murdered. But you've got to calm down."

The table comes whistling out of the darkness, and I

dive to the floor, knocking the breath from my lungs. The table's trajectory changes, cutting sharply toward the ground. I roll to the side with a pained gasp, and the table shatters on the ground next to me. Splinters scatter against my back. A second later, one of the legs hits me in the head.

"Okay, fine," I shout, pushing myself up and brushing tangled strands of hair from my face. "If that's how you want to play, that's how we'll play."

I take a deep breath, ribs protesting, and close my eyes. I reach out, stretching, and the warehouse snaps into view behind my eyelids. The world is lit in blue-white light, psychic energy outlining everything in slowly moving rivers of untapped power. Hovering in the center of the warehouse, only visible in the soft blue glow of Second-Sight, is a young girl. She's just a kid, no older than seventeen, her body thin and coltish. Her hair is dark, hanging in clumps around her head, her eyes shadowed hollows in her baby-round face. Her dress is torn and bloodstained, the wet fabric clinging to her legs. Hands clenched tightly, she stares at me with open hostility. There's an energy to her here that was missing in the morgue. This is all that's left of her now, this transparent facsimile of life, filled with rage and sorrow. Her mouth opens, breath poised on her lips.

I don't want to talk. I want you to leave.

Her voice rings in my head, full of anger and pain. She takes a phantom step forward, and another piece of rubble on the floor lifts.

I get it, I Send, the words echoing within my mind. *What happened to you is awful, but I'm here to help.*

I don't need help, she spits back, fists still clenched. *I need you to go away! I need him to pay for this, for all of this!*

Her hair whips about her face, her gray eyes darkening, black seeping in like spilled ink in water. Rubble whistles through the air and crashes into the wall behind me as more starts to lift from the ground. The air fills with floating pieces of concrete, wood, and metal, all pointed in my direction. I quickly throw a shield up. It flows from my body, expanding into a shimmering hemisphere of light that encircles me. The first chunk of debris that hits it sends me stumbling back, the shield scraping against the ground as I try to absorb the impact. It holds. Barely.

Tell me who did this to you, and I can make him pay, I say.

There's a jarring crash as concrete slams into the shield. It flickers around me and falls away for a brief second before I pull it back up around myself, teeth gritted.

I don't know who he was, she says, stalking toward me. Another piece of rubble pounds against the shield, and I'm pushed back, my feet sliding on the floor.

Priya, a little help would be nice, I think, casting out to my partner. She pops into view by my side, bright blue and translucent, and quickly bolsters my power. The shield glows brighter for a moment with a quick flare of energy as Priya adds her strength to mine. Her expression is determined, her mouth pressed into a tight line as she inspects the ghost in front of us, her dark hair sleek and pulled back from her face.

Kim, I don't know that I can help here, she says, looking from the girl to the pieces of concrete that fill the air. *She doesn't seem to want outside help at the moment.*

I get that, I say harshly, gathering my power, *but I can't keep the shield up and get her to stop.*

I can maintain it but not for very long. Be quick.

I nod, pulling in the psychic energy that swirls around me until it's a writhing pool in my stomach. It fights for freedom, but I keep a tight leash on the white-hot reservoir of power, waiting.

He found me in the night, she says. *He followed me.*

More rubble starts slamming into the shield, piece after piece breaking apart on the glowing sphere around us. Priya winces.

On my go, I say, *drop it.* Priya nods, and I raise my hands.

He grabbed me from behind.

The attack is a steady torrent now, no breaks between each hit. A whirlwind starts to pick up around the girl, whipping dust and gravel into the air. Her eyes are fully black now, and whatever human reason she had left is gone, lost in a wash of anger and frustration. I ready myself, pulling more energy into my body until I can feel it racing over my skin in tiny, stinging sparks. Power races through my blood, ready.

Priya, I say, widening my stance.

He wrapped his hands around my neck until I couldn't breathe, and then he—

"Now!"

The shield drops. Wind pushes against me, and my feet start to slide on the broken ground. Pieces of gravel bite into my skin, leaving shallow cuts that bleed down my face and neck. I duck as a large block of concrete whistles by my head. With a yell, I let the coiled power in my gut spring forward.

It slams into the girl, wrapping around her like a sheet of blue-white light. Everything is cast in sudden, stark detail, the flash of light blinding in the darkness. There are bruises around her throat, and her eyes are black and bleeding. She screams silently, and I hear a window shatter somewhere in the distance. She struggles against my hold and sweat breaks out all over my skin, stinging the open cuts. I grit my teeth and press forward.

One by one, the floating debris in the warehouse starts to fall. The sound of rubble hitting the floor fills the room, echoing in a cacophony as the girl screams again. She falls to the ground, weeping, and I loosen my hold until the light disappears, leaving just a faint glow around her wrists.

I close the distance between us, hesitant. My eyes are open, but I use Second-Sight to find my way toward her. Everything is a dizzying blur of both the physical and psychic worlds for a brief moment, and I fall into the familiar half sight. In the twilight between Second-Sight and normal vision, the girl glows, her head bent so low that her hair nearly touches the floor. I kneel beside her, though she floats a few inches above the ground, and wait.

Why me? she sobs, her hands resting in her lap, the blue-white light of the binding still circling her wrists.

I don't know. But if you help me, there won't be anyone else out there asking the same question.

She raises her head, her now-gray eyes locking with mine. *You'll get him?*

I nod, and she sighs, wiping at her face.

Let me go. Her voice is quiet but steady. *I'll help you, I promise.*

I drop my hold on her and struggle for a moment to stay upright. I'm drained but not done. I raise my hand toward her, palm up. She reaches back, her own hand translucent, and touches my skin with ice-cold fingers.

The Sending is like a punch in the gut. My head is suddenly filled with sights and thoughts that aren't mine. There's a dark figure, a heavy sense of fear. I feel hands biting into my neck, skin giving way beneath my nails. I smell blood and sweat, whiskey heavy on a shuddering breath. I catch a glimpse of a face, just for a moment, and then it all sinks into blackness.

"Emma," I gasp, unable to maintain enough focus to Send it. The building flickers around me, blinking in and out of Second-Sight in a flashing haze. I dig my nails into the palms of my hands and use the pain to distract myself from the sudden urge to vomit. I struggle back into Second-Sight and the semitransparent web of psychic energy slowly materializes in a soft glow around me. The girl stares challengingly back at me.

Your name is Emma.

She nods. *Find him.*

I will, I Send. I take a quick moment to gather myself as her memories slow and settle in my mind.

Are you ready? I ask, unsteady. She nods again, and I fumble for the chalk I always keep in my pocket.

In the dark, it takes me a long time to sketch out the runes and lines that make up the circle. I'm careful to get everything just right, to make sure I don't let anything through that shouldn't cross. The marks are barely visible in Second-Sight, the chalk psychically inert, but as I finish the final sigil, the entire diagram bursts into burning, blue-white light. I can feel the energy zinging along my skin. Emma hesitates, then looks to me for some kind of comfort. I nod slightly, uncertain if it will help. It must do something because she nods back and steps into the blazing circle.

As her bare feet cross into the center of the design, her dark hair lifts around her face into a wild halo. The bruises on her neck fade, her torn dress knitting back together thread by thread. The blood burns away, leaving clean white linen. She looks at me from the center, her mouth lifted in a small, hesitant smile.

Will it hurt? she asks, her voice breaking.

I shrug. *I don't know. I don't think so.*

She falls silent, her smile dimmed.

I take a step back and pull a knife from the top of my boot. It's solid silver and sharp, and I press it into the pad of my finger. A drop of blood wells up, and I place my finger against the edge of the circle, drawing the final mark in a dark red streak. I think I hear a whispered thanks but can't tell.

There's a flash of bright light and then nothing. The chalk and blood are gone. So is Emma.

I quickly fall out of Second-Sight and collapse, shivering and trying not to puke. Priya appears next to me, a softly glowing light in the darkness. I start to feel better almost immediately as Priya bolsters my energy with her own. I smile halfheartedly, nodding my thanks.

That was a bad one, she says, looking over the ruined interior of the warehouse.

"Yeah, it was." I rub my eyes, exhausted. "I think I have enough to get him, though. She scratched him pretty good. I'll talk to the medical examiner in the morning, make sure he got good fingernail scrapings. It's gonna be hard to find him, but when we do…"

Are you going to be okay?

I pause, considering. I'm bleeding and feel bruises forming all over my body. My jeans are torn at both knees and cool air slips through tears and rents in my jacket to prickle against my heated skin. The fight and Burning have left my reserves drained. Emma's memories skate through my mind. I still feel hands around my neck that I know aren't there.

"Yeah," I say, standing up. "Yeah, I'm fine."

It's freezing outside the warehouse, and I shiver, pulling the remains of my coat tighter around my shoulders. My car—an older-model Ford Focus that's a bit worse for wear—is parked on the edge of a parking lot, nestled under one of the few unbroken streetlights. It takes a couple tries to get the engine to turn over, but once it does, I crank the heater to max. I warm my hands and shrug out of my ruined coat before tossing it into the back seat. There's an old sweatshirt crumpled in the passenger seat that I shrug on. It's a little threadbare, but it keeps out the chill the heater hasn't reached. I buckle in and back out of the parking lot. Cutting up Wabash, I head toward Fifty-Seventh Street and duck onto the northbound Dan Ryan.

It's late, well past midnight, and except for a few late-night truckers who speed past me, the expressway is empty. I'm exhausted, and as I drive, the flashing of the streetlights starts to lull me into a half doze. The quiet roar of the city, the sound of car horns echoing around the high-rises, the blur of stoplights and flashing police cars— it all passes around me, muffled and distant.

I'm shaken out of my stupor by the rattle of the "L" passing over my car as I idle at a red light. I'm nearly a block away from my apartment, and when I check the clock, a half hour has passed since I left the crime scene. I shake my head sharply, trying to wake myself up, uncertain how the time has passed so quickly. It's just enough to keep me focused as I turn down my street toward my apartment, which stands on the corner. I pull into the small lot around back, park, and stumble my way inside.

The building is old, the brick and mortar stained dark by the years, but it's sturdy and welcoming in the dead of night. Light fills the lobby and I'm hit by a wall of dry heat that washes over me in a familiar rush. I sigh and feel my shoulders loosen, tension easing from me as I head farther inside. The elevator, a stately old thing that's almost always broken, has a huge CAUTION sign hanging from the front. I barely even bother looking at it before hitting the stairs. By the time I reach the fifth floor, my legs are shaking.

I open my door, step into the dark foyer of the apartment, and close it, leaning my weight against the solid oak. I drop my keys on top of the small table by the door and bend down and slide my knife from my boot, setting it next to my keys. My Glock 22 takes up the rest of the space on the table. I untie my boots and leave them strewn on the front rug. Pushing myself upright, I make my way to the couch on the other side of the room and flop down face-first. The sound of Priya locking the door makes a twinge of guilt twist in my gut. It takes a lot of energy for her to manipulate objects, especially metal. After her help tonight, she must be as drained as I am. I feel her settle like a soft breeze on the ground near me.

"Thanks again for tonight," I say, pulling my face from where it's pressed into the cushion. "I promise we won't be doing that again for a while."

You know I understand the challenges of this life, Priya says, annoyed and tender. *Or have you forgotten what I did before I died?*

I shake my head and close my eyes, sliding into Second-Sight without thought. She's sitting on the ground next to the couch, arms slung over her knees. She's wearing a long tunic with delicate flowers embroidered on the hem and cuffs. Her pants, which look like they're linen, are loose around her legs, her feet bare. Her hair is long, like it was before she died, and a rich blue black. It hangs around her face in shifting waves. I'd found pictures of her after we Bonded, and she'd had green eyes before she died. After, though, her eyes had turned a pale gray like every ghost's, her form shedding color and fading into a blue-tinted grayscale. Her skin is still dark, though, hinting at her Indian ancestry. Sometimes, when it's cold and snowing and the trees are covered in small, white lights, there's a faint tracery of henna on her hands. She doesn't talk about it, and I don't ask.

She'd been a Healer, a Medium with the ability to bind bone and flesh rather than spirits. Priya had been good, too. One of the best in the city, working at different hospitals, moving wherever need had taken her, saving countless lives.

We don't talk about it, her life before. Priya's been dead for almost fifty years now. She'd been on the edge of Turning, of losing her final grasp on humanity and reason, when I'd found her haunting the burned ruins of a house west of the city. I'd heard reports of a ghost who was at turns kind and loving, then dangerous and threatening. I caught her during a brief lucid period, and she'd agreed to Bond with me. It had strengthened my powers, made me a full Medium, and stopped her from losing her sense of reality and falling into madness.

I groan and push myself off the couch, not bothering to turn on the lights, and use the dim glow coming from Second-Sight to get around. Long familiarity with the apartment and sheer stubbornness get me to the bathroom tucked in the back.

There's no window in the bathroom, so I'm forced to flick on the lights. I flinch at the sudden brightness and turn on the shower, letting it run while I wait for the water to heat up. My battered face stares back at me from the mirror above the sink. There are cuts and scrapes across my high cheeks and forehead. An already darkening smudge near my temple will probably blossom into an enormous bruise. The dark circles under my eyes make them a violent, shocking blue. There's a mix of dust, dirt, and dead leaves tangled in my short, golden blond hair. It hangs limply around my face, the messy bob more of a tangle than a hairstyle after the rough night. I stare at myself for a long moment with a puzzling mix of confusion and humor, wondering how, after doing this for over a decade, I'd still ended up battered and bruised from what was supposed to be a simple Burning. Steam slowly clouds the mirror, and I look away with a faint smile and a shake of my head.

I run my fingers through my hair, tossing leaves onto the floor. Once my hair is free of debris, I undress, my jeans and stained long-sleeved shirt sticking to my skin, and climb into the shower. The water stings, just a little too hot. I scrub at the dried blood and dirt on my body and wince through it. My head pounds, and there's a pressure around my throat I can't shake, like fingers pressing too hard. The humor I'd felt earlier washes away as the heavy weight of exhaustion settles over me. I turn off the shower, then clumsily step out. The tile is cold against my feet, and I shiver and reach for a towel.

I barely dry off before making my way to bed, falling onto the mattress, asleep before I even think to crawl under the covers.

I'm in a hallway filled with lockers, some standing open, some shut. A few are missing, the wall stained red where the metal edges have rusted against the drywall. It's nearly pitch black in the corridor, but there's just enough light for me to see a hunched shape at the end of the hallway.

"Hello?" I shout.

The word echoes down the hall. One of the lockers creaks, its door swinging wide, before it falls. It hits the floor, and with a twisted shriek, the locker crashes through the floor and into the story below. My breath hangs in the air in a damp cloud. I shiver and start walking, placing my feet carefully and tensing as the floor groans beneath me. The lockers continue, a jagged line that leads deeper and deeper into the darkness. I don't notice time passing, but my legs start to ache, and the hallway keeps growing longer and longer. The shape doesn't move, and I wonder if there's someone there after all.

"Hello? Are you okay? Do you need help?" I yell again.

As I get closer, the shape shifts and roils like smoke, becoming more distinct as I move closer. It looks like a person, a torso with hunched shoulders and a bent head, legs covered. It's sitting on something, though I can't tell what. The head lifts slowly and turns toward me. Its face is creased with age, its skin cracked like worn leather and so dark, it's almost blue. It's an old man. He has a thick white beard that falls down his chest, and what little hair remains on his head is white, tightly curled, and matted. His clothes are blackened and torn, his feet bare. As he shifts, I hear something clatter against the floor. I take another hesitant step forward, and with a quick jerk that leaves the bottom of my stomach somewhere far behind me, I'm only feet away from him. He looks up at me with light gray eyes and an unreadable expression.

"Can you help me?" he asks, his voice soft but strong. The corners of his mouth twist up into a grimace. "Please?"

I nod and walk closer. "Of course, let's get you out of here."

He's sitting in an old, rusted wheelchair that doesn't look like it could hold much of anything, far less a person. There are broken spokes on the wheels, the tires dry and crumbling. The handles twist loose in my grip as I try to move the chair. With a screech, we lurch forward. I lean in with most of my weight to keep moving. A clammy sweat breaks out over my skin, and my hands slide free of the handles again. I tumble to the floor, knees biting into the broken linoleum in sharp bursts of pain. The old man sighs, hands clenching the armrests.

"Faster," he says, voice cracking. "There's no time."

From the ground, I see chains wrapped around the back of the chair. Unlike everything else here, they're shiny and new. The metal is smooth and ice cold beneath my fingers. There's frost clinging to my skin as I pull my hand back. I stand and grab the handles again and push. The chair refuses to move, groaning and screeching like a wounded animal in the empty hall. The overhead lights flicker as I try to move forward, casting the ground in wavering shadows that seem to lunge toward me. Something grabs onto the cuff of my jeans and starts pulling me back. I shake my leg free, but when I turn to look, there's nothing there. I feel another hand dig into my calf. Denim tears and warm blood trickles down my leg.

"Push!" he shouts, and I give one more shove and fall, my feet sliding out from under me. The ground is hard and unforgiving against my knees. Something cuts deep into my hand as I push myself upright, the stinging pain sharp and sudden.

The shadows writhing around us grow, lifting from the ground in distorted shapes with softly glowing eyes. In the depths of their bodies, I see runes and sigils twisting in unreadable circles. Their hands grab at me, pulling my hair and clothes. A sharp pain shoots from the top of my head, and when I turn, one of the figures is holding a clump of familiar blond hair in its malformed fist. I crawl backward, falling against the wheelchair. The chains bite into the back of my neck, so cold that I can feel my skin freeze. I scramble toward the center of the hallway, trying to get away from the dark, shifting creatures.

The man in the chair screams, the sound louder than what should come from such a frail and broken body. It bounces around the hallway, lockers falling and adding to the din. The shadows begin to keen, a high-pitched, nearly melodic tone that only adds to the growing roar. I clamp my hands over my ears, and I feel something wet and warm pool against my palms.

The man starts to swell, his body expanding in unsettling rises and falls. I scramble back from him and struggle to my feet as I shove away the shadows. They coalesce around him, containing him, pressing in until I can't see anything through their opaque bodies. Slowly, broken bits of light tear through the darkness. There's a flash so bright it burns my eyes, and the shadows are pushed back, howling. In the chair, the man's body is shining and changing. The shrunken muscles on his body are filling, bulging with sudden strength. His hair turns black, the beard shrinking down to stubble. The chains wrapped around the chair cut into his chest and arms, and he starts to bleed. His mouth is too wide and still snarling, his eyes glowing. The creatures surround him—their bodies shift dizzyingly in the light.

I take a step back and start running. The floor gives way beneath my feet, tumbling into nothingness with my every step. I can hear him laughing, can hear tearing flesh and roaring darkness. The sound ricochets down the hallway until it drowns out the racing pulse in my ears. Light starts to pour out from behind me, casting the walls in spotlights. There are runes scribbled on the broken drywall, and as the light hits them, they start to pulse a deep, burning red. I put my hands over my ears again, close my eyes, and scream, trying to somehow drown out the noise.

I wake up sweating, a scream lodged in my throat. Priya is Sending at me to wake up, to say something. She's upset, and knickknacks are floating around the room. I try to calm both her and my racing heart at the same time.

"It's all right, it's okay," I pant. "I had a nightmare, that's all. Calm down, it's going to be okay." I brush at tears clinging to my cheeks, my hands shaking.

That wasn't a normal nightmare, Priya shouts. I hear something break in the living room. *Something was wrong, I could feel it.*

I lean forward, pressing my forehead against my knees as she whirls around me. Something about her behavior brings me back to that hallway, and I start to shiver.

"It was a *dream*, Priya. Just… put everything back and calm down. I'm fine."

She slows, stops. The few items still floating around the room settle onto my dresser and nightstand. She wraps herself around me, warm and familiar. There are comforting hands in my hair, gentle whispers as I shake. It takes a few minutes, the bedroom quiet except for my panicked breathing and Priya's soft words of comfort in my mind. My legs tremble when I finally stand and head toward the bathroom. The lights come on, harsh but welcome.

The blood running from my ear, down my neck, and staining my hands is so bright, it nearly glows.

CHAPTER TWO

I 'm still shaken in the morning. As I pick up the items littering the floor and avoid Priya's questioning gaze, I struggle to remember the dream. The harder I try, the less clear it becomes, and my head starts to throb. Through it all, I remember a shadowed figure and unfamiliar runes and screaming… There's a sharp twinge in the front of my skull, and I wince, the few wisps of the dream disappearing in a blazing wash of pain. The Burning must have taken more out of me than I'd thought, and I wonder if I still have any Excedrin.

I find the empty bottle in the bathroom cabinet and toss it into the trash with an angry groan. Getting dressed takes longer than usual, my body aching and tired from the night before. The jeans and old white T-shirt I throw on are comfortable and familiar, worn soft from time. My back protests when I shrug into my shoulder holster. As I tame my hair with my fingers, I wince slightly. Part of my scalp is tender—just another injury from the night before to add to the tally. The ache fades as I walk through the hallway into the living room. Scattered papers and empty takeout containers litter the floor, and pictures hang at drunken angles on the walls. I start picking up the worst of the mess and slide into Second-Sight out of habit, letting it merge with my normal vision, casting the world in a blue-white overlay.

Priya waits in the living room for me. She drifts toward the front door and waits. Ducking into the kitchen, I stuff the trash in my hands into the slightly overfilled garbage can and head to the door. I slide on an old black leather jacket and grab my gun, knife, and keys from the side table. When I unlock the deadbolt, Priya flips it back.

C'mon, I say, looking at her with a raised eyebrow. *We have to go.*

Not until we talk about last night, she Sends, floating between the door and me. *You should be resting, not going out.*

You know I need to talk to the medical examiner about Emma.

So call him. Abramo knows how to answer a phone, and if he doesn't, the receptionist does. You can leave a message.

I shake my head. *No, I need to go in person. I can't let her down, Priya. I promised.*

Priya frowns. *You need to take care of yourself,* she says, reproving. *You push yourself too hard, Kim.*

I know, I say with a sigh. *I'll rest tonight, I promise.*

I can feel Priya's heavy judgment, but when I unlock the door, it clicks open and stays that way. I give her a quick smile and head out, locking the door behind me.

She doesn't talk to me the rest of the ride to the morgue. My hands clench the steering wheel, and I find myself glancing at her every few moments. Her back is turned, and when she notices me looking, she drifts out of Second-Sight, choosing to manifest a form no longer. I sigh, shoulders hunched, and drive a little faster. When we finally arrive, there's a slight tug in the center of my chest as Priya stretches our Bond. It's just another ache to add to the pains from the night before, but I find myself frowning, reaching for her.

It's okay, she Sends. *I just can't be in the morgue right now.*

I nod, uncertain. *Okay. I won't be long.*

I take a deep breath and brace myself, pouring some power down the bond to strengthen it, before walking into the medical examiner's office. There are some people milling around—clerks, a pathologist I vaguely recognize, the admin assistant—but the hallways are overflowing with the dead. The ghosts move around quietly. They look like the living. Just people sitting in chairs or wandering the halls, waiting for something. If they weren't tinged blue from Second-Sight, their eyes all the same shade of light gray, it'd be hard to notice any difference. Looking closer, though, you can tell. Their clothes and hands are stained. Hidden under their shirts and dirty hair are gaping wounds that never stop bleeding, organs spilling out from burst skin and muscle. But they walk around like normal, like nothing's wrong. They try to talk. They reach for people when they need comfort. If you have the aptitude and the urge, you can have entire conversations with them about the weather or how the Cubs are doing or who they're going to vote for in the next election. After a while, though, the ghosts start to notice that something isn't quite right. They can't touch things, can't always communicate. That's when they start to Turn, start lashing out at the people around them. They become filled with rage and grief, and they take it out by breaking windows or trashing rooms. Over time, they escalate, moving onto assault, arson, murder.

The ghosts here never hang around long, though. They're confronted with death every day, and most come to terms with it after a couple of months. The few who hang on, who refuse to leave, are taken care of by Mediums who make their way through the morgue. Still, being surrounded by the graphic reminder of so many deaths is hard for me to handle, even on a good day.

After the night I had, this is not a good day.

I head to the glass-enclosed reception area and give my name to the woman behind the counter. She dials the phone with her pen and idly taps her desk as the phone rings. There's a brief exchange and some nodding and affirmative sounds on her end before she hangs up.

"The medical examiner will be ready to see you in a few minutes. He's finishing up an autopsy. Just make yourself comfortable. There's coffee and this morning's *Tribune*."

I thank her and sit in the hard plastic chairs lining the edges of the room. I let my eyes close, leaning my head against the wall. I tried going back to sleep last night but ended up tossing and turning until morning. Priya refused to settle, hovering over the bed. Normally, that would've helped, but it felt uncomfortable and too close. I gave up on sleep around four. Hours later, I fight against the urge to doze, then sit forward with a quiet groan when I hear footsteps coming toward me.

"Detective Phillips, how can I help you today?"

Dr. Frank Abramo is standing in the center of the waiting room, wiping his hands on a paper towel. He's not a large man, but his short stature and square frame make him feel like one. A dusting of gray hair peppers his temples and the short beard he grows every winter. His thin-framed metal glasses slide down his nose, and he pushes them back up after throwing away the paper towel.

"Dr. Abramo," I say, standing. "It's good to see you. I'm here to talk about a Jane Doe who was brought in a couple of days ago. She was found in a warehouse, young, dark hair? COD would've been strangulation."

He nods, looking slightly puzzled. "I know the case, yes. I thought Cross was lead?"

"Yeah, he picked it up. But I'd been hearing things about the crime scene. Rubble flying around, people getting attacked, a persistent sense of cold and unease…"

"I think it's safe to assume you went looking for her, then?"

"Yeah, last night. Her name's Emma Murphy." I pause for a second, concentrating. "Date of birth is June 18, 2000."

Pain lances through my head, an electric discomfort that's a clear sign my power reserves are still far from full. Recalling the Sending is a struggle, and the harder I try, the worse the pain gets. I shake my head slightly, trying to stop the slow, aching beat that grows in strength behind my temple.

"Sorry, she didn't focus on her personal details when she Sent me her death." I sigh and shake my head again. "I know you'd have checked her nails for scrapings already, but she's definitely going to have skin and blood from her attacker. You might be able to get fingerprints off her neck, too, if you haven't already. The guy grabbed her pretty hard." I reach up and run a hand over the unblemished skin around my throat and shiver.

"Sorry, she didn't focus on her personal details when she Sent me her death." I sigh and shake my head again. "I know you'd have checked her nails for scrapings already, but she's definitely going to have skin and blood from her attacker. You might be able to get fingerprints off her neck, too, if you haven't already. The guy grabbed her pretty hard."

I reach up and run a hand over the unblemished skin around my throat and shiver.

"We got usable samples, yes, and a thumbprint. We weren't planning on it, but we can run those through CODIS and IAFIS, see what comes up if your gut's telling you he's already in the system?"

I nod. "Yeah, I'm sure."

"You know how cases like this can go, though," Abramo says, looking over the top of his glasses that have already slipped back down his nose. "If you don't have a suspect, there's not much we're going to be able to do over here."

"I'll try not to get my hopes up," I say.

Abramo nods and pushes his glasses back in place. "Have you talked to Cross yet? He's going to need to question you if you took the time to Burn her."

"I'm headed to district HQ right after this to get it squared away. You'll let me know if anything else turns up?"

"Absolutely," he says. "Keep yourself out of trouble, okay?"

"I'll do my best." Smiling softly at the familiar reminder, I turn and make my way to the car. Priya waits inside, arms crossed.

Look, I get you're pissed. But we've got to go talk to Cross before we can go home.

She doesn't say anything, but her unhappiness comes down our Bond loud and clear. I sigh, shift into reverse, and drive toward headquarters.

Detective Riley Cross has been a detective in the CPD homicide unit for the last five years. He's by-the-book, detail oriented, persistent. It makes him a great detective, but it also makes working with him a chore. A few years ago, he and I were assigned to a task force to cut down on gun violence in our district. For me, it had been a simple matter of getting guns off the street. Bag 'em and tag 'em, move on to the next report. But Cross? He spent hours tracking down manufacturers, gun dealers, gang leaders. He reconstructed filed-down serial numbers to find original owners. That whole three months, I don't know that I ever saw him well rested. On his own, he charged more people than the rest of the task force combined. He was tenacious and unyielding. He did great police work, but it put the rest of the team to shame. He got away with it, though, with quick, easy smiles and a charm that has always rubbed me the wrong way.

I can't say I'm looking forward to the upcoming confrontation. Detective Riley Cross has been a detective in the CPD homicide unit for the last five years. He's by-the-book, detail oriented, persistent. It makes him a great detective, but it also makes working with him a chore. A few years ago, he and I were assigned to a task force to cut down on gun violence in our district. For me, it had been a simple matter of getting guns off the street. Bag 'em and tag 'em, move on to the next report. But Cross? He spent hours tracking down manufacturers, gun dealers, gang leaders. He reconstructed filed-down serial numbers to find original owners. The whole three months, I don't know that I ever saw him well rested. On his own, he charged more people than the rest of the task force combined. He was tenacious and unyielding. He did great police work, but it put the rest of the team to shame. He got away with it, though, with quick, easy smiles and a charm that has always rubbed me the wrong way.

The district HQ parking lot, usually packed during the week due to limited spots on the street, is empty this morning. Sundays tend to be slow. There are only a few officers inside, and I—unsurprisingly—see Cross as soon as I walk in, all loose-limbed confidence. His dark hair is slightly rumpled, but it somehow manages to still look professional. He's chatting with another detective, half-sitting on a desk while he flips through a case file. His shirtsleeves are rolled up to his elbows, and his tie is loose, collar hanging open to show a glimpse of smooth muscle and the hard jut of his collarbone.

Kim, Priya says, voice teasing, *you're staring.*

Shut up, I Send back, walking toward Cross. He looks up as I draw closer and smiles. My cheeks warm, and Priya shoots me a smug grin.

"Phillips," he says, getting off his desk and standing to meet me. "I thought you had the weekend off?"

"I do." I grab a chair near his desk and swing it around to sit, my legs spread around the backrest, arms resting on top. "But I Burnt someone last night and you've got the case."

"The Jane Doe I got Wednesday?"

"Yeah," I say. "You got a minute?"

"For another cop investigating *my* case?" He pulls out a chair and sits down, frowning. "Yeah, I've got a couple."

His desk is pristine, everything lined up on ninety-degree angles. He opens the bottom drawer and slides his folder into its exact, alphabetized slot. His long fingers flip through the rest with familiar ease, and he pulls out another folder.

"I don't appreciate you stepping on my toes." His tone is slightly reproving as he opens the folder and leans back in his chair with a sigh. "But I could use the help."

His mouth quirks into a half smile that's somehow both charming and frustrating, and he slides the folder to me across the clean surface of his desk. "Not a whole lot to go on here. Jane Doe, discovered on the south side in an abandoned warehouse, strangled, signs of sexual trauma. No identifying marks or ID on the body. No cell phone, either, but that could've been stolen. A prospective buyer for the property found her a day or so after she was killed. The owner says he hasn't been there in at least six months, but it looks like we have regular foot traffic in the building."

I pick up the folder and flip through crime scene

photos. Emma's body is facedown, her hair spread about her head in a tangled mess, her dress bunched up high around her waist. I shake my head, unable to reconcile the angry, powerful spirit with the broken, lifeless corpse in the photos.

"CSI found signs of some squatters," Cross continues, his green eyes watching me closely as I continue to look through the case file. "Probably homeless looking for shelter now that it's getting colder. There were also a couple sets of tire tracks that looked recent, but the techs couldn't get any good impressions. Other than that, and the physical evidence on the body, that's pretty much all we've got." He raises his eyebrows, looking down his nose. "So what have the spirits revealed to you about my case?"

I can feel my headache coming back.

"Her name's Emma Murphy," I start, passing the folder back to him. "She didn't know the guy who attacked her and, unfortunately, didn't get a good look at him. But he was bigger than her, had dark hair. He smelled dirty, a bit like booze. He could be one of the squatters you mentioned. I wouldn't be surprised if he has a prior criminal record or other victims we haven't found yet." I pause and rub my neck. "I think he'll attack someone again. There was something... off about him in the Sending."

"You have anything to corroborate this with?" Cross asks, leaning back in his chair and kicking his feet up on his desk.

"Identity, sure. You can check for her dental records. I've got a DOB that I already passed on to Abramo earlier today. If I try, I might be able to get an address or her parents' names. She didn't give me a lot of the basic details, just what she saw before she died."

"Well," Cross says slowly, "that's something to start with, at least. I'll need to get that all written down, add it to the file. And we'll need to go back to the scene to do a walk-through, see if it meshes with what our techs found."

"I don't know if that's going to help much." I fold my hands together to stop from fidgeting. "She wasn't happy to see me the other night, and, well... Let's just say, a walk-through is probably a waste of time."

Cross frowns and takes his feet off the desk. "Are you saying you tampered with a crime scene?"

"Of course not, no," I reply carefully, brushing a loose strand of hair behind my ear. "There were forces beyond my control that caused significant physical damage to the scene, but I was in no way responsible for what transpired."

Cross groans and opens his desk. He pulls out a couple sheets of paper.

"Fill these out while I get a room ready for your statement. You'll have to explain what happened at the scene in detail, and we're *definitely* going to need to do another walk-through."

I nod and take the unfortunately familiar forms from him, pulling a pen from my jacket pocket. It's basic stuff: who I am, what I was doing, my affiliations. I fill in the details, jotting down my badge number and my Medium credential, a unique ten-digit identifier assigned by the federal government. Trying to explain what happened takes a bit longer. I write out the basics of what Emma—I pause, then shake my head—*Murphy* Sent me, focusing on as many specifics as I can. Sometimes it helps to replay the Sending, but hers is so disjointed, it's hard to sort through what's admissible and what isn't. The laws surrounding spiritual testimony are stringent, and nothing's allowed in front of a jury without physical evidence to back it up. Right now, the only things I have to work with are her fingernail scrapings and the vague images of her attacker's body.

I hear Cross call my name from across the room. He's in one of the interview rooms, lounging against the doorframe. He's rolled his sleeves back down and straightened his tie. Frowning, he looks off toward the front of headquarters, his mouth a tight line. Something about his distracted expression draws me in. I wonder what it would be like to smooth the wrinkles around his eyes away... whether the skin of his jaw would be warm beneath my hand.

You're staring again. Priya's voice is loud and sudden, and it brings me back to reality in a jarring rush.

I grab the forms, unsettled and embarrassed, and head over to where Cross is waiting.

"Let's get this over with," I say, squeezing past him into the room. "I've got things to do."

He's staring, too.

Priya, you're not helping.

I hear her cackle again as the door shuts. A steel table and large two-way mirror that takes up the back wall dominate the otherwise barren room. Cross is already sliding into a chair, dropping a pad of paper and a tape recorder onto the table. I sit, wincing as my chair screeches against the concrete floor.

We spend the next hour rehashing what Murphy had Sent me. Cross is meticulous, making me go over the events again and again. It wears on me, especially after everything that happened last night. I'm exhausted, and I don't like being on this side of the table. Answering questions always puts me on the defensive, reminds me too much of when I was growing up and trying—and failing—to stay out of trouble.

My headache comes roaring back about thirty minutes in. It builds the longer we go, the energy it takes to revisit Emma's Sending draining me faster than usual. I fight against the feeling of phantom fingers on my neck, to not gag on rancid breath long since exhaled. Priya comes in halfway to boost my energy, but I can feel her fading, too.

Cross looks like he's going to ask another question, and I raise my hand, stopping him. I rub my eyes, wincing.

"I need a break," I say, trying to think past the pounding in my head. "Can you give me five?"

"We've got to get this right," he says, stopping the recorder. "There're some holes in your story that need patching up."

"I get that. I just need some air."

I push back from the table and stand. My vision goes dark around the edges, and I fumble for something to hold onto. I fall back into the chair, and Cross is by my side in seconds. I brush him off, leaning into the table.

"Hey, you all right? C'mon, breathe for me," he says,

pushing my head down between my knees. Blood pounds in my ears, drowning out his words.

"I'm fine, I'm fine. Five minutes, and I'll be good to go," I murmur, unsure if it's more for his benefit or mine. After I take a deep breath, the room steadies. I stand, hand pressed hard against the table.

Kim, are you okay? Priya hovers close by. I can feel her brushing against me, a wind against my overheated skin. *I told you, you need to rest.*

I nod and blink my eyes open. There's a little gray still clinging to the edges, but my vision slowly clears.

"When'd you eat last?" Cross asks, moving closer. I take a step back and feel better when I don't stumble.

"Breakfast, and I'm *fine*. I've got it, give me a minute. I just need to get outside."

My skin feels too tight as he casts me a look of complete disbelief, and I make my way to the door. The walk through the main room of headquarters feels like miles instead of the few hundred feet it is. As I get closer to the front door, the gray starts creeping back into my vision. There's a ringing in my ears that's getting louder and louder, and my pulse races. Cross comes barreling out of the interrogation room after me, and heads start turning. I make it outside and lean my head against my car, trying to stay conscious and not vomit.

"Phillips! Wait up!"

It's November in Chicago, and the metal of the car frame is cold and soothing against my forehead. I shut my eyes and breathe slowly and evenly until I can focus enough to slide fully into Second-Sight. Priya runs her hand over my back, and her power seeps in through my skin. My nausea disappears, and the world stops spinning. Thank God for having a former Healer as a partner.

"Detective, what's going on?" Cross asks, standing next to my front bumper. He frowns and shifts his weight from foot to foot. He looks both concerned and pissed, and I don't quite know what to do about it.

What do I tell him? I ask Priya.

The truth, probably. She keeps rubbing my back. I take another deep breath and lift my head from the car.

"Just a rough Burn and not enough sleep," I say. "I'll be fine once I get some rest."

"Look, if you can't handle this, I can call someone else in." He takes a step toward me, stops, then stuffs his hands in his pockets and looks away.

"I'm not incompetent or emotional, just tired." I glare at him, standing straight and fighting back another quick wave of dizziness that overtakes me.

Maybe he has a point, Kim. This isn't normal, Priya says. I move away from her, and Cross follows my movement with skepticism.

"Maybe you shouldn't have come in on your day off," he counters, taking another step forward.

"I owe it to the victim to see this through. I'm not going to sit at home with my feet up and let some child's murder go unsolved." I fumble for my keys, pull them out of my pocket, and jam them in the lock. "We can finish up the interview later, right? I'll go home, drink some tea, *rest*," I bite the word out, "and I'll be back to normal in no time. I'm not dropping this."

"All right," Cross says, still frowning. "Just make sure you get your head in the right place first."

"I'll call you later," I say as I open the car door. He stays outside, watching until I pull out of the parking lot and he quickly disappears from view.

I don't want to admit it, but they're both right. Even with the heat on full blast, I can't get warm, and my headache keeps getting worse. Something is wrong, but I don't know what.

The drive home is quick, everything rushing past in a blur. I stumble into my apartment, exhausted and still shaky. Groaning, I lie down on the couch. I keep an old quilt my grandma made draped across the back and pull it down, wrapping myself up in the musty, familiar fabric.

I roll onto my back and close my eyes… count my breaths, focusing on the slow motion of air against my lips; it flows past my throat and into my lungs and I exhale through my nose. Slowly, I start to drift. The world around me shifts, and with a long sigh, I'm floating outside of my body.

Astral projection is difficult, requiring a careful balance between meditative state and active awareness. From there, depending on what you want to do, that difficulty increases. Seeing yourself using Second-Sight is near the top of the list. There's something about walking the line between living and dead that makes everything unclear. It leaves you vulnerable and weak, open to attacks both physical and psychic. Trying for it now, when my reserves are as low as they are, is a risk.

Are you sure this is safe? Priya asks, joining me.

I need to see what's going on, I say.

I turn to look at myself. No one ever looks exactly like their normal selves in Second-Sight. It's always the potential of the person rather than what's contained in their physical body. In the real world, I'm tall and lean with short, golden blond hair that brushes the bottom of my chin. I have high cheekbones, a wide mouth, and an impish nose that has always seemed out of place.

In Second-Sight, I look more rugged, more chipped at the edges. My skin is tougher, my hands more calloused and rough. It's a truer reflection of what I've done and seen as a Medium and as a cop. There are scars that don't show on my skin, some that I take pride in and others I don't know how I survived. Now, there are bruises around my neck in the shape of fingers. There's also a coating of darkness circling in slow, undulating waves around my entire body, coalescing around my neck and chest. I watch my body as it breathes in, and the darkness tightens, closing around my throat. I feel an echoing tightness that only loosens when my body slowly exhales.

That's not good, I say, floating down to brush my fingers against the writhing mass. It snaps back at me, trying to flow up my hand. I pull away quickly and frown.

Any ideas? I ask Priya. Her fingers pass through the darkness like fog. It clings for a second to her but sluggishly returns to swirl around my neck.

It's keyed to you, she says.

I concentrate, pulling my power around me. My other self starts to glow, the light that forms my psychic body brightening until it's almost too much to look at. I hold my hands in front of me and start sketching runes. My fingers leave traces of light in the air, the symbols falling slowly to land on the now-writhing blackness. I feel the smoke fighting and I push harder. I watch as it slows… and then stops. It solidifies into a dark crystal, and I suddenly can't breathe. My vision starts to dim, and there's a sharp tug as the connection between my body and my astral self tightens. I sketch one final sigil, a symbol that ties the power together and directs it, and the crystal shatters, exploding outward. I throw my arm up to protect my eyes, but the shards pass through me harmlessly.

I fall back into my body, my energy depleted. I open my eyes and groan as pain races from the base of my skull to overwhelm my head, centered directly over my right eyebrow, sharp and stinging and deep. I roll over and press my face into the cushions of the couch, blocking out as much light as I can.

Is there anything I can do to help? Priya asks, hovering nearby.

Just don't let me sleep too long, I say.

Priya nods, then shifts so she's sitting next to me. She's cool against my skin, and I feel her using her power to ease the ache behind my eyes. I try to tell her to save her strength, but she must be doing more than just Healing because I fall asleep with the words on my lips.

I don't dream, not in any concrete sense. Instead, I'm dogged by a sense of darkness, of something clawing into my soul and sapping my strength. I feel lingering hands around my throat. I hear a young girl's screams and a man's laughter.

I see nothing.

CHAPTER THREE

I wake up an hour later, still a little groggy and unnerved. The headache is better but still hovers behind my right eye, waiting. I grab a quick bite to eat and pop an Excedrin before heading back out. By the time I climb into my car, I start to perk up, the cool air refreshing against my skin. As I back out of my spot, my phone pressed between my shoulder and my ear, I wait for the call to connect.

"Detective Cross. How can I help you?"

"Hey, it's Phillips," I say, pulling out from the parking lot and onto the street. "Do you want to try to do the walk-through today?"

"You're feeling better?" He sounds disbelieving.

I want to sigh, but fight the urge. "More or less, but I'm good to go. Just needed to grab a quick nap. I'll meet you out there?"

I hear Cross typing for a moment, then silence. "Yeah, give me twenty minutes."

It ends up being more like thirty-five, and I try to not let my impatience show when he finally arrives. He steps out of his car, locks it, and walks toward me. I'm leaning against my car, hands in my pockets, and I raise an eyebrow as he draws closer. He quickly runs a hand through his hair and nods.

"Sorry, I got hung up at HQ."

"It's all right." I shrug. "C'mon."

We head toward the warehouse, which looks the worse for wear in the harsh light of midafternoon. Sunlight filters in through the holes in the ceiling and walls. It's brighter than last night, but there are still patches of persistent darkness clinging to the corners. The pile of debris in the corner is likely what Murphy hurled at Priya and me last night. There's a smooth area where my circle was, but otherwise, gravel and debris litter the concrete floor. If any signs of Murphy's murder remain, they're buried now.

"Well, this is great," Cross says, exhaling. "I'm pretty sure that chunk over there was part of that wall when we came through earlier." He points to a large piece of concrete resting against the far wall. On the opposite side of the building, there's a conspicuous section of wall missing, rebar poking out at odd angles. He stares at it for a long moment, then shakes his head.

"Want to walk me through what happened?" Cross

asks, pulling a pen and a small notebook from his jacket pocket. He flips the notebook open and looks at me, eyebrow raised.

"It was straightforward, really." I kick a loose rock, sending it skittering across the floor. He glares at me.

"I heard through the grapevine that there was some new activity here, and I knew about the murder, so I came by to investigate. And before you get your panties in a bunch," I say as he starts to open his mouth, "I cleared it with the Lieutenant before I came out."

I walk to the center of the warehouse, my footsteps echoing through the empty space. I close my eyes and try to remember what, exactly, happened last night.

"We came in through that door." I walk toward the entrance and turn to face the main space. "Didn't see anything that interesting. Priya and I cast around for the ghost, didn't get any response. I almost left before she let us know she was here." I let my feet and memory guide me, pausing. "It wasn't until I got right around here that she started to act up."

I bend down and brush some of the gravel away. There's a thin line of white that comes away with my fingers. I sweep more of the dust and grime out of the way, slowly revealing some hastily scribbled runes and sigils. They're imprecise, clearly drawn by an inexperienced hand, but I recognize them immediately.

"I'll be damned," I whisper. "She was a Medium."

"What? Why do you say that?" Cross comes walking over, hunching down next to me. I keep brushing away the gravel and dirt, trying to keep the chalk line intact. He joins me, and in a few moments, we've cleared away enough of the scattered gravel to see the whole thing.

"This is a circle, the kind Mediums use when we're working with a spirit. You see this right here?" I say, gesturing at the symbol in the center of the design. "That's for improving communication. And that right there"—I point again— "is a protective sigil. It helps keep anything nasty from coming through. But this is all wrong."

"What do you mean?" he asks, peering closer.

"This stuff won't work together. There are other symbols that you need before you start getting to these specifics. Like, if you want to use this"—I point back to the first rune—"you also have to include another rune that specifies the type of communication and who you're trying to talk to. Then, if you tie in the one for protection, you have to again specify what kind of protection you need and for how long. Most of those are missing from this circle." I shake my head, sighing. "I mean, I've never even seen this mark before."

It's a circle with a crude eye drawn in the center, the pupil filled in with another eye. It's unlike any sigil or rune I've seen, and I wonder if Emma came up with it on her own. All in all, the circle looks like someone playing at being a Medium, more than someone who knew what they were doing.

"Whoever Murphy was, she was a Medium, but she was still in training."

"So, she comes out here looking to talk to a spirit, one that she wanted protection from. Wouldn't she have needed her mentor to do this?"

I shake my head. "Not necessarily. She could have drawn this out just as easily as I can. Her mentor would have known how to fix it. Taka, my mentor, would've never let me try to summon or bind anything with this, much less on my own. There's no way it'd work. But that's obvious. The circle's still here."

"What do you mean?"

"Here, let me show you." I grab my chalk, draw a quick circle, and scribe a rune and sigil pair on the ground near it.

"Circles are used to channel energy that you can't necessarily use yourself. You know how all Mediums have an Affinity? These symbols, when scribed in the correct way, allow us to tap into the Affinities we don't have. It's still not going to be as good as someone with the actual Affinity, but it's better than what I can do on my own. This one here works kind of like a Reader, only it shows what happened in a small area in the past. Depending on how I draw it, I can set how far back in time it goes, though that's also dependent on how strong I am. But before it can work, it has to be drawn correctly, and I have to put power into it."

I slide my knife out, nick my finger, and scribe a symbol. It bursts into light, and inside the circle, images flicker by. Cross jumps back, surprised, then leans forward to watch the scene playing out in the small, glowing circle. We can see the edge of my boot slide into view and a piece of rubble comes tumbling through before the light flickers and dies. There's nothing left on the concrete afterward, just a space clear of rubble.

"When it works, there's nothing left," Cross murmurs. "She would've known immediately that there was something wrong."

"Basically," I say, shaking my head. "If I'd been her, I'd have run."

Cross pauses for a moment, looking thoughtful, then glances at me, the fringe of his hair hanging in front of his eyes. "Couldn't we use something like this circle to see who killed her?"

"It doesn't work that way," I say. "I'm Reading what the concrete saw, so I'm limited to its field of influence."

"So Read further," he presses.

"I *can't*," I say, getting frustrated. "Reading is also tied into the emotional investment in the thing. The only reason I can get this much is because it just happened, and I was keyed up during the Burning. This memory will be gone in a few more hours, a day at the most. Murphy was killed on Wednesday, right? It's too far back."

"Even though she was murdered?" Cross asks, slightly incredulous.

"Would you care about a patch of concrete if someone was trying to kill you?" I say, eyebrow raised.

Cross sighs and runs his hand through his hair again. "Couldn't you make a circle large enough to get the whole warehouse? Cover everything, get something usable from that?"

I laugh. "Not without killing myself. I power the circle with my blood. Something that big? I'd run out before I had enough power to see even a second."

We stop talking for a moment, both of us lost in our thoughts.

Poor child, Priya says, skimming low over the malformed circle and kicking up a bit of gravel.

Cross frowns, looking slowly around the warehouse. "So, she's alone, trying to communicate with something dangerous, and lacking the proper training to handle it. That's not a good combination." He pauses and runs a finger around the edge of the circle, staining the tip white. "You said someone attacked her, though. A person, not a spirit?"

"Yeah," I murmur, eyeing a poorly drawn rune. "She wasn't killed by a ghost."

"Then this may be connected to why she died, or it could be that she was just in the wrong place at the wrong time. Maybe she was distracted while scribing the circle, and whoever killed her snuck up," Cross says, looking around the warehouse.

"Maybe. You have to concentrate when you're scribing, especially if you're not familiar with it. And this definitely isn't a place for a girl her age to be at night. I don't even know how she was able to get over here without her mentor knowing. I mean, she looked old enough to drive, but there wasn't a car left here. Taka always kept track of me when I was that age, especially if I was trying to do anything that involved ghosts."

Cross stands up and looks around the warehouse again. "It may end up just being a run-of-the-mill murder," he says, "but do you think you could find out who her mentor was? I want to make sure we cover all our bases even if it doesn't lead to anything."

"Absolutely. I'll reach out to Taka, see if he might have known her or someone who would." I stand, brushing dirt from my knees.

"While you work on that, I'll see if I can track down any cabbies who were in the area. Might explain why there wasn't a car."

"Seems strange that a cabbie would drop off a teenager in this neighborhood, especially in the middle of the night."

"And you think it's normal to talk to ghosts," he says with a grin. "You may not be the best judge of 'strange.'"

I roll my eyes, but he has a point.

"So, what happened after she let you know she was here?" he asks, pen skittering across the page.

"The usual," I say. "She threw stuff at me, made a big mess. I had to trap her to get her calm enough to talk to me. Then she Sent me her last moments, and I went home."

"Nothing else?"

I consider telling him about the dream I had, the ominous feeling that hung around the halls of that empty, unknown place, the darkness that clung to me, but I shake my head instead.

"No, nothing else."

Kim... Priya says admonishingly.

"I'm going to get this documented, head back to the station to do some follow-up" Cross says, tucking his notepad into the inside pocket of his jacket. "Let me know what you find out."

"Yeah, of course. Do you have her photo on you?"

Cross nods, slides a photograph from his pocket, and passes it to me. It's from the morgue, labeled "DOE, JANE" in large, block letters near the bottom. Murphy's pale face stares back at me and I stuff the photo into my pocket, suddenly cold.

"Thanks. I'll talk to you soon."

He nods, already preoccupied, and walks out of the warehouse ahead of me. We go in opposite directions, him speeding toward headquarters, me heading toward Taka's.

Taka lives on the west side of town. I'm on the southeast side, so it takes about forty-five minutes to get to his place. I'm zoned out, barely paying attention to the familiar roads in front of me, when Priya starts talking.

The nightmare, she starts. *You need to tell me what you saw.*

I sigh and shake my head, trying to pull the details together, but they won't coalesce into a clear picture. I try harder, but it just makes it worse. There's a sharp throb behind my right eye, and I stop, rubbing my temple until the pain disappears.

I can't remember the specifics, I say. *I was in a dark hallway and there was a… person. He needed help. Then things got weird and I woke up.*

Why were you bleeding?

I don't know, I say, still shaken.

And the black spirit? The one that you had to Burn. Where did that come from?

I don't know, I say.

I just… I want you to be safe, Kim. This isn't like anything I've ever seen, and now this girl is a Medium… It scares me.

It scares me, too. I say, sighing. *Taka will know more. Just hold your questions until we get there?*

Priya nods and sinks into the passenger seat, her body disappearing from Second-Sight.

I pull into Taka's driveway about a half hour later. He lives and works out of a small brick bungalow in Forest Park. I spent five years of my life here, squeezed into the spare bedroom between bookcases and packing boxes. Somehow, between the cramped space and the endless training, it became home.

I lock the car and head toward the front door. My fingers twitch in simple, memorized patterns that disable the wards Taka etched into the concrete steps years ago. They fire against my fingertips like static electricity. I barely have the opportunity to knock before Taka opens the door. His hair is thinner than the last time I saw him, sprinkled with more gray, and the laugh lines on his face seem to have spread. He's thin, but his arms are still lean and corded with muscles as he opens them wide, welcoming.

"Kim! *Okaeri!*" He's grinning as he pulls me in for a quick hug, my feet tripping on the doorframe.

"*Tadaima.*" My throat tightens at the welcome. "How are you doing, Taka?" I step into the house, Taka's arm still wrapped around my shoulder.

"I'm doing well, quite well. Though it's been too long since you last visited. Three months or so?" He scowls faintly.

My cheeks go warm as I bend down to untie my boots. "I know. I've been busy." I toe off my boots and walk into the living room.

Brightly colored cushions are spread across the floor of the room, surrounding a low table. Taka motions for me to sit while he heads into the kitchen. I can hear him bustling about, cups clinking in the cupboard. I'm transported through the years by the familiar sound, suddenly feeling too old and too young at the same time.

"I've seen you in the papers quite a bit," he says as he walks out of the kitchen, a tea tray balanced in his hands. "You've been doing a lot of good work."

"I try." He passes me a teacup. It's *genmaicha*, my favorite, and I take a deep sip. The flavors of green tea and roasted rice settle on my tongue with a familiar, comforting warmth. Taka pours himself a cup, his movements quiet and sure. I cradle my cup while he drinks, enjoying the heat seeping into my hands.

"What brings you here, Kim?" He looks at me through the steam curling up from his cup. "You're not one to visit for just sentiment's sake. And while it's been too long since you last visited and I'm happy to have you here, you seem... burdened."

"I Burnt a young girl last night." I pause, not ready to share the news. The heat from the cup stings my fingers and I shift it in my hands. "She was a Medium. Or at least an apprentice."

Taka's face pales and he leans back. He shakes his head and sets his tea down, running a hand over his face. "I assume you're here for my help, then?"

I nod, my throat tight.

"Give me a description of the girl."

I run through her basic description and slide the morgue photo over to him. He picks it up and nods.

"That's a shame." His voice is unsteady, and he shakes his head again. "A damn shame. She's a very nice, very energetic young girl. She's training to be a Seer, working with Ruth. Ruth Peterson."

I nod, immediately recognizing the name. Ruth Peterson is one of the strongest Seers in the US, not just in Chicago. She and Taka were friends when I was younger. He had her over a couple of times for tea, but I didn't pay much attention to it while in training. At the time, she was just another of Taka's Medium friends, a vaguely unsettling older woman who seemed to see more than what was there. Now, I recognize the strength of her Affinity and the power that it brings. Murphy must have had some real natural talent for Ruth to mentor her directly.

"I'll need to talk to her," I say, taking the photo back and putting it in my jacket pocket.

"Of course, of course. I've got her number, hold on."

Taka stands, and I think I hear his knees crack. It's a painful reminder that he's not as young as he used to be—that *I'm* not as young as I used to be. I finger Murphy's photo, remembering who I was at that age and feeling incredibly old.

He comes back from the kitchen with a well-worn address book, small slips of paper and a couple business cards hanging out the sides. He's holding a card, which he passes to me.

"Here," he says, "go ahead and keep it, just in case. She knows who you are. You shouldn't have any problem getting through."

"Thanks." I slip the business card in next to Murphy's photo.

"Can I ask you…" Taka starts, but trails off. "No, never mind."

"What is it?"

"The girl," he says, "Was it…?"

"I can't talk about the specifics of the case with you," I say, wincing, "but it was quick."

The lie sits heavy on my tongue. I hope he can't tell, that I don't somehow give it away. Death is hard, even for us. He nods, then sighs and sits down next to me.

"It's always hard to lose one of our own, especially so young."

"I didn't even know she was a Medium," I say, fiddling with my teacup. "Not until we did a second walk-through of the scene. She'd drawn a circle. Looked like she was trying to capture something or communicate with someone. I don't know." I swallow, my chest tight. "Afterward, I… I had a dream. Almost like a vision."

"Are you all right?" Taka asks, resting his hand on mine.

I shake my head.

"There was something dark hanging on to me. Priya and I were able to Burn it, but it's left me off-kilter. I'm not even sure where it came from or what it was."

Taka hums quietly and sets his tea down on the table. He closes his eyes; I do the same. In Second-Sight, he looks younger, his hair thicker and darker. His skin isn't as wrinkled, and his arms are solid and strong. Here, he still looks like he did when I first met him, powerful and confident. Over his shoulder, his ghost partner, Claire, hovers, face creased with worry. Taka looks at me with bright white eyes and frowns.

"Your energy is pretty low," he says, reaching out and tracing a quick sigil in the hollow of my throat. I'm hit with a sudden force, and my breath leaves my lungs in a quick, painful burst.

"What'd you do?" I gasp, inhaling sharply. There's a low thrum of energy coursing beneath my skin, and I suddenly want to move. My leg starts to jitter, knee bouncing against the underside of the table.

"It's just a boost to your energy that I learned a few years back," he says. "It won't last for long or take care of the problem entirely, but it should help you get through the rest of the day. You said there was a dark spirit clinging to you?"

"It wasn't hard to get rid of, not really," I say, nodding. "But I have no idea where it came from. I wonder if she pulled something in before or when she died, if she opened a gate of some kind. But then again, I know what that feels like, and there's no way I would've missed it."

"Perhaps there wasn't any intent. Dark things can

sneak over without our knowledge, and they tend to cling to the living."

"Maybe," I say, setting my now-empty teacup down on the table. "Whatever it was, it's gone now."

"Good. Now, tell me more about what's going on in your life."

"I'd love to," I say, "but I have to go follow up with Ruth as soon as possible. Let's meet for dinner and catch up. Soon?"

"Yes, absolutely. No more disappearing for months," Taka says with a smile, though a hint of disappointment clings to the corners of his mouth. "You know you're always welcome here."

I give him a tight hug. As I hurry down the steps toward my car, Taka waits on the porch, waving briefly. Once inside my car, I jam the keys into the ignition and pull my cell out, dialing Cross's number before the engine kicks to life.

"Cross," he starts, but I cut him off.

"I've got a lead," I say, heading back onto the main streets.

"What d'you got?"

"Her mentor. A Seer named Ruth Peterson. Pretty sure you've heard of her."

"Well, shit. You headed there now?"

"Yeah," I say, taking a hard left as the light changes to yellow. "You want to meet me there, or should I take this solo?"

"I'll be there," he says and hangs up.

CHAPTER FOUR

I t takes me about twenty minutes to get into the Loop and another fifteen to find parking. I refuse to use parking garages. The prices are always too high, and so far this year, I've had to Burn three ghosts while looking for my keys. I eventually find an open meter—a veritable unicorn on a weekend and in the middle of the afternoon—about three blocks from Ruth's building, so I park, pay, and start walking.

Her building is in the center of the Loop. The lobby is a monument to money and marble, huge columns supporting the heavy, ornate ceiling. The floor is polished to a mirrored shine, and my boots squeak as I walk toward a desk labeled "Security." Suddenly, the casual T-shirt and jeans I'd thrown on this morning seem ill-advised. I shrug my jacket forward on my shoulders and try to stand up straight.

There are two guards—one blond, one bald—who look more like black op soldiers than rent-a-cops. I get my badge out and lean forward on the counter. After the bald one looks up at me, raises an eyebrow, then he lowers his head again.

"Good afternoon, gentlemen."

Neither of them responds to my greeting, still checking the monitors tucked behind the desk.

"My name is Kim Phillips. I'm a homicide detective with the Chicago Police Department. I'm here to see Ruth Peterson."

The bald one looks up at me again and raises the same eyebrow as before.

"Do you have an appointment?"

"It's in regards to an active investigation," I say. "Can you page her, please? It's urgent."

The other eyebrow goes up.

"You'll need an appointment, ma'am. She doesn't take unscheduled visitors." He starts looking down again, dismissing me.

"Did you not get the part where I'm a cop?" I ask, showing him my badge again.

"Yes, ma'am. You still need an appointment," the other guard says, eyes still on the monitors spread out behind the desk.

"Will you page her, or do I need to start pressing obstruction charges?" I ask.

The bald guard starts typing, pressing each key with slow exaggerated motions. I stand back up, hands on my hips, when Cross comes into the front lobby. He makes a beeline for me and glares at both security guards.

"What're we waiting for, Detective?"

"I'm waiting for these *gentlemen* to page Ruth Peterson." I frown, not sure how to press the issue. "They don't seem to be handling this with the urgency the situation requires."

"Officers," a young woman says from behind us, looking at Cross and me like we're unruly children. "There's no need to page. Mrs. Peterson is expecting you. Follow me, please."

I shoot the bald guard a cocky grin. His eyebrows fall, forehead deeply furrowed. He hunches his shoulders as he returns to work with a mumbled apology.

The young woman, probably a secretary or personal assistant of Ruth's, is wearing a white blouse and a dark pin-striped skirt with black patent leather heels. As we turn from the desk, she starts walking toward the center of the lobby, her steps sure and steady even in stilettos. I straighten my spine as Cross straightens his tie, and we follow her to a bank of chrome elevators. She swipes a card and presses the call button. We wait in awkward silence while the floors count down. After what feels like much longer than a few seconds, the doors chime and slide open.

"She's on the top floor," the woman says, reaching in to push the highest button before she steps out. "Have a nice day."

The doors shut, and Cross sighs audibly. We ride up in silence, both focused on the case.

Murders aren't always hard to work, especially if there's a clear suspect, but this case feels like a ticking time bomb. Mediums make good news, especially if they're involved in crimes. If they're the victims, even better. Most people think we're invincible, but a dead Medium proves the exact opposite. Add a high-profile mentor, a lack of solid evidence, and a dead, pretty white girl, and it's only a matter of time before someone at the *Trib* or the *Sun-Times* takes this and runs with it.

Best-case scenario, we work the case fast and well and find the killer before it gets bad. I remember the vague shape of Murphy's killer, the slope of his cheek, the tilt of his head. All indistinct, blurred, faded. I doubt this will be anything close to a best case.

"Before we head in there," Cross breaks the silence, "you are feeling okay, right? I know this hits close to home, what with… I just… If it's too much or if you need a break…"

"Riley," I say, using his first name so I know he'll shut up, "this isn't the first time I've investigated a Medium's death, and it won't be my last. I can handle it."

"And earlier, when you nearly passed out at the station?"

"I told you already, that wasn't related to the case." I cross my arms and lean against the elevator wall.

"Are you sick?"

"I was," I say, shrugging, "at least, in a way. But I took care of it and I'm fine now." I lean my head against the wall and look at him under raised eyebrows. "While I appreciate your concern, I know my limits, and I know when I can and can't do my job. Just trust me, okay?"

He puts his hands in his pockets, shifts his weight back a little, and sighs.

"Look, I *do* trust you. We've been working in the same building long enough that I know you can handle yourself.

But I'm depending on you here, and I need to know you're on your game."

"I'm *fine*,"

"Fine," he says. He doesn't look me in the eye, just keeps his hands in his pockets and his eyes on the display showing the floors.

The elevator opens straight into the penthouse. There are floor-to-ceiling windows overlooking downtown Chicago. The view's gorgeous. I can see sparkling slivers of Lake Michigan through the spaces between the towering high-rises. There's a large desk at one end of the room with bookshelves lining the wall behind. On the other end, there's a sitting area with plush, dark blue chairs and a low glass-topped coffee table. Ruth is seated in one of the chairs, body slumped with obvious fatigue. Even exhausted, she's a well-put-together woman, her white hair in a tight bun. Her dark gray suit fits her well and sets off her light blue eyes, but it's rumpled. It looks like she's been wearing it for longer than this morning.

"Officers," she says, rising, visibly pulling herself together. "How can I help you?"

"Ma'am, I'm Detective Riley Cross. Detective Kim Phillips."

"Taka's Kim Phillips?" Ruth asks, starting to smile.

"Yes, ma'am," I say.

"It's a pleasure to meet you," Ruth says. "Taka has such wonderful things to say about you. Would you like some coffee, tea, water?"

"Ma'am," Cross interrupts, "we have a couple

questions for you related to a homicide investigation."

"Oh," she says, face quickly falling back to a polite mask. "That's... I Saw that you were coming, but not what about. Please, have a seat."

She directs us toward the sitting area, settling onto a love seat as Cross and I sit down in the chairs.

"Now, I have a photo I need you to look at. It may be a little difficult for you to see, but let me know and I can put it away." Cross motions to me. I pull the morgue photo from my pocket, laying it facedown on the table, and slide it across to Ruth.

"Take your time, and let me know if you recognize the person in the photo."

Ruth's hand is steady when she flips the photograph over, but it starts shaking the longer she looks. The low, keening cry that comes breaking out of her makes my blood run cold.

"It's her," she says, the words choked with grief. "That's Emma. Oh God." She bends over, resting her face in her hands, the photograph pressed against her forehead.

Cross and I wait for her to calm down. His fingers are laced together, thumbs rubbing his skin. I keep my hands on my knees. This part never gets easier.

Ruth composes herself slowly. She takes a shuddering breath, then meets our eyes.

"Tell me what happened. Please."

Cross gives a quick rundown of the case, glossing over the more difficult details. Even then, Ruth still flinches. When we get to what we found in the warehouse, I take over.

"She drew a circle," I say, leaning forward. "It looked like she was trying to talk to a ghost, one she didn't trust completely."

"She's been having visions lately," Ruth says, shaking her head. "Dark ones. I told her to not go looking into them on her own. That anything like that needs to be handled with care, but you know how kids are at her age. Tell them to not do something and it's the first thing they do, just as soon as you aren't looking." She gives a pained smile. "She's always like that, so headstrong." She closes her eyes, tears leaking from the corners.

"These visions, can you be more specific?" Cross asks, his notebook at the ready.

"She didn't like to talk about them," Ruth starts, sniffling. "They left her unsettled, weak. All she would tell me was there was a man who needed her help and that he kept trying to talk to her, but she couldn't hear him. She told me that they'd stopped, but I could tell she was lying. There was something bothering her, something she didn't feel like she could talk to me about."

"When was the last time you saw Emma?" Cross asks.

"It was a couple of days ago, maybe Tuesday? I'm not sure," Ruth says, shaking her head. "Before you say anything, this isn't the first time she's disappeared. Her background isn't a good one. Emma's parents weren't very understanding of her powers. A lot of terrible things happened to that girl when she was younger, and she sometimes needs her space. She usually goes to see her aunt—she's a Medium, too. She's been disappearing more frequently lately, but she always calls me after a few days and comes home. This is the first time I didn't hear from her after she ran off."

Ruth takes a deep breath and exhales in a slow sigh. "You can never really tell with Seers. What's a vision and what's just a dream, I mean. I was going to teach her how to protect herself and how to better communicate with spirits, just to be safe. To think that she was killed by one before I could—"

She bites her lip and shakes her head.

"According to Detective Phillips," Cross says, tilting his head in my direction, "the suspect wasn't a ghost."

I nod. "From her last Sending, she was attacked by a person."

"His face," she says, sitting forward. "Were you able to see his face?"

I shake my head, and she slumps back into the chair.

"She wasn't able to give me much, but it's enough," I say, leaning forward. I take a deep breath, then meet her troubled eyes. "Mrs. Peterson, I hate to ask this, but do you know of anyone who might have a grudge against you? Someone who might hurt those you care about in order to send a message?"

Ruth pales, shaking her head back and forth. "I've made enemies over the years, it's true, but only political ones. No one who would go to these kinds of lengths. No one who would hurt a child."

Cross frowns. "You're sure about that? There must be a few people out there who'd like to see you knocked down a peg. You have a lot of power, a lot of influence."

"That's why they don't fight me, not directly." Her eyes spark briefly with power, a crackling of blue-white light that fades into the depths of her eyes.

Silence stretches for a few seconds as Ruth's eyes lock with Cross's. He holds her gaze, quiet and stone-faced. She's the first to look away, staring down at her hands for a long moment.

"Maybe you have a point. I'll have to think about it and try to get a list together for you."

"And Emma," Cross presses. "Was there anyone in her past who might want to hurt her?"

"No," Ruth says with finality. "Her parents caused her the most pain and they've been out of her life for a long time. Once she came to live with me, she left that behind her. She was cleaning up her act, trying to make friends at school. No one would've wanted to hurt her, not those who knew her."

"I'm sorry," I say, feeling the inadequacy of the words as they spill from my mouth. "We'll do our damnedest to catch whoever did this." My tone is gentle, but there's steel in the words.

"She was the daughter I never had," Ruth says as she meets my eyes. "I see—*saw* so much of myself in her."

"Would you happen to have her aunt's contact information?" I ask gently. "If Emma told her anything about the visions or how she was feeling, we might be able to learn why we found her where we did."

"Yes, absolutely. Just give me a moment."

Ruth walks over to her desk and grabs a pen, writing on a Post-it Note.

"Here," she says, handing it to me. "Her name's Rachael Franklin. They're related on Emma's mother's side. That's her address and phone number. She's a freelancer and usually home in the afternoon."

"Thank you." I give her hands a quick squeeze and smile reassuringly.

"We'll do our best to make sure she gets justice," Cross says. He stands up, and I follow his lead. Ruth joins us, though more slowly. She steps close and clasps my hands in hers, then leans in.

"Get him," she whispers harshly. "For her and for me."

"You can count on it," I respond.

"We'll keep you up to date on the case. In the meantime, if you think of anything else or if you See anything, please give us a call." Cross passes a business card to Ruth.

"I'll make it a priority," she says, holding the card tight in her hand. I pass her my card as well, squeezing her fingers again. Her hand tightens on mine for an instant, and then she drops it and turns to face the windows. Her head falls as we leave, her shoulders tense and bowed.

As soon as the elevator doors close behind us, Cross sighs.

"You know we don't have a whole lot to go off of with this case," he says. "We may not be able to close it."

"I know," I say, shaking my head. "But she's just lost her apprentice, and you don't know… I can't see her suffer like that. I had to tell her something."

He shrugs but doesn't comment. We ride back down to the lobby in silence.

"I want to go over everything with you one more time, if you're up for it," Cross says as we head toward the front door.

"The Berghoff's a couple blocks away," I say, turning west. "I could use a drink."

Cross nods and we start walking. It's getting dark, the streets hidden in subtle shadows. There's a hint of exhaust in the air, burned rubber and sewer gas rising from the warm asphalt. The roads and sidewalks swarm with people on their way home. Everyone is moving at that specific speed you need to catch every light, their strides long and purposeful. A few tourists, who can't keep up, get stuck waiting at corners with the locals who impatiently check their watches or phones for the time. Cross doesn't say a word and I figure it's for the best.

It's crowded when we get to the Berghoff, a group of investment bankers filling up the entryway. Cross and I squeeze our way in, pressed up against pressed suits, and find a table tucked into a back corner. There are empty glasses and napkins stuck to the wood from the last customers. We clear it up as best we can, slide the tip to the edge of the table, and sit down. A waiter comes by, takes our orders, and Cross pulls out his notepad.

"So, we've got a young girl, running around at night in

a dangerous neighborhood. She ends up getting raped and murdered by an unknown assailant." He sighs and leans back in his chair. "Also turns out she's apprenticed with one of the highest-profile Mediums in the US and may have been trying to communicate with or trap some unknown spirit that had her pretty freaked out."

"If someone were trying to get to Ruth," I say, "taking out her apprentice would be a good way to go about it."

"We don't have any evidence supporting that, though."

We sit quietly, both lost in our thoughts when the waiter comes back with our beers. I take a deep sip, then reach across the table to grab Cross's notepad. He shakes his head and leans back in the chair.

"Go ahead and look." He takes a long drink. "If you can make anything else out, I'd love to hear it."

His handwriting is blocky and precise, covering the main details of the case. He's labeled and carefully arranged everything, but none of it helps straighten out the mess in my head.

"Maybe it's unconnected," I say, frustrated. "Maybe she wasn't targeted. If it's just a coincidence that she's a Medium, that she was out there to communicate with something, it could be a random attack."

Cross slides the notepad into his inside pocket before taking another sip of beer.

"I don't like chalking things up to coincidence," he says, "but I also don't know what else to consider."

"What's the next step?"

"We'll start canvassing the area, see if we can find any

of the bums who might be living in the warehouse. Do you think you could sit with a sketch artist, try to get something down from what she showed you?"

I take a drink and nod. "Yeah, I can do that. I'll get something scheduled in the morning."

Cross's food shows up, and he eats quietly while I keep working through the case.

"So, how'd you get into this?" he asks, jarring me from my thoughts.

"Into what? Homicide?"

"No, the whole"—he waves his hand in a circle—"Medium thing, I guess. I've never had the chance to ask."

"I don't know that I ever 'got into' it," I say, grinning. "I was kind of born this way."

Cross rolls his eyes. "You know what I mean. When'd you figure out you were Gifted?"

"When I was a kid." I shrug. "My folks just thought I had an overactive imagination. We'd be at the grocery store, and I'd just start talking to the displays or to nothing in the parking lot. Once they figured out what was really going on, they did what they could to get me help. They didn't know what they were getting into. The last Medium in our family was my grandmother, but she didn't talk about it much. When I turned thirteen, I apprenticed with Taka. I found Priya when I was eighteen, and then I went to college."

"How'd you figure out you were a Burner?"

"I don't know," I say, running a finger around the rim of my beer glass. "I just knew, once I started learning about the Affinities. Burner… It called to me, I guess."

"Never wanted any of the other Affinities?" Cross asks with a lopsided grin. "I could imagine you as a Shaker, picking shit up and throwing it all over the place."

"If that's a dig at how I left that crime scene," I say, mouth twisted wryly, "I am going to be the better person and pretend I didn't hear it."

Cross laughs and shakes his head. There's a pause, and his expression shifts, becoming more serious. "And you were never afraid?"

I pause, considering. "You know, I don't remember being afraid as a kid. When I was older and knew what I was dealing with, knew what kind of dangers there were, yeah. But as a kid? I just thought they were my friends. Now, I know better. Sometimes it's routine, but sometimes…"

Cross nods and pushes the last of his food around on his plate.

"What about you?" I ask, trying to break the silence. "What made you want to be a cop?"

"When I was in elementary school"—he leans back in his chair—"my older brother went missing. It ended up not being anything dangerous. He'd just wandered off and eventually wandered home again, but I remember the police officer who found him. I thought he was the coolest guy I'd ever met." His mouth crooks up at the side, just this side of charming. "I ended up being a cop every year after that for Halloween."

I laugh. "Seriously?"

"Yeah." His mouth quirks up in a self-conscious smile. "When I applied to the academy after college, no one was surprised."

"And then homicide?"

"And then homicide. I got interested in it when I was a beat cop and when the opportunity came, I took it."

"You're good at it," I say.

"Thanks. I try to do my best." He jokingly salutes me and I laugh.

"You ever think about what you'll do after?"

Cross shrugs. "Not really, no. I'm only thirty-six. I've got plenty of time before I need to even think about retirement."

"I'd like to move somewhere warm," I say. "Don't get me wrong, I'm a Chicago girl, born and raised, but every time November rolls around, I start thinking about moving to Fiji."

He laughs, eyes crinkled in amusement. I find myself unwittingly captivated, eyes tracing over the planes of his face, the slight dimple on only the right side of his mouth, the gentle curve of his lips.

Kim, Priya says, *you're staring.*

I am not, I reply, frowning and looking down at the scratched tabletop.

"Fiji doesn't sound bad," he says, "but then you'd miss the snow and the lights and the windows on Michigan Avenue."

"Parking's probably better," I say, tracing a deep gouge with a nail.

"Probably," he says.

I look back up to see him waving down the waiter. I finish my beer and crumple my napkin idly, trying to keep my hands busy.

Cross must pick up on my awkwardness, or the pause in the conversation is too long. He gives me a searching look, smiling softly. I swallow, afraid to move or acknowledge whatever this moment is or could be. His face slowly falls, and he leans back, closed off and serious again. Part of me is thankful that he's taken charge of this, that he's moved us back to familiar ground.

Another part of me—the part that gets lonely at night, that wonders what it would be like to feel a warm body against mine—aches.

"So tomorrow," I say, pushing the words past the sudden tightness in my throat, "I'll talk to the sketch artist, and then I can help you or the uniforms with canvassing."

He nods and signals the waiter over. "Sounds good. I'll call you if I go back to the crime scene. I've got a couple other cases I need to work on, but I'll be following up for a little bit tomorrow."

"All right. I have some stuff I need to work on, too. Few cases I need to get paperwork together for."

I reach for my wallet and pull out a ten, tossing it onto the table. As I stand, I reach out for Priya through our connection. A few seconds later, she materializes next to me, frowning.

"I'll see you tomorrow," I say, grabbing my coat from the back of my chair and fleeing.

I'm halfway to my car when Priya finally speaks up. *You want to talk about it?*

Not really, no. I sigh and fumble for my keys. *There's nothing to talk about, anyway.*

This case is more than what it seems, she says. *If you don't want to talk about it now, that's fine, but you're going to need to talk about it eventually.*

I know, and when that time comes, you're going to be the first person I talk to. I sigh. *Just right now? I don't even know where to start.*

Reaching the car, I wrestle with the door for a second before it finally pops open.

At least you got dinner with some nice eye candy, Priya says, sinking through the roof of the car to sit next to me. *Do you remember when you were dating that guy a couple of months ago? Rob?*

I thought we weren't going to talk about Rob, I sigh, starting the car.

Just an example. We can talk about Brandon instead.

I laugh. *Oh, c'mon. Low blow. He tried to blow up my* car, *Priya. I had to arrest him.*

I'm just saying, it's been awhile since you've been on a real date, and you could do worse than Cross.

You're kidding, right? I ask, starting the car. *Just because a guy is attractive and breathing doesn't mean he's a good dating prospect.*

You get where I'm going with this, though. You at least know *Riley. And he's definitely not going to commit a felony.*

I shake my head, but I'm smiling. *I appreciate it,* I say,

flicking on my turn signal. *But I'm okay. I'll start dating when I'm ready. In the meantime, let's focus on solving this murder, okay?*

All right, she says, sounding disappointed. *I just want you to be happy, Kim.*

I am, I say. I try to ignore the part of me that might say otherwise.

CHAPTER FIVE

I walk into HQ the next morning, bleary-eyed, with a lingering sense of uncertainty about the Murphy case. I'm about halfway to my desk when I hear my name. Lieutenant Walker stands in the doorway to her office, arms folded.

"Phillips, get over here," she says again, turning and walking into her office. I groan and follow her, shutting the door behind me.

Lieutenant Leanne Walker is an intimidating woman. She's been working for the CPD for twenty years, at least, and has been running this district since I was in the academy. I don't think, in the entire time I've known her, that I've ever seen her looking anything but perfect. Not a hair out of place, dress shirt neatly starched, creases sharp and constant. And while I wouldn't say I'm afraid of her, not outright, there's a healthy dose of fear mixed in with the respect I have for her.

She's just sitting down behind her desk when I walk in, her hair a little grayer than when I started in the department but no less carefully arranged. She waves toward the chair opposite, then waits for me to sit.

"How was your vacation?" she asks, leaning back in her

chair, arms crossed.

"Fine," I say, hesitantly.

"You get some time to relax, kick back?"

"Yes." I can see where this is going.

"So, I shouldn't be concerned that half of the district saw you stumbling out of here yesterday or the fact that I've gotten *three* separate e-mails from detectives this morning asking after your health?"

"No, ma'am."

She sighs and runs a hand over her face.

"Kim," she says, leaning forward. "You're a good cop. A hard worker. You get your cases closed. And I know for a fact that you freelance during your downtime because you want to help people. But you can't keep going twenty-four seven like this. You're gonna burn out."

"I've got Priya to keep me in line," I say, fidgeting.

"And if something were to happen to you?"

I shrug, unsure of how to answer the question.

"Now, I know you've resisted having a full-time partner since Bob retired, but I'm assigning you someone. You've worked with him before, and you both did a good job. Kept each other on your toes." She passes me a manila folder with a piece of paper taped to the front.

I pick it up as she waves someone into the office. I'm staring at the bold words at the top of the page as Cross walks in.

"Ma'am," he says, standing in the doorway.

"Seriously?" I ask, looking back up at the Lieutenant. "You're partnering me with Cross?"

"You make that sound like it's a bad thing," he says, frowning.

"You need someone to keep an eye on you, and since you were willing to use your free time to look into another detective's case"—she raises her eyebrows, judging—"you can at least work with him on it. And on any other cases that you're assigned."

"Yes, ma'am," I say, fighting back my irritation.

"You can move your desk to the open one across from him, too."

I nod, then quietly storm into the main room, Cross close on my heels.

"You need help with any of that stuff?" he asks, pointing his thumb toward my desk. It's cluttered, to put it mildly. Papers are falling out of folders, a squadron of empty disposable coffee cups takes up one corner of the desk, and a half-eaten sandwich from a few days ago is tucked near a notepad. I shake my head.

"No, I've got it. I'm pretty sure some of that stuff is a biohazard."

He gives my desk a long look and takes a step back.

"Yeah, probably. Just try to keep the mold to your side," he says, frowning slightly as he walks back to his desk.

"There's no mold," I mutter, not sure if I'm lying or not.

It takes about an hour to shift all my stuff to my new desk, and there is mold, but only in one of the coffee cups. I have to knock an alarming number of crumbs out of my keyboard, but other than that, it's not too terrible. Cross watches the whole spectacle carefully, pushing my coffee cup away with his pen when I put it near the gap between our desks. I can feel my face flushing, and I shoot him a glare as I put the cup back where it started.

I comfort myself with the fact that at least nothing's gained sentience while it's been incubating on my desk. The stuff that's irredeemable gets thrown out, and I settle into my new desk to sort through and organize paperwork. By the time I'm done, it doesn't look as neat as Cross's, but it's better than it used to be.

After I finish and get a fresh cup of coffee—shooting Cross a glare as I pick up my cup—I make a call to the sketch artist we use and set up an appointment for later in the day. With the downtime in between, I look up Emma Murphy's record. There's not much in the system. A couple of reports for truancy, but those disappeared after she turned thirteen and started apprenticing with Ruth. After that, there's nothing for anyone named Emma Murphy.

The sketch artist shows up a couple of minutes early, and I spend another half hour working with him to get a sketch put together of the man who murdered Emma. All things considered, it's not that great. I don't have a clear picture to pull from, so the sketch ends up looking like a generic homeless man, someone who most people will see in a million different faces. It's better than nothing, though, and I make a copy of the drawing to show around later. The artist promises to mock up and send out a poster we can pass around the neighborhood where Emma was found. I give him the fax number for the district headquarters and he leaves.

I take some time to look over my other active cases, updating notes and contacting witnesses for follow-ups. It's nearly one in the afternoon before I get a break and eat quickly. Cross keeps looking at me surreptitiously as I dig into my sub.

"What?" I ask, mouth still slightly full.

"Nothing," he says, shaking his head. "Just wondering if I need to get you a bib and a mat to put under your desk."

I roll my eyes and stuff the last of the sandwich into my mouth. He frowns and passes me a tissue.

"You're disgusting," he says, his expression a mix of disbelief and humor.

"I try," I respond, delicately blotting the corners of my mouth. He grins, quick and unexpected, and turns back to his computer monitor, face calm.

"You have any plans for this afternoon?" I ask, tossing the tissue and the sub wrapper into the trash can under my desk.

"Yeah, I've got a couple other things I need to follow up on." He looks away from his screen. "Why? What're you thinking of doing?"

"Going to interview Emma's aunt. I have her address, and Ruth said she should be available in the afternoon."

"Do you need me on it, or can you handle it on your own?"

"I'm fine on my own," I say, irritated. I lock my

computer and grab my badge and wallet. "Just wanted to make sure you felt like part of the team, *partner.*"

"No problem, *partner,*" he says, turning back to his computer screen. "Just let me know what you find out. I should be here, and you've got my cell number otherwise."

"I'll give you a call if anything comes up," I say as I pull my coat on. "Stay out of trouble."

"No promises," he says with a quick grin.

I huff out a reluctant laugh and head out. The air is brisk outside, nipping at my cheeks, and I slide into my car quickly, waiting a moment for the heat to flare to life before I hit the road.

It's not a long drive from the district headquarters to Rachael Franklin's apartment; it's on the same side of town, just a short drive north. I park a couple of blocks away from the place, a brown brick building in a long line of other brown brick buildings. The street's clogged with cars. *The hazards of living in Chicago*, I think as I walk down the leaf-covered sidewalk. When the wind picks up, it cuts through my jacket and sends shivers up my back.

I walk up the crumbling steps and search for Franklin's name on the buzzer panel. She's near the bottom, apartment 2B, and I press the button hard. After a moment, the door buzzes, and I push my way in. It locks behind me loudly, and I make my way up the central staircase. I find her apartment rather quickly, the door propped open as I go to knock.

"Hello?" I call, the door swinging open slightly.

"Come on in," I hear someone call from inside. "I'll be right there!"

I push my way in and feel a sizzle of energy race painfully over my skin.

Wards? I ask Priya, shivering as electricity crackles between my fingers in blue sparks.

Looks like it, Priya says, frozen on the other side of the doorway. *I can't come in.*

Brilliant, I say, sighing.

"Miss Franklin?" I call again, and a woman comes out of the hallway, wiping her hands on a dish towel. I see the family resemblance immediately. She has dark hair like Murphy's, curly and cut to frame her face. There's something about her eyes that reminds me of her niece, something about the calculating look she shoots me that brings back the angry young woman throwing tables and concrete with enough force to kill. I pull out my badge and she holds out a hand. I pass it to her.

"It's Rachael," she says, peering closely at the badge in her hand. "What do you want?"

"Detective Kim Phillips," I say as she hands the badge back. "I'm here to talk to you about your niece."

"Oh God," she says, throwing the towel onto the coffee table in the center of the room. "What'd she do now? Do I need to bail her out or something? She knows to call me if anything happens."

"Ma'am," I say, feeling awful—but unsurprised—that I'm going to have to have this same conversation again today. "You might want to sit down."

I sit on the couch across from her and start explaining. She takes the news surprisingly well. I can't tell if it's shock or numb acceptance, but Franklin just sits heavily on the couch, sighs, and asks what happened. I run through the details of the case as carefully as I can, leaving out the more gruesome aspects.

"And you've talked to Ruth?" she asks, shaking her head. "This is going to kill her."

"Yes, I've already spoken with Mrs. Peterson. She directed me this way. From what she told me, Emma had been having visions lately?"

"Yeah," Franklin says, tucking her hair behind her ear. "Some dark shit. It was really messing with her. She was upset about it."

"Ruth said Emma wouldn't talk about it with her, but that Emma confided in you fairly regularly. Would you be able to tell me anything about what she was Seeing, specifically?"

"A lot of it won't make sense if you aren't familiar with being a Medium," Rachael starts, and I shake my head.

"I'm a Burner. Feel free to be as technical as you need to be."

"Me, too, actually," Rachael says with a smile that's more of a wince. "It runs in the family, or at least it used to. Hold on a moment, I had her write the details down for me."

She stands up, walking to a desk tucked in the back corner of the room. I see her grab a journal, cradling it for a moment, letting her fingers trail over the spine. She walks back and hands it to me, her hand lingering for a long moment before letting go.

"I used to have her write down her thoughts. She had a hard time talking to people. You know how it is. She'd write it all down, and I'd write back. It was easier for her that way."

I look at her understandingly and open the book. There are words in a girlish scrawl covering the first page, the letters wide and curved. It's dated about six months back, and as I flip through, I watch as the letters slowly lose their curves, getting harsher and more jagged.

"They were really starting to get to her, weren't they?" I ask. Rachael nods and reaches for the journal. I hand it back to her. She opens it toward the back and returns it to me, pointing to a passage.

"Here's where she finally told me what she was Seeing. It's some fucked-up shit."

I pull my notepad out and tear off a piece of paper, tucking it into the page. I start skimming, making note of where the handwriting falters and skips. There's a whole section that's been scribbled out in dark, cutting swatches, the page torn in some places and the writing underneath illegible.

hes coming hes coming cant stop it cant do anything no no no wont cant i wont let him

"When'd you see her last?" Unsettled, I set the journal on the table between us.

"Sometime last week. Tuesday, maybe?" Her tone is uncertain and pained. "I guess right before she…"

Franklin swallows, then continues.

"She'd had another vision, only this one… It was really bad. She was sick for a couple of hours. Couldn't breathe, kept throwing up. I told her she needed to talk to Ruth about it, but she said that was impossible, that Ruth wouldn't understand. It's hard to explain to a kid that telling the people in charge is sometimes the best thing. That was Emma, though. Once she got it in her head that something was one way, it was almost impossible to change her mind. She, uh… She wrote most of it down, but she told me some of it. Said there was something evil following her, that it'd taken over her body once or twice. Made her do things she didn't want to. I taught her some protective runes, just simple stuff to stop ghosts from possessing you. She was talking about getting them tattooed…"

"Would you mind showing me what you taught her?"

Rachael nods, and I pass her my notepad and pen. She scribbles a couple of symbols on the paper, and I recognize at least one of the protective runes from the circle Emma had drawn in the warehouse.

"I kept telling her to talk to Ruth, that she needed to trust her mentor. I guess whatever she was seeing, she thought it was too dangerous to share. I don't really know what she was thinking." She shakes her head, her mouth twisted into something like a grin and a grimace. "Dumb fucking kid."

Silence grows in the small apartment. Rachael's head is bent; she stares sightlessly at the table in front of her.

"I'm going to take this if that's okay." I say, reaching

for the journal.

She nods, and I tuck it into my jacket.

"I'll make sure to return it once we finish the case."

"Yeah, thanks. I'd… That'd be nice."

"If you think of anything else or have any questions, please call." I pass her my business card, and she nods, worrying it between her hands.

"Thank you for your help."

"You're welcome. Sorry about the wards," she says, following me to the front door. "You never know who you can trust these days."

"No, you can't. I'll call if I have any questions."

"Okay. Thanks for letting me know. If I, uh, if I wanted to claim the body? Get funeral services arranged?"

"Just call the city morgue." I scribble the number down quickly. "They'll be able to walk you through the rest of the process."

"Thanks." Rachael holds onto the paper and my card like a lifeline. I walk out of the apartment, the wards snapping uncomfortably over my skin again. The door closes behind me quietly. I think I hear Rachael start to cry, and I head toward the stairs quickly, letting her grieve in private.

This part of the job never gets any easier, I think, shaking my head as I step outside into the crisp November air.

CHAPTER SIX

T he sidewalks fill with people clad in business suits heading home from work. Some nod at me as I walk past, but most keep their eyes straight ahead, focused on getting home after a long day. I'm jealous that they're nearly there, while I'm still looking at a few more hours of paperwork and procedure. Not to mention going over Emma's journal with Cross back at HQ. I wonder if he'll be able to find something in the scrawled words that I can't see.

I'm about halfway to my car when something catches my eye. Farther up the street, backlit by the slowly sinking sun, is a figure on the top of an apartment building. I squint and raise a hand to my brow as I try to block the light. Something makes me pick up my pace, and I find myself falling into a jog.

As I draw closer, the figure becomes more distinct. It's a young man, slightly scruffy, wearing a baggy T-shirt and jeans. He's looking out over the rooftops, and I wave, trying to get his attention. I can't tell if he makes out what I'm shouting as I scream at him to step back, but he turns in my direction, then stills. He's precariously close to the edge. If it scares him, there's no sign. He's motionless. Waiting. For a brief moment, it appears he's going to move back, but then his eyes lock with mine, he takes two careful steps forward and falls.

I break into a sprint, mindless, rushing toward him. I know I can't catch him, can't stop his fall, but part of me hopes that I'll be able to make a difference, somehow. His body turns as he falls, and he lands on the pavement two blocks ahead of me—faceup, eyes still on me—with a sound like a carton full of milk dropped on the ground.

Priya flies forward and presses her hands to the guy's body, trying to heal his injuries as best she can. I run, unable to keep up with her, my feet pounding against the sidewalk while pedestrians scream and back away. Someone fumbles with their phone, holding it up to shakily record what's happening, but I'm too distracted to tell them to put it away. I turn back to the guy, looking for any sign of life.

"Back up!" I shout to the growing crowd as I fall to the pavement next to him. Blood's everywhere, spreading out in a pool around his body. It seeps into my dress slacks, warm and nauseating. His neck is twisted, head broken open. Bits of his skull are embedded in his brain, and bile rises in my throat. His eyes are glassy and vacant. Priya looks at me and shakes her head, pulling her hands away. I let my head drop, hands resting on my thighs while I catch my breath.

I pull out my phone and dial 9-1-1. The operator picks up and asks for my emergency, and I start running through procedure. Badge number, location, situation.

"I'll have a team to your location as soon as possible," she says. I can hear her typing in the background, the clacking keys like softly breaking bones. I shiver, then glance back at the corpse. People are starting to gather around the body, a few folks holding others back when they try to get close. I sigh, uncomfortable with the growing crowd.

"There's a crowd forming," I say, throat tight. "I'm going to need that team here soon if I'm going to be able to keep the scene under control."

"Understood, Detective. I'll do what I can."

"And I need you to get Detective Riley Cross out here, too," I add quickly. "He's my partner."

"Can do, Detective. I'll make sure he's on his way."

I hang up the phone with a murmured thanks and turn to the victim. He's a college kid, way too young to be lying faceup and dead in the middle of the sidewalk. His shirt is faded and gray with some kind of logo emblazoned across the front in flaking letters, though blood is soaking into the worn fabric and obscuring most of the details. His head lolls away from me in an unnatural position against the ground, too loose on his neck, twisted past where the muscles and bones should let it go. His mouth is slightly open, blood staining his lips. It drips slowly onto the sidewalk, leaving a thin rivulet of red on his skin that joins the spreading pool beneath him. His eyes are open, the eyelids only slightly drooping. I shake my head and look back at the crowd.

As I start to stand, something grabs at my arm. I turn, puzzled then horrified at the bloody fingers tightly grasping my wrist. I think I hear someone scream, but I can't take my eyes from the broken fingers holding me in place. There's still warmth in the kid's body, the blood coating his hand hot and slick against my skin. I try to pull away, but his grip tightens, holding me still. The kid's head turns deliberately, muscles convulsing and bones cracking, and he looks up at me, smiling with broken, red teeth. The whites of his eyes are black, from blood or something else, I can't tell. His other hand twitches against the ground, spreading blood in erratic circles and slashes.

"Hello, Kim," he says, his voice crackling and wet with congealing blood. Priya flares, her hair whipping up in an unseen wind, and her eyes start to swirl with black streaks. She rushes forward, but stops suddenly, hands pressed against an unseen force. I can hear her screaming, but it's muffled. The sounds of the street fade, the now-speaking corpse the only thing I can hear, its grip on my wrist burning.

"It's a pleasure to meet you," it says as blood continues to seep out of its ears, eyes, and mouth. "I've waited so long to find you."

"What the fuck?" I ask, my throat tight.

"Oh, Kim," it says with a wet laugh. Blood flecks its lips, and it slowly licks it away, leaving a red smear behind. "It doesn't matter. I would have found you some way or another. I've been looking for you for a long time," it says, then starts to cough. Warm blood mists on my face. I wipe at my cheek with my free hand, body numb and sluggish.

"This vessel is failing. Find me. I can answer all of your questions then." The corpse tightens its grasp on my wrist for a second before it lets go and lunges for me. Its fingers scrabble at the collar of my jacket, then find purchase and pull me in close with unnatural strength. Broken bones shift, a quiet grating that I can feel more than hear, and my hand lands hard against the sidewalk to stop myself from falling onto the body.

Blood and decay taint the corpse's breath as it speaks again. "*Find me.*"

I finally wrench free, the corpse's hand falling limp to the ground, and tumble back onto the bloodstained sidewalk. Priya shrieks, shoving her way between me and the corpse, whatever was holding her back suddenly dissolved. For a split second, I see a darkness rise from its mouth. I blink and it's gone.

Sirens wail down the street, but they're muted. I wipe my bloodied wrist, trying to get the rust-stained streaks off my skin. The people behind me speak in hushed, frantic voices. Slowly, still wiping at my wrist, I clamber to my feet.

"Step back," I say, eyes unable to leave the body, its head tipped back toward me with vacant eyes. "This is a crime scene. I need you all to step back."

I turn, finally, and watch as the crowd moves away from me hesitantly. There's more than one cell phone up, pointed in my direction. I take a step forward and they move back, stumbling away.

"I'm a police officer," I say, pulling my badge from my jacket with numb, bloodstained fingers. "I need everyone to move to the other side of the street. Now."

A few heads nod, a few phones disappear, but most of the crowd stays still, staring.

"What was that?" The man's eyes are wide, watching

me with poorly disguised fear. He's wearing a black sports coat and khaki pants, a briefcase dangling from his hand.

"A suicide," I say, unable to keep his gaze for long. "Please, sir, I need you to move."

He stares at me in disbelief, then takes a step back before turning and crossing the street with the rest of the crowd.

Two cop cars pull to a stop in front of me, lights flashing and sirens screaming. The uniformed officer behind the wheel of the first car climbs, his partner joining him.

"Ma'am, I need you to join the rest of the crowd on the other side of the street."

"Detective Phillips," I say, showing him my badge, my voice somehow muffled in my own ears. "I called it in. Get the area cordoned off and do something about those people."

"Yes, Detective." He motions to his partner, who heads to the trunk of their car. He starts pulling out police tape, and I turn back to look at the corpse on the sidewalk, the still-growing pool of blood turning black as the light fades.

The ambulance shows up a few minutes later. Paramedics arrive and swarm around the body, and I feel a strong hand on my arm, pulling me away.

"Phillips, are you hurt?"

I turn toward the voice. It's Cross. His green eyes change to dizzying colors in the flashing red and blue lights of the squad cars.

I shake my head slowly. "No. No, I'm fine."

"Come with me, okay? I think you might be in shock. I'll help you get cleaned up."

I nod and follow him toward the back of an ambulance. The sirens cut off, though the lights are still flashing. Cross motions for a paramedic, who makes me sit on the tailgate of the ambulance. The paramedic hands me a damp cloth, and I start to absently clean off my face and wrist.

What was that? I ask Priya, still trying to process what just happened.

A dark thing was inside that man, she says, hovering close to me. I shiver.

Cross steps closer. "Do you need a blanket?"

"No," I say, wiping my face one more time. The cloth is stained a light red, and I set it down next to me quickly, then push it farther away.

A dark thing like when I was a kid? I Send to Priya, curling into myself under Cross's watchful gaze.

No, not like that. Whatever attacked you back then was a predator, something out to kill and hurt. This was a scavenger. Something that preys on the weak and the dead.

How did it know my name?

She doesn't answer, just hovers closer.

It's going to be okay, she says. She quickly brushes my hair back, tucking it behind my ear. *It's gone now, and those things can't just cross over. There are specific times and places where they can, and even then, not for long.*

"Phillips," Cross says, leaning in close to my face. He

raises a hand to my cheek, his fingers warm against my chilled skin. His thumb rests on my cheekbone for a long moment, palm cupping the curve of my jaw. I start to lean into it, a subconscious reflex to the comfort his touch offers, yet the moment is broken as he swipes his thumb over my skin and pulls his hand away.

"You missed some," he says quietly, grabbing the discarded cloth to clean his hand. "How is it that trouble just seems to find you?"

I shake my head and look away, ignoring his words and letting his familiar voice wash over me for a moment. Still a little shaken, I sense the numbness of shock fading; the weakness that accompanies it frustrates me. Priya settles next to me, concern radiating from her in soft waves.

Are you going to be all right?

Probably, I say, standing up and pushing my way past Cross, *but not right now.*

CHAPTER SEVEN

U sing a pair of gloves the paramedics gave me, I carefully remove Murphy's journal from my now-ruined pocket. Cross comes after me, grabbing my arm. I remember the feeling of broken fingers against my skin and shake his hand loose with more force than needed.

"What's wrong, Phillips?" he asks, pulling his hand back, face creased in a deep frown.

"Nothing." I turn and walk toward one of the uniformed police on scene.

"I need an evidence bag." I hold up the journal. "This is for a different case, but it's got blood on it and I need it bagged."

"Yes, ma'am," the officer says, heading toward the back of his squad car. He rummages through the trunk as Cross confronts me again.

"There's obviously something wrong," he says. "You just saw a man jump to his death. You're shaken up an—"

"That's not the problem," I say, turning on him. The shock gives way to a deep-seated fear, a cold emotion that roils in my gut and spreads out to my hands and feet in numbing waves.

"Talk to me," Cross says, stepping closer.

"It talked to me," I say, the words rushing out before I can stop them.

"What?" His voice rises an octave, his confusion evident.

"*It* talked to me."

The uniform interrupts us to hand me the evidence bag. I drop the journal in, then fold the top down a few times until the bag and book are a small, compact package.

"Where's your car?" I ask Cross, walking away from the scene, needing distance.

"Right over here"—he follows closely—"but you need to stop and explain to me what you meant. The jumper was still alive when you got to him?"

"Is it unlocked?" I ask as I try the door handle for the passenger seat. It pops open, and I throw the paper evidence bag inside.

"Goddammit, Phillips," Cross says, pushing me away from the door and slamming it shut. "What the hell is going on?"

For a moment, it seems like I can't breathe. Cross is furious and confused, his body taut with anger, face creased with worry. My hands start shaking, and I pull the latex gloves from my fingers with a stinging snap. As I try to figure out what to do with them, Cross grabs them from me, tosses them to the street, and goes back to staring at me.

"That guy... He wasn't alive," I say, folding my arms across my chest, holding tight so I won't shake. "He was dead. There was bone in his brain, I could *see it.* There's no way he would have been able to move or speak. But... Cross, there was something *in* him. A spirit or... or something, and it took over his body and spoke to me. It knew my name."

I can't stop the stream of words coming from my mouth. Panic is heavy on my tongue, and I can feel the tattered remains of my calm falling to pieces around me as I speak.

"How did it know my name?" I ask, looking up at him for an answer I know he can't provide.

"Slow down." Cross opens the car door again. "C'mon, get inside."

I climb into the car and he shuts the door behind me. It's warmer inside than out, the heat still hanging around from his drive to the scene. I watch as he walks around the hood and pulls open the driver side door, falling inside, the motion somehow graceful and careless at the same time.

"All right," he says, turning the ignition and cranking the heater. "You're going to take a deep breath, try to calm yourself down, and then you're going to tell me what happened."

I bristle at the slightly condescending tone. "I don't need you taking care of me," I say, voice biting, and he grins.

"That's the Kim Phillips I know. Tough as nails, takes no shit. Now"—he leans back to rest his body between the seat and the door, giving me space—"tell me what happened."

With a nod and a deep breath, I try to explain what

took place. Cross keeps his eyes on my face, expression thoughtful, until I finish. The heat from the car and his calm regard help me stay centered, but my hand trembles a little as I brush my hair away from my face.

"I'm guessing from your reaction that this isn't something that happens a lot in your world?"

"No," I say, shaking my head. "Possession happens, but it's generally people the ghost knew or was connected to in life."

"Did you know the guy? The jumper?"

"No, I've never seen him before."

"And the spirit," Cross asks, "it just asked you to find it?"

"Yeah, and that's the weirder part," I say, frowning.

Cross raises an eyebrow. "Weirder than a corpse talking to you?"

I roll my eyes. "Kind of. Most spirits, they don't have anything to *find*. Unless they're Turning, they stay with their body or in the place where they were killed. If this spirit knows where it is and knows that it wants me to find it, why not just tell me?"

"You're sure it's a spirit?"

"I don't know what else it might be," I say, confused and a little scared.

"What about a Passenger?" Cross asks, and my eyebrows shoot up.

"Look who's been doing his homework," I say.

He shoots me a glare. "Seriously, though. They can do that kind of stuff, right? Take over someone? Possess them?"

"Yeah, but the closest one I know of is in Ohio. No way he'd be able to Ride—sorry, possess someone in Chicago. The distance is too far."

"Your powers," Cross starts, voice tentative, "it's all dependent on how powerful the Medium is, right? A strong Reader gets more out of an object than a weak one, right?"

"Basically. It depends on the Affinity."

"So a more powerful Passenger could possess someone from farther away than a weak one."

"And for longer," I say. "But this is all moot. Passengers don't possess the dead, and that guy was definitely dead."

"Maybe," Cross says, frowning. "We're going to have a hell of a time writing this all up."

I balk. "How do we write it up? Corpse talked to detective on scene? Corpse scared the shit out of said detective?"

"I don't know," he says, sighing loudly, "but we can't *not* write it up. It's significant. If this guy was possessed by *something*, that means it may not be a suicide. It's got to go into the report."

"I know." I kick my feet up onto the dash. "I just... None of this makes sense."

Cross doesn't answer, just watches me for a long, quiet minute. Blue and red lights still flash around us, glancing off the surrounding buildings and the crowd that still, persistently, hangs around. It cuts through the night, somehow comforting, and I feel my shoulders sag.

"Fine. I'll write up the report. You look it over and add what you can. But not now. Tomorrow morning. I need to go home, get this blood off me…" I shudder, looking at the red stains on my knees.

"You need me to walk you back to your car?" Cross asks, sitting up and reaching for the keys.

"No," I bite out. "I do not need you to walk me to my car. I'm fine."

There's a quick flash of a grin, and he's reaching past me to pull open the passenger door. I'm still slightly leaning against it, and it gives way quickly beneath my weight. I catch myself and glare at him.

"Get your ass home, Phillips." He grins widely as he buckles himself in. "I'll see you in the morning."

"Bye," I say, tone less than pleasant. I grab Emma's journal from the floor of the car, then slide out before slamming the door shut with enough force to rattle the glass in the window. I check in with the uniforms on scene, as well as the crime scene unit that showed up while Cross and I talked. We go over the details briefly, noting that the victim's body is bagged and ready for transit.

"Get it to Dr. Abramo," I say, "and make sure he knows it's my case. I'll need to talk to him later."

I hold onto the journal, setting it down on the passenger seat of my car as I climb in and drive away. When I make it home, I start stripping the moment I enter the living room. Each bloodstained piece of clothing goes into the kitchen trash until I'm standing in just my underwear and socks. I head to the bathroom, take a perfunctory shower, and collapse into bed.

I open my eyes, and I'm in the abandoned building again, the locker-filled hallway stretching out before me. Slowly, that first nightmare comes back in jagged, painful pieces. I start to curse and turn, heading away from the hallway. Glancing behind me, I try to see the man in the wheelchair. There's only the creaking sound of the building shifting and my too-loud footsteps echoing around the hallway.

I close my eyes and reach out with my senses. After a long moment, I feel a creeping darkness moving toward me. Somewhere in this place is something that sets my skin crawling. I sense it reaching back and I quickly pull away. There's a dark spirit here that's shielded or warded, but aware. Awake.

I start walking again, heading away from where the figure last was. The building is falling to pieces, literally. Acoustic tiles hang from the ceiling; dark gaping holes open into the upper structure of the building. Light fixtures hang from tangled wires, swinging gently as I move past. I glance around the walls, all covered in scrawled marks that look like runes or sigils. Some flare to life as I pass, flashing bright blue-white for an instant, then dying. At the corner of two intersecting hallways, there's a white sign that says "ward" in faded letters.

It must be a hospital, I think, brushing my fingers against the sign. They come away covered in dust, but the letters are as faded and unclear as they were before.

I speed up, heading toward a set of double doors. I'm running as I reach them and burst into a large rotunda, clearly the entryway to wherever this place is. There's a desk with scattered papers, and plastic chairs are spread around the room. I head toward the front door, sprinting, and slam into it, my palms out. The door rattles but refuses to move. I try putting my shoulder into it, but I can't get it to budge.

Spotting a glass pane in the top half of the door, I scrawl quick runes—ones of breaking and shattering, of destruction—and tie them with a sigil and blood.

The window lights up, then shatters into spider webs. I go to reach through the empty frame, but my hand stops, fingers and palm pressed against the empty air as if the glass were still there.

"Shit," I say, stepping back from the door. I pace, letting my fingers run through my hair and feel a smudge of blood on my forehead.

Whatever wards are holding the spirit at bay, they must cover the entire building. Looking around the room, I spot papers scattered everywhere. When I pick one up, though, it crumbles to dust. The other pages that lie on the floor are illegible, the text long since faded.

A breeze kicks up in the front entryway. Soon, it speeds up and my hair whips around my face, the papers scattering into the air in a whirlwind.

Something is coming.

The doors I'd come through blow open, crashing off their hinges to slam into the far wall. Slowly, the man in the wheelchair rolls out into the entryway. His eyes shine bright red when he looks up, and his mouth splits into a familiar and broken grin. Writhing behind him are the shadow creatures, their bodies filled with shifting and changing runes. They circle him but are pushed back by unseen hands, their dark bodies tearing into ragged strips.

"Welcome back, Kim," he says, and it sounds like rocks grinding together, like the earth shifting, like bones breaking against concrete. I cringe and reach out blindly for my power, desperate for protection of any kind.

And then I wake up.

Priya hovers over me when I jerk out of bed. She quickly runs her hands over my shoulders and down my arms, lingering over my sweating hands. The coolness of her brings goosebumps to my skin, but it calms me down and I can breathe again.

Another nightmare? she asks, still running her hands over my skin.

"Yeah. I think it was the same place." I say it aloud, relaxing into the solidity of my voice in the dark apartment. Head resting on my knees, I sigh. "I'm fucking tired," I groan.

Priya runs her hands through my hair, soothing. She doesn't say anything, but her presence is comfort enough.

It's dark outside, but the street is brightly lit against the black of night. The light casts shadows in the hallway that seem to shift and dance to my too-tired eyes. It takes me a moment to gather the courage—feeling like a child again, scared of things I can't see—but I eventually lie back down and push my feet to the end of the bed.

My eyes slowly adjust to the darkness. I can hear the city just outside my window, cars and people bustling around even though it's late. The sheets are warm around my legs, but I can't shake the coldness from my bones, the pounding, aching fear that was coursing through me as I woke. Even working hand in hand with death for a decade, I still fear it. The primal, primeval part of me, the hindbrain, which keeps me breathing and my heart beating even while I'm asleep, is scared to die, scared to go into that unknown world that we all eventually fall into. Being a Medium doesn't help. If anything, it makes it worse, because I know exactly how bad things can turn out.

When I was fourteen and going out with Taka on our first Burning together, I saw how bad it could get. I was excited, ready to take on a ghost who'd been tormenting an apartment building on the southwest side. From the research Taka had done, the guy was a World War II vet who died in the building. He had a lot of built-up anger and was becoming increasingly violent. Breaking windows, trying to throw people down the stairs. He broke the elevator while it was full, sending it careening down until the safety brakes screeched to life.

There's a point where you just can't let ghosts hang around any longer, when they Turn into something dark and dangerous. It's different for each one and depends on who they were before they died and where they linger. It took Priya nearly fifty years before she started to Turn. This guy didn't last half that long. Once a ghost starts to Turn, there are only two choices: to Bind or to Burn.

The Burning started normally. The ghost was quiet, so Taka and I were able to get in and set up uninterrupted. I drew the circle, made sure that everything was perfect. Taka was nervous and wouldn't stop pacing. A Medium's first Burning is always the most dangerous. More than one apprentice has been burned out, too. They reach too far, too fast, and end up losing their powers and their connection to the afterlife.

Taka was halfway through checking my work when the ghost arrived. He was angry and confused, and everything quickly got out of hand. Wheeling around the room, the ghost created a massive cyclone of wind, kicking debris into the air. Taka and Claire, his partner, tried to control it, to protect me. I remember my hair whipping around in the wind so hard, it left welts.

Taka screamed at me to activate the circle, pushing me forward in one giant rush. That first time, I'd cut too deep, too hard. Blood poured out of my finger, staining the floor. It activated the circle, which Burnt the ghost, but the blood that was outside of it, the blood that broke those carefully drawn lines, was just enough to let something else through.

There's power in a Medium's blood. It's part of who we are, part of what makes us able to speak to the dead, to channel their power into ourselves and change the world around us. Blood alone is enough to let things through that shouldn't pass the barrier between life and death.

What clung to me after Burning Emma, what may have clung to that poor man after he died, was just a little thing, a scavenger looking to gain brief access to life. That day, so many years ago, hunched on my knees, hair tangled around my face, I spilled enough blood to cross the line from scavenger to predator.

I don't remember everything from that moment on. There was a shooting pain up my arm, a darkness crawling beneath my skin. I clawed at my arm, trying to pull it out. I screamed my throat raw.

Taka had to hold me down. I was convulsing by that point. Whatever I'd let in tried to take control of my body. Claire reached into me, held the core of my soul in her freezing hands, as he wrestled with the dark thing that invaded my body. Some nights, I can still feel it. Like something writhing beneath my skin, looking for the chance to escape.

I close my eyes to the streetlight seeping into my room, body aching and mind spinning. I start to drift, falling into exhaustion. There's a soft, cool wind above me, and phantom but familiar fingers brush my hair back.

I'll keep watch, she murmurs. *I'll keep you safe.*

I quietly fall into dreamless sleep.

CHAPTER EIGHT

District HQ is nearly empty the next morning. It's early Tuesday and most of the officers have yet to arrive. Cross is hunched over his desk, a half-forgotten bagel sitting to the side of his keyboard near a cup of coffee. I pull my chair back from my desk and sit heavily. He gives me a quick nod and goes back to typing. After pecking out my password, I wait for Windows to load up. I have paperwork to catch up on, including the report on what happened yesterday, and a few other cases I need to follow up on. There's an e-mail from the Lieutenant marked high priority. Its bright red exclamation point glares at me from the monitor. I minimize the program, then stare blankly at my screen for a long moment.

Cross finally drags his attention from his computer to frown at me. "Where've you been? You're in late."

"Coffee took too long to brew," I say, placing my arms on my desk and laying my head on top of them.

After a beat of silence, I hear Cross shift in his chair.

"You all right?"

"Yeah, yeah. I'm fine," I say, trying to get control over the small ball of panic that's still living in my chest. The nightmare and the jumper have me shaken, though one is indistinct, hazy, and the other is as vivid as spilled blood. I take a deep breath to steady myself and lift my head, sitting up. "What'd you find out?"

"Not much more on Murphy, but we've got a potential suspect. I was going door-to-door with some uniforms yesterday, passing out copies of the sketch you helped with, and a couple of people recognized him. Said his name's Jerry or Barry, something like that. The beat cops I talked to said he's been in and out of trouble the last couple of years, but all minor stuff. Disturbing the peace, minor shoplifting, those kinds of things. From the way the residents described it, though..."

"I'm guessing not good," I say.

"Not even slightly." Cross shifts his weight, leaning forward. "Now, I don't know if any of this is pertinent or not, but from what most of the people working in that area said, he's a nuisance. Breaks into cars, steals packages off porches, sneaks into buildings, that kind of stuff. One of the women I talked to said he followed her home and tried to get into her garage. She called 9-1-1, but he left before the police could get there, so there's really nothing on the record about it. And besides a couple of complaints filed by folks in the neighborhood, there's nothing on the books about the guy."

"Has anyone seen him recently?" I ask, feeling the first stirring of hope since we started working the case.

"That's the funny thing," Cross says, leaning back and crossing his arms. "No one's seen him in the past two days. It's like he just vanished."

"Brilliant. So, what're we going to do?"

"I've got the beat cops on the watch for him. If this guy shows up anywhere, they'll detain him and give me a call."

I nod.

"I also came across some info on our jumper." He passes me a folder. "Name's James Moore. He was a Shaker, in town for graduate classes at the University of Chicago. No idea how he ended up in Archer Heights. No one remembers seeing him leave, but they also don't remember seeing him that morning. We've contacted his next of kin and they're coming out here to get the body in a day or so. There's no history of mental illness, depression, or suicidal tendencies. The medical examiner's sent out for toxicology, but we probably aren't going to hear back on that for a couple of weeks at the earliest."

"You said he was a Shaker?" I ask, opening the folder.

"Yeah, a good one, apparently. He was still in school, but he'd made the local news at least once. You remember that bridge that collapsed in Cleveland a couple months ago?"

"Yeah," I say. "Some Mediums saved a passenger train, kept the track under it until it crossed a ravine, right?"

"Right. Apparently, he was one of them. He'd just been offered a job to do work on a deep-sea drilling platform off the coast of Africa. Pretty lucrative work. You've got to wonder why he'd jump."

"Yeah," I say, closing the folder and sliding it to Cross. I pinch the bridge of my nose.

He pauses, then coughs. "Could it have been that... thing that you saw? That talked to you?"

"No," I say, shaking my head. "From what Priya could tell, it wasn't a powerful spirit, just something jumping into the kid after he died."

"So you don't think he was possessed?"

"I mean, he could've been"—I shake my head—"but he was a powerful Shaker, and ghosts tend to possess the weaker people out there, ones who aren't fully Mundane, lacking in powers but who aren't fully Mediums. The people in between."

"And Moore definitely wasn't in between. So, what, something tried to take over his body?" Cross looks aghast, his face paling.

"It can happen sometimes, especially with Mediums who pass suddenly or unexpectedly, but it doesn't last long and whatever takes residence is generally weak. We Burn the more powerful spirits or Bind them. They don't have a chance to hang around or take over bodies."

"The more you tell me about this shit," Cross says, his skin still slightly ashen, "the more I think I should be seriously worried."

"No. You're completely Mundane. I've never picked up even a hint of any power in you. You're about as safe as it can get."

Cross sighs, but he still looks troubled.

"Oh, and there's this," I add, pulling the evidence bag containing Emma's journal from my desk. I hold it out to Cross, who frowns and takes it.

"I saw it last night. What is it?"

"A journal that Emma kept with her aunt," I say.

Before he opens the bag, he eyes me questioningly. I nod, and he pulls it out. He immediately flips to where my bookmark is and starts reading for a quiet moment.

"This sounds like what Ruth Peterson was telling us about," he says, passing the journal over to me, his finger resting on a line. "Read that part."

I can't get rid of him, no matter how hard I try, I read. *He's trying to get in my head, trying to take over. I can't let him. Something bad will happen if I do, I know it. I don't understand how I know it, but if I let this thing in, I'm going to die.*

I shiver and pass the journal back.

"Maybe she found a ghost, one who was about to Turn," Cross continues. "This thing hounds her. She goes to her aunt for help because she doesn't want her mentor to find out. Maybe she's convinced her mentor will drop her, who knows? Murphy tries to communicate with this thing, to stop it from bothering her anymore, and bam, it takes its chance."

"Whether she was being dogged by a ghost or not, someone flesh and blood still killed her," I say, shaking my head.

"You think it might've been trying to possess her? She was still in training."

I shake my head. "It's hard for ghosts to possess people with any kind of Medium training. We know what to look out for, know how to stop it, even at the beginning. People with power who are untrained are the ones ghosts target. If a mentor thinks you're going to be a full Medium, they make damn sure that nothing is going to crawl inside you and take up residence."

"Then maybe one of the bums, this Barry guy? Could explain why she was killed by a person and not a ghost."

"That'd make sense," I say, "but he'd have to have some kind of connection to the afterlife."

Cross tilts his head, thinking. "So, we look for this guy, see if he has any scratch marks and some kind of connection to the afterlife, even minor, compare his DNA to what we found on the victim, and we've got our killer."

"Except, if our killer was a Turned ghost, putting this guy in jail isn't going to help."

Cross leans back in his chair. "Good point." He sighs and shakes his head. "That's why I hate working these kinds of cases. This supernatural shit gets confusing real quick."

I sigh and let my head drop back, staring at the ceiling.

"So, first things first, we find this guy and question him. In the meantime, we do follow-up on our jumper. You have a report to write if I remember."

"That I do," I say, scooting closer to my desk and launching Word.

It's a couple of hours before we're able to head over to Moore's apartment. We nearly call a judge for a search warrant, but Cross finally hears back from Moore's next of kin. The car ride over is fairly short—Hyde Park, just a quick drive from district HQ. Cross turns on the news, and the first story is about a jumper in Archer Heights.

Silently, we share a look and I turn off the radio.

We pull up to an older brick building with a small courtyard and park in front. A low set of stairs is nestled between the wings of the building, and Cross waves me ahead of him as he locks up the car.

"C'mon, let's get inside." His breath frosts in the cold air.

There's a small alcove in the center of each wing, and we head toward the one on the left. Cross buzzes one of the apartments listed next to the door, which clicks open a second later. We walk in, Cross shaking his hands out and muttering about getting better gloves, when an old, hunched man comes toddling down the main hallway toward us.

"You the folks who called earlier today?" the super asks, voice scratchy and surprisingly high.

"Somewhat, sir," Cross says, pulling his badge out and passing it to the man. "I'm Detective Cross, this is Detective Phillips. We're here to see James Moore's apartment."

The old man furrows his brow. "That's right, that's right. His cousin called me, said you'd be coming."

He turns and toddles back the way he came. A few moments later, he returns with a heavy set of keys jangling in his hand. Pushing past Cross and me, he slowly makes his way up the stairs.

Moore's on the third floor, and it takes a long time to get there. The super doesn't move quickly, placing first one foot then the other on the same step. When we finally get to the apartment, he fiddles with his large key ring. He jams a key into the lock, gives it a sharp twist, and pushes the door open, waving us inside. The door shuts loudly behind us, and Cross flips on the lights.

Dirty laundry litters the floor, a pile of old pizza boxes takes up a side table, and a large TV fills one full wall. Moore's apartment looks like it's out of a prime-time comedy show about bachelor men in their early-twenties. Video games and DVD cases line hand-me-down bookshelves, and the few books that I can see are covered in yellow "USED" stickers. Most of them have to do with deep-sea drilling, but as I finish making my walk-through of the main living area and head into the small room leading off the kitchen, I'm surrounded by piles of stuff on Mediums. Legal pads are scattered about the table, as well as books still open to dog-eared pages.

"What was he looking up?" Cross asks as he walks in behind me.

"Not sure," I murmur, leaning in to read a highlighted passage.

"These are library books," Cross says, sounding scandalized.

I roll my eyes and slip on a pair of gloves before I flip to the front cover. A small pocket has been glued to the inside. A bar-coded list is tucked into it, with a date from last week printed to the side.

"And there are a lot of them," I murmur, opening the book back up to where Moore left it. After a moment, I flip the book to the front cover again.

"It looks like he's researching his family... or at least people with his last name," I say, looking through the table of contents quickly, then opening back to Moore's marked page. "He's highlighted a lot of stuff about a Caroline Moore."

Cross leans in to look at the book over my shoulder. I can feel his breath on my neck, suddenly, painfully aware of how close he's standing, and I shiver. He reaches his arm out, brushing against me, and lays his fingers on the page near mine. I pull my hand away after a long moment and step out of the cage of his body.

"Who's Caroline Moore?" he asks, stepping forward to fill the space I just left.

"No idea," I say. "Judging by this, she was a powerful Shaker from about a century ago. I'd have to do some research to find out more."

That name sounds familiar, Priya says, leaning closer to the book. *Very familiar. Are there any pictures in here?*

No idea, I say. *Take a look for yourself.*

The pages in the book start to turn on their own, Priya's fingers flicking over the edges just enough to move the paper. Cross takes a step back, then quickly gains his composure.

"Could it be a genealogy?"

"Maybe," I say, picking up another one of the books. A brief look shows more highlighted passages about Caroline Moore.

"Doesn't really tell us why he jumped off the roof, though," Cross says, straightening and heading into the small kitchen.

"I don't know," I say, flipping idly through the book.

"If I had to research my family, I might consider it."

"That bad, huh?" Cross asks, looking through the kitchen drawers.

"You could say that."

He lets my statement go, then keeps searching the kitchen. I head toward the back of the apartment. The bathroom smells faintly of mildew. There's a towel crumpled on the floor, along with dirty laundry. I open the medicine cabinet and find an old Taco Bell wrapper, but otherwise nothing unusual. There's cold medicine, Band-Aids, some Q-Tips, and a thin layer of dust on most of it. No prescriptions, nothing that might clue me in to what was going on in this kid's head.

His bedroom is farther down the hall, and it's more of the same. Dirty clothes, unmade bed, nightstand with an alarm clock and a small lamp. There are more books on the floor, a journal tucked underneath them. I open it up and flip the pages idly. Most of his notes are about his family history, where they settled, who married whom. Toward the end, though, the notes start getting disjointed. I walk out of the bedroom with the journal to find Cross looking through Moore's other notes.

"Well, the bathroom was a bust," I say, handing him the journal after he looks up at me. "But this might be useful."

"What is it?" Cross asks, opening the book and flipping through quickly.

"More of his research. Starts out talking about his family history, but it takes a pretty sharp turn toward the end."

Cross opens to the back, then starts reading. I sort through the rest of Moore's research, looking at the books left open on the table. There's more and more about Shaker history, but buried under a pile of papers and Post-its, there's a plain book, its title in gilt on the cover: *On the Summoning and Capturing of Spirits through the Use of Inscribed Circles by Jefferson Moore.*

I open it up, thumb through it quickly. A lot of it is pretty basic stuff, things I studied during my apprenticeship, though a little old-fashioned. The topics become increasingly esoteric the farther into the book I go. The last chapter is simply titled *On the Binding of Mediums.*

I frown. Pulling out a chair, I sit and turn to the back of the book.

Occasionally, it reads, *a Medium must be Bound. There are dark temptations that taunt and beckon us all, and those who give in to their call are stained and forever marred by them. These Mediums, who have trespassed into the dark realm and therefore lost some of their humanity, become darkness themselves. In order to stop them from bringing their darkness into the world, they must be Bound.*

The passages after that start talking about how to scribe the circle, what items are needed, and the Mediums required to perform the ceremony. I don't recognize most of what the book talks about, and I turn to the front of the book to check the publication date.

"This thing is ancient," I say, shocked. The original printing is from the early 1800s, with subsequent editions printed until the early 1900s, when the dates end.

"Why was Moore looking into circles?" Cross asks, closing the journal and sliding it into an evidence bag.

"The book was written by one of his ancestors, or at least it looks like it was," I say. "He must have found it while he was doing his genealogy research. It's pretty interesting once you get past the basics. There's stuff in here that I've never heard of before. I can understand picking it up for the hell of it."

"I still don't see anything that tells me this guy was looking to kill himself," Cross says. "So, why'd he jump?"

"No idea." I shake my head.

As I stand and prepare to put the book down, something glints off the back cover and catches my eye. In the corner, embossed on the worn cover, is a circle, with a line dividing it into two halves, another arcing up across the center.

"Cross, look," I say, pulling the book closer.

"What?" He peers over my shoulder.

"I've seen this somewhere before." I point to the mark. "But I can't... I don't remember exactly."

"Could it be a printer's mark or some kind of branding for the publishing house?"

"Maybe. It's an old book, it could've been custom bound or the mark could've been added later. I'm going to hold onto this, do some research and see if I can figure out what it is."

"Sounds good. Maybe you can find out why this guy was looking into his family."

"If you've got this, I'll head out now," I say, tucking the book against my side.

"Yeah," Cross says, distracted. He places his hands on

his hips, then settles his weight back on his heels, frowning. "I just don't get it."

"Me, either."

He sighs again, then nods toward the door. "C'mon, let's go."

We step through the doorway, turning the lights off behind us. A shiver races up my spine, and I turn back toward the dim interior of the apartment. I sense something's watching, waiting. When I drop into Second-Sight, though, there's nothing. Just more darkness.

CHAPTER NINE

A fter Cross drops me outside of HQ, I get into my car and head toward the Newberry Library. The roads are clogged and slow, weekday tourists and students filling up the streets. It takes me awhile to find parking, but I manage to squeeze my car into a spot near Washington Square Park. I cut through the park, walking past couples holding hands and groups of women drinking coffee and laughing. Everything is awash in color, with leaves changing on the trees and littering the ground. It smells slightly of car exhaust and something burned, and the wind nips at my nose and cheeks. I pull my coat tighter around my neck as a gust of wind works its way into the gaps of my collar to tickle my skin with icy fingers.

There's a smaller building attached to the main library, and I push my way inside, thankful for the warmth. While the Newberry itself focuses on a wide variety of subjects, including the history of Mediums in and around Chicago and the Midwest, the Victoria Carter Memorial Library focuses solely on Mediums and our history. It's one of the most expansive libraries on Mediums in the US, and, thankfully, after years of making the right kind of contacts, I've got access.

The librarian, a woman I've worked with for years whose name I've never managed to learn, looks up from the front desk and smiles.

"Detective Phillips," she says. "What brings you in today?"

"I'm doing some research for a case I'm working. I need to look up any Mediums with the last name Moore from around the last century."

Her eyebrows creep up toward her hairline. "That's going to take me awhile to hunt down. Do you know if the family line had any sort of Affinity, or were they a more scattered lot?"

"The few I'm aware of were Shakers. One was named Caroline Moore?"

"Ah, yes. That will help immensely. It's always easier to find the rarer Affinities—fewer resources to search through, and names always help. Now, if you were looking for a Burner, we'd be here all week." She smiles, then motions toward the hallway. "Go ahead and make yourself comfortable in the reading room and I'll bring you what I find."

"Thanks," I say, heading deeper into the building. The hallway splits into a T, a wide set of dark wood doors directly in front of me. I push my way inside. The reading room is a wide-open space with well-lit tables spaced out in neat, orderly rows. The walls are paneled in the same wood as the doors, giving the room a sense of historic grandeur. It's easy for me to imagine the people who used to spend their time here as a few of them still hang around as ghosts. Today, the room is nearly empty of the living and the dead. My footsteps echo loudly on the marble tiled floor. For a second, I'm taken back to the warehouse where Murphy was found, the ricocheting sounds reminding me of that empty and abandoned place. I shake it off, then sit down at one of the computers along the edge of the room, signing in and powering up Google.

A quick search for Caroline Moore pulls up a stub article on Wikipedia with a few external links. Some of them are broken, leading me to 404 pages with frowning emoticons, but one checks out. I'm about halfway through reading a basic biography when the librarian comes back, pushing a cart laden with books.

"You got lucky," she says, kicking on a brake on the cart. "The Moores were apparently a well-known family, especially that Caroline."

"Great, thanks."

Most of the books are general histories of Mediums in the Midwest. According to them, the Moores were a large family that settled in Ohio during the early 1800s. In the years leading up to the American Civil War, they started being more active in the abolitionist movement, becoming some of the leading Medium voices for the cause. During Reconstruction, they headed to a ravaged Atlanta to help rebuild. Most of them were Shakers.

I knew that name was familiar, Priya says. She starts flipping pages quickly, and I see the librarian stand up, looking concerned.

Priya, you're gonna get us kicked out of here, I say, trying to get her to stop.

Just hold on a second, she says. The pages slow, but she

keeps flipping through them until she reaches a full-page photo of the Moore family.

That woman, she says, pointing to a younger woman in the front row. *I know her. She was much older, but that's her. That's Caroline Moore.*

The photo is grainy and faded, but I can make out the woman's characteristics. She looks like James, at least a little. Her name is in small print under the photo.

Why's she so important? I ask, flipping to the back of one of the general reference books, looking through the index for her name.

She was extremely powerful, Priya says, helping me flip to a brief biography of Caroline. *And very well known. Even though she wasn't a Burner, she played an integral role in helping deal with some of the more powerful Turned ghosts in the Midwest. I met her in the last couple of years of my life, and she was still quite strong. She was an important figure in the community.*

And she was related to James?

It should be relatively easy to find out, she says. I nod start pulling books off the cart to look through. Priya and I end up falling into a quiet rhythm, exchanging information as we go.

It looks like he was *related to her. I think he was her grand or great-grandson.*

Do you think this could be a vendetta? Like it might be with Murphy? That thing that was in him, can Mediums call those?

Priya loudly closes the book she's looking through. *You know better than to ask about the darker side of our powers, Kim.* She sighs and settles. *Harnessing those spirits is dangerous and difficult. For those who attempt it, there's a cost, one that other Mediums can sense almost immediately. It takes part of your soul to try to manipulate those things. It leaves you twisted, and it only gets worse over time, whether you call any more spirits or not. There's a residual darkness left from working with them. Most Mediums won't try to attempt it, and the practice has thankfully almost entirely died out. There were a few people in my time who practiced it, but they were... taken care of.*

But it can be done.

I've heard of it happening, yes, she says begrudgingly.

Priya, there are two Mediums dead within days of each other, both of them connected with some unknown dark spirit and a potential for a grudge. We need to find out if there's any connection between Murphy and Moore, see if they knew each other or if they were acquainted in any way. This could lead somewhere if we're able to prove that someone had a reason to go after both of them.

I don't know, she says, closing another book. *Moore was certainly possessed* after *he died, but there's almost no chance that he was possessed before he died. It's hard enough for ghosts to take over someone with Medium training. I can't imagine doing it to a Shaker, especially a powerful one, would be even remotely possible.*

I sigh and lean back in my chair. *There's more going on than what we're seeing. I just feel like there's a connection here, somehow.* I shake my head and close out of the browser. *Maybe the tox report will come back with something we can use. If he was drunk or high, it might explain why he was on the roof or why he got so close to the edge.*

It's going to take time, Priya says.

I know. But it's the only thing we've got right now. If he was depressed, no one else knew it, and there certainly weren't any signs at his apartment.

I run my hand over my face and pull out my phone. It's later than I expect, and I close up quickly. I wave to the librarian as I walk past her, and she waves back. I pause, then turn around.

"Can you do me a favor?" I ask.

"Absolutely, Detective. What do you need?"

"Can you find out if there's anyone in the Moore family, the one you pulled for me earlier, who's high profile? Just anyone in the family who's connected to the government or money or anything?"

She frowns. "I'll check with our genealogy department, see what they can find out. It'll take some time, though."

"That's fine, thank you." I pull out a business card and scribble my cell on the back. "You can reach me at this number whenever, just call me if you find something."

She smiles and tucks the card into her desk. "Will do."

It's overcast when I step outside, the gentle gusts of wind from earlier now cutting and sharp. I open my car and dial Cross.

"Hey, Phillips," he says. "What d'you got?"

"Moore," I say as I pull into traffic. "His family's basically all Shakers, some pretty big ones, and..." I pause, still uncertain, but going with my gut. "I think there's a chance that this may have been some kind of vendetta, like with Murphy."

"Except we don't have any proof that Murphy's death was an attack against Ruth Peterson, and James Moore jumped off the top of a building of his own will. You have anything to prove your theory?" he asks.

"Maybe." I scrub my hand over my face. "Okay, likely not. If the tox screen comes back and there's nothing there, we really aren't going to have anything to point to for why he decided to kill himself."

"I don't know, Phillips," he says, sighing into the phone. "You know if you can't find the evidence to support your argument, you aren't going to be able to bring it in as motive. And even if it ends up being a vendetta, how are you going to find out who did it?"

"I don't know," I say. "There's just something about this that's telling me the two cases are connected."

"Well, if your gut can provide some evidence, then I'll start considering your theory. But what I see right now are two unconnected deaths. I know Moore's suicide was rough to watch and I'm sorry you had to go through that, but people kill themselves all the time."

"Yeah, I know. You're right." I shake my head, sighing. "Sorry, it's probably because they're both Mediums, you know? We're a small community; it's hard to lose one person, much less two."

"I know."

"I'm headed down to the morgue. I want to see if I can get anything off Moore's body. You want to join me?"

"No, I've got stuff to do at HQ. Paperwork to fill out, people to call, journalists to chase off, the usual. Let me know what you find?"

"Yeah, can do. I'll swing by before I head home for the night."

"Sounds good. Take care of yourself, all right?"

"I will," I say, smiling again.

The medical examiner's office is fairly quiet. It's late, the roads clear of traffic, and there are only a few people milling around in the lobby, mainly uniformed officers and medical staff. I head to the receptionist and quickly give her my credentials.

"I'm here about James Moore," I say, taking my badge back.

"Down the hall," she says. "First bay on the left."

"Thanks."

I head toward the bay slowly, the stress of the past couple of days laying heavy on me. As I push the door open, I see Moore lying on the slab, body pale white and waxy where it peeks out from beneath the sheet that covers most of him. There's a box by the door with purple nitrile gloves, and I slide on a pair, then remove the sheet.

Abramo hasn't performed the autopsy yet, so Moore's chest is still in one piece. Or, at least, it's stubbornly trying to stay in one piece. His torso bulges in places where it shouldn't. His skin is shockingly white, but the places where his ribs have burst through are a dark red that's nearly purple, sharp pieces of yellow-white bone breaking through bruised skin. There are still tracks of blood around his mouth, nose, and foggy, hazel eyes. They bulge in their sockets, his head deformed, the skull crushed in the back.

The major bones of his body are broken so badly, it's twisted his frame into a gut-wrenching approximation of a human shape, and his arms and legs, though arranged carefully by some lab assistant, aren't perfectly straight. His left foot lies flat on the table, though his leg is rotated slightly inward, his knee pointing toward the ceiling. The sight should nauseate me, but as I stare at the body and it fails to speak to me, fails to turn its eyes to meet mine, I find myself quiet and detached. Perfectly calm.

I drop into Second-Sight to examine the body. Even after death, there's still some remnant of the soul that inhabited it. If the person turns into a ghost, that remnant will solidify and slowly separate itself from its body. If they pass, it dissipates, disappears into the afterlife. I expect to see something like that with Moore, some semblance of the guy still lingering, but fading. Instead, I'm forced to squint, his body flaring into sharp, unexpected light.

All over his body are sigils and runes, lines connecting them into a complicated circle. Most of the symbols are centered around his throat, wrists, and chest, but they spread outward, covering nearly every inch of his skin. And unlike chalk circles or the general cast of Second-Sight, these symbols glow golden and clear, even after a violent death.

Like his body, the lines are malformed and twisted, but I can make out the general intent of the circle. Protection, mainly. Some for strengthening power, for focusing it. Symbols crowded around his wrists and hands seem to hint at communication or enhancing knowledge. All told, it shows someone who was trying to strengthen himself for a fight, one that he desperately wanted—and failed—to be prepared for.

Out of Second-Sight, the bright light of the markings disappears, though I have to blink their ghosts away. Once the spots clear from my vision, I lean in closer to Moore's body. This close, I can clearly see the slightly raised edges of scars from where the ink went in. Most of his tattoos aren't visible. Whoever the tattoo artist was, they were careful. But right over his heart, I see a circle, cut down the center with a line, another arcing up across the middle, the scar subtle but raised when I run my fingers over it.

That was on his book, Priya says, floating closer to Moore's body

You've never seen that symbol before today, right? I ask Priya, fingers still on the raised mark marring his skin.

No. I've seen ones that are similar, but they only have three lines or it's a half circle.

What are they used for?

Binding, mostly. But it's for the bigger spirits, ones that are an imminent threat. The marks are powerful but imprecise. It's like a shotgun rather than a rifle.

I drop back into Second-Sight, diving deeper, looking past the blinding designs on Moore's skin. Once I force myself to see past the light covering Moore, I catch a swirl of darkness. It coils around his chest, something about it reminding me of a predator stalking its prey. When I reach out, it passes through my fingers like smoke, then settles closer to Moore's body.

That looks familiar, Priya says.

Yeah, I say, trailing my fingers through the smoke again. *I wonder if that symbol is keeping it here?*

Why would Moore try to pull something dark, then cover his body in symbols to dispel it? Priya asks. She drags her hand through the smoke, too, and it roils, twists, and coalesces again. *It seems counterproductive to me.*

I sigh and start sketching runes over the darkness. It swirls faster and faster, then solidifies into a crystal. With a final glittering mark, it shatters, disappearing into nothingness.

At least we can tell he was possessed. I say, shaking my head. *Poor guy. All this work to protect himself and his corpse is taken over.*

I drop out of Second-Sight and pull the sheet over Moore's body, covering his face. I snap the bright purple gloves off my hands, toss them into a biohazard bin by the door, and dial Cross's number.

"Detective Cross."

"Hey, it's me."

"Hey. What'd you find?"

"Well, he was definitely possessed by something after he died. I found some kind of darkness on him, similar to what I saw on myself after I Burnt Murphy. And that symbol I found on the back of that book? He had it and a bunch of others tattooed all over his body."

"Is that normal?" He sounds a little shocked, a little confused.

"Not really, not anymore. Maybe a hundred years ago, you'd find people who would use tattoos to protect themselves." I shake my head, though Cross can't see it. "But that was a rougher time, back when we were isolated and had to use whatever tools we had to defend ourselves. If people do it now, it's mainly for show. Moore's tattoos are only visible in Second-Sight, and they're pretty heavy-duty protections."

"What does it mean?"

"I have a feeling the tox report will come back clean."

There's a long pause. I can hear Cross tapping something against his desk and the soft background noise of HQ.

"Those tattoos, can you tell if they're new?"

"They're all healed pretty well if that's what you're asking. I'd have to check with Abramo to get any real idea of their age."

He lets out a quiet sigh. "I can't see a guy getting a bunch of new tattoos, much less protective ones, then killing himself while they're still fresh. If those are new, then I think you might be right."

"And what about it being connected to Murphy's killing?" I ask, heart starting to pound.

"I don't know about that," Cross says. "You've got a lot of work to do to convince me that they're related. The tattoos don't do it for me, not by themselves. Let's focus on figuring out if this guy offed himself or if someone else did it for him. The cousin'll be here tomorrow. I'll check with him, see if he knows anything. Maybe Moore mentioned something about Murphy to him."

"And I'll interview Ruth Peterson again," I say,

stepping out of the autopsy bay, "find out from her if Murphy may have known Moore. They're close enough in age that they might have been friends or something."

I rub my eyes and head back toward the parking lot.

"This is a fucking mess," Cross says, his voice breaking on a huff of air. "What the hell is going on?"

"I have no idea," I say, frustration turning to exasperation and an uncertain, but persistent, sense of dread. "I have no fucking idea."

CHAPTER TEN

My phone goes off early in the morning. I fumble for it in the dark, then quickly answer the call when I don't recognize the number.

"Detective Phillips," I say, rolling onto my back. I lay a hand across my face and rub the sleep from my eyes. "What's up?"

"Detective," an unfamiliar voice answers, "this is Officer Williams, from the second district? We apprehended an individual tonight who was trying to get into a crime scene for a murder you're investigating. I believe he may be a person of interest in the case."

"What's he look like?" I ask, waking up quickly.

"Older guy, maybe in his mid to late forties, it's hard to tell. Dark beard, bad teeth, and he's got some pretty deep scratches around his neck. Name is Jerry Richardson."

"He's in custody?"

"Yes, ma'am. He's at the second district HQ right now, but we can get him transferred to the seventh if you'd like to interview him in-house."

"No, that's fine. I have to grab my partner, and then we'll be over. Should be about an hour?"

"All right, we'll hold him for you."

"Thank you, Officer."

I hang up and quickly dial Cross. His voice is rough, low and heavy with sleep.

"Cross. What is it?"

"It's Phillips. We've got a suspect, a guy trying to break into the Murphy crime scene. They're holding him at the second district for us." I hear him groan quietly as I rummage around for a pair of slacks. "I told them we'd be there in about an hour."

"All right," he says. I can hear sheets rustling quietly in the background. "I'll meet you there?"

"Sounds good. Bring coffee."

I hang up and dress quickly. My shirt might be a bit wrinkled, but I'm presentable enough for the hour of the day. The walk to the car is icy cold, my breath clouding the air in front of me. With the roads nearly empty and lit only by flickering streetlights, it's a peaceful and quick drive to the second district. There are a few lights on in the front of the building, and I see Cross's car pulled up in the small lot before the covered doorway. I grab Murphy's case file from my passenger seat and head inside.

Cross is sitting at a desk, two cups of coffee in front of him. He looks tired but stands up when he sees me walk in.

"Here." He passes a cup of coffee to me. "You look like you need it."

"You're not looking too hot yourself, partner," I say, smirking. I take a grateful sip and smile. "Thanks."

"C'mon, let's get started."

Cross waves over an officer. He's young, with dark hair and a warm smile. The name Williams is stitched in gold thread on his chest, and he reaches out to shake my hand.

"Officer Williams," he says. "Thanks for coming down. We've got him in interrogation room one. He's already been Mirandized, and he said no to a lawyer. Camera's all set and there's an audio recorder running, too."

"Great, lead the way."

I pause when Officer Williams opens the door, sizing up the man sitting at the small table filling up the room. Jerry Richardson is unkempt, dirty, and massive. He's wearing a coat that's threadbare at the elbows and collar, covered in stains of unknown origin, and straining around the shoulders. He barely fits in the small chair, and his shoulders are hunched forward, large hands resting close to each other on the table, forced together by cuffs. His hands are dark, dirt worn into his cuticles, leaving a black circle around each nail. I can tell he's too warm, sweat beading on his forehead, but he shows no sign of discomfort. The scratches on his neck are visible above his collar and have scabbed over. There's a dank smell to the air that seems to emanate from him... like laundry left in the washer overnight. The reek is familiar. I can feel it on my face, feel those dark and stained hands around my throat. I swallow, the muscles of my neck shifting and contracting. I have to remind myself that I'm not Emma, that this moment—my moment—is not hers.

I pull out a chair and sit down, setting the Murphy case file on the table. Richardson reaches for it, then pauses, hand hovering, and pulls back.

"Good morning," I start, pulling the folder a little closer to my side of the table. "My name is Detective Phillips. This is my partner, Detective Cross. We're here to ask you a couple of questions. I know the officer has already informed you of your rights, but I have to go over this one more time. Do you understand that you've waived your right to an attorney?"

He doesn't say anything, just looks at me. There's an emptiness in his eyes, something blank staring back out.

"You don't have to say anything," I say, opening the file and slowly spreading crime scene photos out on the desk. I make sure to push the photos of Emma's body closest to him. "I just have a few things I want you to look at."

When I look up, he's still staring at me, eyes locked on my face.

"Can I get you a cup of coffee?" Cross asks, leaning forward in his seat next to me. "Something to eat?"

The silence drags on, the only sound in the room Richardson's slow, even breath. His eyes never leave mine. I fight the urge to lean into his stare, to turn it into a show of dominance. Instead, I shift my weight, throwing my arm over the back of the chair, affecting disinterest and cocky assurance. I don't break the stare.

"You have the right to remain silent," Cross starts, "but that doesn't mean you can't talk to us. You answer a couple quick questions for us, we'll get you some food, maybe a new jacket? Maybe we can find a shelter with an extra bed, get you in there and off the streets…"

"I don't want to talk to you," Richardson says quietly,

his voice surprisingly clear and strong. "I want to talk to Kim."

"All right, Jerry," I say, trying not to let his use of my first name—which I never gave him—and dead stare get to me. "Talk to me."

"You know what I want to talk to you about," he says, blinking slowly. He presses his hands against the table.

"Emma Murphy," I say. "Tell me about her."

"No, not the girl. You know who I want to talk about. He told me about you," he says, leaning forward slightly. "That you knew better than any of the others, that you would understand."

"I don't understand," I say, pushing one of the photos of Emma's autopsy closer to him. "I don't understand why you would kill and assault a young girl."

"I didn't kill her," Richardson scoffs. "He killed her."

"Who killed her, Jerry?" Cross asks. "If you can give us a name, we can—"

"He said you'd understand. About the darkness. About the... the voices."

That doesn't bode well, I think, pausing. I make a note, then press again.

"What I understand is that we have a dead girl, Jerry, and it seems like you might know something about it."

"He said you'd be able to help me," he continues, eyes wide. His fingers flex against the table, fingertips turning white. "He said you'd make it stop."

"My partner and I, we're going to step outside until you're ready to talk to us about this dead girl, okay?"

"No, you don't get it," he shouts, standing suddenly and knocking over his chair. The chain on his handcuffs clanks loudly against its anchor on the table. Though he's hunched over, tied to the heavy table, I still reach for the gun at my waist.

"Officer Williams!" I shout, standing up and moving toward the door, Cross close by. "We need backup in here!"

"You don't understand!" Richardson continues to yell, wrenching his hands back and forth. The table lifts and clangs against the floor. Blood runs from around the edges of the cuffs where they cut into his wrists. The table tips to the side, resting on two of its four legs, as Richardson lurches toward me.

"They're always there! I see them all the time. They talk to me, and no one understands, they don't! He said you'd make it stop, that you'd make them go away."

Williams and another officer rush into the room. Williams slams the table onto the ground, wrenching Richardson's wrists down and causing him to hunch over at the waist. The other officer dashes around the table and grabs Richardson. The officer's arms stretch tight around Richardson, and in an awkward hold, he manages to pin Richardson's arms to his body and stop him from struggling. He looks at me, bent over and panting, pleading.

"Please," he says, shoulders heaving, "he said you'd understand."

"I do," I say, shaking my head. "We're gonna get you the help you need. Cross, c'mon."

Richardson yells behind us as we leave the room. Another pair of officers rushes past us. I hear more clanging, the sound of a chain against metal, then someone's shouting, "Taser!" There's a pained yell and then blessed silence.

Officer Williams comes out of the interrogation room holding Murphy's case file. Some of the pictures are bent when I flip through it, but everything's still there.

"Sorry about that," Williams says, shaking his head. "We didn't know he was unstable."

"Should've been better prepared," Cross says. "Guy like that, you don't know what you might have to deal with."

"It happens," I say. "No one was hurt and I don't think we'll get much else out of him anyway. Let's make sure he gets printed and that we get samples for DNA testing. With those scratches on his neck, I think we've got enough probable cause for it."

"Yes, Detective." Williams turns and walks back toward the interrogation room while I tuck the case file back under my arm.

"You think he's the guy?" Cross asks, raising an eyebrow.

"I don't know, maybe? He seems familiar, but Sendings aren't perfect. It's close enough that I think it's worth a shot."

"And what about your vendetta theory?"

I frown. "That"—I gesture toward the interrogation room—"kind of shot it all to hell. It's not clear to me that he's connected to reality. Talking about voices and seeing people all the time? Could be that he has a bit of Second-Sight. Or he's schizophrenic. Either way, I think if he were targeting someone specifically, it would be spontaneous, not well planned or thought out." I shake my head, frustrated. "Maybe we'll find something that links him to Murphy besides her death, but right now, I don't see that happening."

"Same," Cross says. He at least has the decency to look sympathetic. "What about possession, like Moore? If this Richardson guy's got a bit of the Second-Sight, a ghost might be able to take him over, right?"

"Maybe," I say, "but I'm not sure. I didn't pick anything up from him, and when you've got the Sight without training or control, you tend to broadcast the power."

"I guess we've got some interviews to do, then," Cross says, looking back toward the now quiet interview room.

"I'll call Ruth Peterson's office," I say, "see what her schedule is like today and do some follow-up. You have any idea when the cousin's getting in?"

"Yeah, sometime this morning. The ME is supposed to call me when he arrives."

"All right. You want to grab something to eat before things pick up?" I ask, heading toward the door. Cross is about to respond when my phone rings. As I pull it from my pocket, Cross's starts chiming, too.

"This is Detective Phillips," I answer, raising my eyebrow at Cross as he answers curtly.

"Kim, it's Lieutenant Walker. We've got another one."

"What do you mean?" I ask. Cross is frowning and speaking low into his phone. He shakes his head at me, then turns away.

"Looks like it could be another Medium. It's pretty bad. I need you and Cross on scene as soon as possible. Someone's calling him right now, and I'll text you the address, but you need to hurry. It's bad."

"I'm with him right now," I say. "We'll be there as soon as we can."

"Understood, Detective. I'll let the officers on scene know you're on your way." She pauses, then sighs. "Kim? I know you've been doing this for a while, but be ready. The victim's unrecognizable."

"Yeah, Lieu," I say, tilting my head toward the door to get Cross to follow. "I understand."

"No, I mean you can barely tell the body is human. Just get here as soon as you can, okay?"

"Yes, ma'am," I say, shaken. I reach the car just as Cross opens the passenger side door. He looks at me, brow furrowed.

"You okay?"

"I don't know that it makes a difference," I say, sliding into the driver's seat. "Let's go."

CHAPTER ELEVEN

"Goddamn," I say, standing in the doorway of the apartment.

Even from the hall, I can see it's an absolute mess. There's blood everywhere. It covers the walls in large sweeping strokes. It's spattered on the ceiling, small droplets that must have come off the end of the murder weapon staining the popcorn texture with tiny splashes of red. The blood's path is evident, painted around the room in grisly brushstrokes. A heavy scent of iron, copper, and death wafts out of the apartment, and I gag slightly, ducking my face into my sleeve to cough. An officer just inside the door passes me a pair of gloves and shoe covers, grimacing in sympathy. I slide them on, still focused on the gore within. He also offers me a container of Vicks VapoRub, but I wave it away, adjusting to the smell of violent death.

Cross brushes past me to approach a uniformed officer standing to the side while I scan the apartment, my eyes tracking the blood trail. What probably used to be a nice sectional in the center of the room is now stained dark with blood. A coffee table lies on its side with a mess of papers on the floor next to it. As I walk around the edge of the sofa, placing my feet carefully, I finally see the victim.

The body lying in the center of the room is almost unrecognizable as human. Open bloody sockets stare back at me in the middle of what used to be a face, which has been left hanging in tattered strips of flesh and skin. The scalp is intact, though the victim's hair is stained black with blood. I see white bone at the cheeks and jaw, and I taste bile at the back of my throat. The tattered remains of a shirt and skirt cling to the body, all stained a muddy brown. Through the slashes and tears of the shirt, I can see more lacerations and stab wounds crossing the chest and collarbone. Lower, there are organs spilling out onto the floor in dark loops, and I swallow hard.

Crime scene techs and people from the ME's office swarm the area. Camera flashes and small numbered photo markers fill the room. I make my way past them carefully, then kneel to look more closely at the body. The smell is nearly overpowering here, a mix of iron and excrement. I'm starting to regret not putting a little of the VapoRub beneath my nose to block the smell when I hear footsteps behind me. I look up to see Cross, frowning.

"According to the uniform at the door, the lease is in the name of a Stephanie Casey. It looks like we're going to have to use dental records to confirm that she's the victim, but they found a purse in the kitchen with her ID."

"Any signs of forced entry?" I ask, looking around the apartment. For the level of violence against the victim, there's little else that's broken or disturbed. Besides the knocked-over table and the blood, it appears to be a normal, tidy apartment.

"No, it looks like she let whoever did this in." He

moves closer to the body, crouching down next to me.

"So, why does the Lieutenant think this is another Medium? What's the link?"

"The murder weapon," he says, waving to one of the techs. She comes over with a paper evidence bag and hands it to Cross. He carefully unrolls the top, and I peer in. There's a large silver knife inside, still covered in blood.

"Is that what I think it is?" I ask, looking more closely. My gorge rises, and I fight it back.

"Depends on what you think it is," Cross says, rolling the top of the bag back so I can see more of the knife. There are runes engraved into its handle and blade, looping over the silver with a delicate craftsmanship that speaks of age, money, and power.

"I think it's a Medium's knife," I say. I reach into my boot and draw out my own knife. While smaller and less ornate, the symbols are the same.

"That's what they told me." He sighs and passes the bag back to the tech. She carries it off.

Kim, Priya says, voice shaking, *who would do something like this?*

"Is this a thing that happens? You ever hear of anyone being killed with one of those?" Cross asks, standing.

I shake my head. "No, I haven't." I remain crouched on the ground. "The knives are generally expensive, and they take on a nearly religious significance to the Mediums who use them. I wouldn't be caught without mine, and I wouldn't think of using another Medium's for any reason, much less to kill them. On top of that, they're generally made from sterling silver, which doesn't keep an edge well. I'm surprised the blade stayed sharp enough for this."

"It didn't."

I look over my shoulder to see Dr. Abramo walking toward me, clipboard in hand.

"You can see as the wounds go farther and farther away from the head and face, the edges get more ragged, more torn." He points to places on the body with a pen as he talks. "The knife was definitely dulled by the end of the attack."

I look back at the body, but the torn edges of skin and muscle look the same to me. The fingers and hands are also damaged, the nails hanging off at the quick. There's a muted glint of gold on one of the fingers. A ring, marred by blood.

"You have any idea when this happened?"

"Well," Abramo says, frowning, "it's hard to tell with the state the body is in. There aren't any obvious signs of rigor, but there's so much tissue damage, I'm not sure I can tell. The legs are stiff, so that means time of death was probably within the last twelve hours, but I can't be positive. Body temp isn't going to be a good way to estimate, either. This much damage, the temp's going to drop faster than normal. I'll be able to tell you more once we get the body back to the morgue. Same for angle of attack. If you don't mind"—he steps toward the body— "I've got some more notes I need to take."

I stand, making way for the medical examiner. He moves in closer, looking over his clipboard. I leave him and join Cross, who's moved to the other side of the room.

"Casey, do we know if she's a Medium?"

"I'm not sure, but they haven't found anything to say otherwise," Cross says. "There weren't any credentials or anything lying around, unfortunately, but judging by her library, she was at least interested in the subject, if not practicing."

"Maybe she was sensitive or just an enthusiast," I murmur, moving toward a line of bookshelves on the far side of the room.

There isn't much blood on them, but the techs have marked a few drops carefully. The books range from trashy romance novels to Shakespeare. There's one entire bookshelf, though, that's dedicated to Mediums and Medium studies. I see a couple of books that I read while in college, as well as some that I've never seen before.

"This is some pretty obscure stuff," I say, running my gloved finger over the spines. "Most of this would be useless to anyone but a Medium."

"Would she be able to do anything with them?" Cross asks, reaching past me to grab a book from the shelf.

"If she's a Medium, sure. But if she's not? She'd kill at Trivial Pursuit, but that's about it. This level of information, it's worthless to someone who doesn't actually have the power to do something with it."

Looking closer, I notice a bit of paper protruding from the top of one of the books, an older leather-bound volume. I slide it free from the shelf. The cover is plain and undecorated, with the title in large gilt letters.

On the Summoning and Capturing of Spirits through the Use of Inscribed Circles.

It's in slightly worse condition than the one at Moore's apartment, but it's the same book. I open it to the small slip of paper tucked between the pages and discover diagrams of circles, the same ones Moore was looking at.

Priya, this is the same book, I say.

She comes over, her fingers brushing against the pages like a soft breeze. The corners flip up for a moment, and I have to hold the pages down while she looks.

What's it doing here? she asks, still lightly touching the book.

I don't know. I shake my head. *I never even heard of this thing until this week. How in the hell did they both have a copy?* Priya doesn't answer.

"Cross, look at this."

Cross closes the book he's holding, leans over, and frowns when he sees what I'm holding.

"Isn't that the same book you found at Moore's?"

"Yeah," I say, showing him the diagram. "She was reading the same stuff that he was. Binding Mediums, rather than ghosts."

"Would she have been able to do anything with this, though?"

"I don't know. We'll have to wait and see who the victim is. If it's Casey and she ends up being a Medium, then maybe. What worries me more is that we'll have three dead Mediums in a week, two in the last three days that just happen to have been reading the same chapter of the same book."

"So maybe your connected case idea isn't as farfetched as it seems."

"There's gotta be something else here," I say, frustration heavy in my voice. "This looks like an obscure text. I've never heard of or seen it before, and now we've got two copies. This one even has notes written in the margins."

"So, besides the book, what's the connection?" Cross's eyebrows knit together. "Why would they both be looking into binding Mediums? I've never heard of Mediums going after each other or needing to do something like this."

I shake my head. "We don't fight each other now, but historically, it happened. The Hatfields and McCoys are probably the best-known examples, but the practice died out as Mediums started becoming less and less common."

"It could explain what they were doing, though. Getting themselves ready to take someone out or"—he frowns, looking around the blood-spattered apartment—"stopping them before they could act."

"No, not with this ritual," I say, flipping from the diagrams to the explanation of the binding. "You have to have one Medium of each Affinity to do this. Unless they were working together and had four other Mediums working with them, it wouldn't be possible. And some of the Affinities are nearly impossible to find, especially Passengers."

Cross shrugs. "It was just a thought," he says as he takes the book from me to flip through a couple of pages. "It's certainly an interesting read."

He hands the book back to me. I turn it over to look at the back cover. There's a small circle pressed into the leather, a line lying tangent to the top, then turning to bisect it. Another unfamiliar rune in the same place the other had been. I let my fingers trace it for a moment, then sigh.

"I want them to be connected," I say. "And I'm worried that that's going to cloud my judgment. I don't want three people to have died for no reason."

"I understand, Phillips. We'll figure it out."

I nod and hold the book tighter.

Kim, Priya says, appearing next to me. Her expression is drawn, eyes sad. *You need to look more closely at the body.*

I frown, then turn. The corpse is still spread in the center of the room, still only the tattered remains of a person. I drop slightly into Second-Sight and gasp. "Oh, you've gotta be kidding me," I say aloud. "Cross, she's in the middle of a circle."

I grab my notebook from my jacket pocket and fumble for a pen. "Pen, Cross, quick!"

He passes me one, confused, and I start frantically scribbling down the runes and sigils I can make out through the blood. The floor is carpeted, the lines written with poured streams of chalk dust. Not as quick as writing on stone, but solid, strong. Most of the circle has been smudged out by a struggle, which explains why it's still here, inactive. There's certainly more than enough blood to have powered the thing, especially if the victim was a Medium. As soon as I finish writing, I open my eyes again and look down at the pad of paper.

Apart from one or two symbols, I have the circle roughly scribed out. It's for summoning, with protections woven throughout in complicated patterns. It's intricate, detailed, and very well crafted.

"If this is Stephanie Casey," I say, passing the notepad back to Cross, "then she's definitely a Medium."

"I thought these things disappeared when you activated them," Cross says, frowning down at the page.

"They do," I say. "But this one was damaged, probably when whoever killed her attacked. It's just chalk, so you have to be careful. And you never know how a circle is going to react to too much blood. They get unpredictable."

"So, you think this is Casey?"

"We'll have to wait for the dental records," I say, though my gut is screaming at me that, *yes*, the mutilated body on the floor is Stephanie Casey.

I pull one of the crime scene techs over and explain what I've found. He listens patiently and bends down to look more closely at the ground around the body.

"Yeah, I can see the dust," he says. "Not sure how much we're going to be able to get documented, though. The blood's ruined a lot of it."

"Well," I say with a sigh, "do your best. It doesn't have to be perfect as long as you get some clear pictures."

"I'll try my best, Detective."

"Thanks," I say, patting him on the back and heading toward the front door where Cross is waiting.

"What'd Casey do?" I ask, looking around the apartment.

"You mean, what's her profession? According to the uniform," he says, dragging out the word as he flips through his notes, "she works at the Field Museum doing archival work. Her boss reported her missing this morning, said she's never taken a sick day or shown up late. He seemed pretty worried." Cross pauses, looking over the room. "Apparently with good cause."

"Do you know what she was working on, specifically?" I ask.

"No, but we can talk to her boss and find out more."

I nod in agreement and head downstairs to the lobby, Cross close behind.

We walk out of the building, heading toward my car, but I find it hard to pay attention to the street in front of me, my mind still focused on the crime scene, the rank smell of death still clogging my throat. Something about this case, about all of these cases, just doesn't want to let go. Whose body is in the apartment, I wonder, and if it *is* Casey, what happened to her in her final hours? And if it *isn't* Casey, then what was the victim doing in her apartment and why was she attacked so viciously? And by whom?

"Hey, Phillips!"

I stop, shaken from my thoughts. I turn toward the voice—it's Cross's—then realize I've walked past my car. He's leaning against it, grinning slightly.

"Right here," he says, letting his shoulder rest against the frame. "You want me to drive?"

"Might not be a bad idea," I say, still shaky. "Sorry, I'm just..."

"I understand," he says, reaching a hand out for my keys. "You're not the only one trying to figure this out."

"I know." I slide into the passenger seat. There are a few quiet minutes while he heads toward the expressway to district HQ. It's nearing midday, the sun bright in a way it only is during the fall. It blankets the city around us, highlights everything in sharp corners of glinting glass and metal. Even with the glaring sun and the heater on full blast, I still feel cold.

"Does your ghost friend have any thoughts on this?" Cross breaks the silence.

Priya? I ask. She materializes next to me, her body coming out of the center console. *What do you think?*

The knife was old, she says, *as was the book. If that was Casey, and I believe it was, she may have been researching both as part of her job. If I had to prioritize things, I would go to the museum and talk to her supervisor. Even if they can't give us any more insight into who may have killed her, they will likely be able to tell us what she was researching. That may connect the murder weapon, the book, and her death.*

I pass the message along and Cross looks thoughtful.

"So we've got Moore's cousin, Ruth Peterson, and now Casey's boss to talk to. You think you can handle two interviews today?"

"Yeah, probably," I say, looking out the window. "But before we talk to anyone at the Field Museum, we need to find out whose body was in that apartment."

Chapter Twelve

We arrive at district HQ and split up, Cross heading back out to talk to Moore's cousin while I sit at my desk, pen and paper at the ready, and call Ruth Peterson. Her assistant answers on the first ring, informing me that Mrs. Peterson will be busy until later in the afternoon. I set a meeting for 3:30 and hang up. Next, I quickly call the medical examiner's office and leave a message for Abramo about the Jane Doe in Casey's apartment.

"Just give me a call as soon as you're able to identify the body," I tell the answering machine. "You've got my number."

Frustrated and without much left to do except wait for someone to call me, I pull up my case notes for Murphy's murder. I add today's date and Richardson's name, then start typing.

Initial interview was unhelpful. Suspect had poor hygiene, appears to be homeless. Was initially nonresponsive, though he started speaking as the interview continued. It is unclear if suspect is mentally sound. He displayed erratic and violent behavior during questioning, which could be indicative of an underlying mental health issue or latent Medium abilities. He had to be subdued by officers on scene. The interview was ended at that time.

I pause, then add more:

If he did kill Murphy, it wasn't because he'd planned it. Waiting for blood typing to come back for initial assessment. Will send further samples for DNA confirmation if blood type from Murphy's nails and suspect's blood match.

I pull out my case file for Moore's suicide, along with my notes from Casey's apartment. Once I spread everything out on my desk, I start trying to piece everything back together.

Murphy, a young Medium in training, murdered by an unknown assailant. She'd scribed a partial circle before her death, including a rune that I'd never seen before, but there were no signs of supernatural activity before or after her death.

Moore, a full Shaker, about to start a new job and without any signs of mental health issues, jumps to his death. He's possessed by an unknown spirit for a moment after his death, but that's likely unrelated. His body is covered in protective runes, tattooed into his body for constant protection. He also owns an uncommon book on binding, with another unknown rune embossed on the back cover.

Finally, an unidentified victim, killed with a Medium's knife in the center of a well-crafted circle for binding and protection. The same book as Moore's is on the bookshelf, a third unknown rune on the back.

If there are any obvious connections between the cases, besides the book and the unfamiliar runes, I can't find them. I'm quietly talking to myself, trying to tie the cases together, when Cross comes back in and sits at his desk. He looks tired and a little frustrated, and his typing is louder than usual. I wait a moment, but when he doesn't say anything, I clear my throat. He hits the enter key a little harder than he needs to and looks at me, brow furrowed.

"I'm going to guess your interview didn't go so well," I prompt, leaning forward.

"No, not really," he says. He looks back at his computer, clicks a few times, and slumps his shoulders. He rubs his fingers into the corners of his eyes, his brow furrowed.

"I guess they were close—small family or something—and his cousin didn't take the news well. He also said there was no reason Moore would've killed himself. They talked the day before he died, and Moore was excited about his new job, didn't seem at all upset, certainly not to the point of suicide."

"You ask about the tattoos at all?"

"Yeah, I did," Cross says. "The cousin didn't seem to know anything about it but said that Moore had always been interested in Medium history, especially the aesthetic aspects of it. He wasn't exactly surprised when I told him. Said it sounded like something Moore would do."

"And the book?"

"More of the same," Cross says, frowning. "No clear idea, but it sounded like Moore. The only thing he kept insisting on was that his cousin wouldn't have taken his own life."

I grip the arms of my chair, frustrated. "So nothing helpful?"

"Not quite. He did give me some of Moore's friends' names to follow up with. Maybe they knew Murphy," Cross says, leaning back in his chair. "You talk to Ruth Peterson yet?"

"No," I say, "not yet. I've got a meeting with her in about forty-five minutes. If you think of anything you want me to ask her, let me know."

"What's your plan?"

"Find out what Murphy was into, who she was friends with. Maybe she had other journals or a blog, something we can use to find out more about her state of mind before she died. Maybe we'll get lucky, and she'll know Moore."

"Homicides don't generally come with lucky breaks," Cross says, mouth quirked up at the corner.

"Definitely not with these cases," I say. "Still, a girl can hope."

He smiles, genuine and stunning. It makes his eyes light up, even as the wrinkles around his eyes deepen. I feel an unexpected tightening in my gut and freeze. If Cross notices anything, it doesn't show. He turns to his computer and gets back to work while I struggle to find my equilibrium again. I push back from my desk and stand, grabbing Murphy's file from my desk.

"I'm going to get an early start, try to get around traffic," I say, attempting to act normal. Cross barely glances up from his screen.

"Sounds good," he says.

"See ya." I turn to leave.

"Hey, just a second," he says. He looks a little uncertain, hesitant. It's not an expression I've seen from him before, and I feel my throat tighten, sudden tension making it hard to breathe.

"You still want to grab a bite to eat?"

I must look confused because he sighs, then starts speaking again. "This morning, you asked if I wanted to get something to eat?"

I nod, not sure if I feel relieved or disappointed.

"I'd like to go over your interview, see if we can piece anything together from what you learn. I'll order some Chinese, and we can go over our notes tonight?"

"All right, that sounds fine," I say, feeling uncomfortable and ready to leave. "I'll meet you back here?"

"Yeah, sounds good. See you when you get back."

I head out of the building, my face warm. The autumn air is cool and soothing against my skin, and I climb into my car hurriedly, trying to feel like I'm not running away from something.

CHAPTER THIRTEEN

I don't have any issues getting past the security desk this time, as I'm met by the same well-dressed woman from my last visit. She leads me to the elevators, swipes her card, and smiles at me as the doors shut.

Ruth Peterson's office is as opulent as I remember, but she seems like a different person. The grief is still in her eyes, but there's a strength in the way she carries herself that wasn't there before. A steel to her spine, a hardness to her gaze. And while I can tell she's been crying the last couple of days, her face drawn and tired, she meets my eyes with an unflinching regard that reminds me of who this is: one of the most powerful Seers in the world.

"Detective," she says, standing from behind her desk. "I'm glad to see you again. Please, have a seat."

She gestures to one of the seats before her desk, and I walk over and pull my notepad out.

"Mrs. Peterson—"

"Ruth," she interrupts, "please."

"Ruth," I say. "I'm sure your assistant already told you, but I have a few follow-up questions to ask you about Emma. Now, I understand this may be hard to talk about, so if you need a moment…"

She shakes her head. "No, I'll be okay. Please, ask anything you want. Whatever I can do to help…"

I flip to a blank page in my notepad and get ready to write. "First, you mentioned that Emma had a habit of visiting her aunt. Do you know if there were any other Mediums that she knew or spent time with, anyone else she might have turned to for advice?"

"No, not that I can think of. She'd met some of my closer friends, but I would be surprised if she felt comfortable enough with them to seek them out. She didn't trust people easily. There were a few kids at school who she was close with, but I don't know that any of them were Mediums."

"What about people slightly older than her, around my age? Maybe a little younger?"

Ruth shakes her head again. "No, she was an introvert, a very quiet kid. I've met most of her friends, and they're all high schoolers. Emma is," she pauses, swallows, "*was* a handful, sure, but she kept to herself."

"What about anything relating to circles or scribing them?" I flip to a new page and draw the symbol I found at the crime scene, a circle with an eye within an eye. "She drew this before she was attacked as part of the circle she was trying to scribe."

Ruth pulls the notepad close and frowns. "I've never seen that before," she says, passing the notepad back to me. "Do you know what it is?"

"No." I take it from her. "I was hoping you might be able to shed some light on it. If Emma was doing any research on her own, it might help us understand what she was doing before she died."

Ruth shakes her head, looking suddenly tired. She takes a deep breath, then answers. "I don't know that she was doing any research into circles, but she was looking into her family history, especially on her mother's side. Her aunt is her only living relative, and I think she felt that lack strongly over the last few months, though I'm not sure why."

"She was an orphan?"

"Yes," Ruth says, shaking her head. "It was a tragic accident about a year into her apprenticeship. There was a drunk driver, and both of her parents were killed. Emma wasn't close with them, but their deaths devastated her. I think because they never apologized for failing to understand her and because she was never able to apologize for fighting them so hard. The last few months, she was researching their history, trying to find out more about them." She pushes her chair back from the desk, then reaches down. "I was going through her things and grabbed some of it for your investigation. I thought it might help."

She pulls a box out from under her desk, one that was used to carry paper. Now, it's full of books, notepads, and drawings, carefully stacked and organized. Ruth puts it on top of the desk and pushes it toward me.

"She had a journal at her aunt's," I say, taking the box from the desk and laying it in my lap. I carefully scan through the contents, shifting things around. I recognize the handwriting scrawled across the pages as I flip through them quickly. There's smudged pencil, dark ink that's been scribbled out, but no circles, no runes. Nothing that looks like the journal I found at her aunt's.

"Is there anything like that at your home or in this box?"

"I'm not sure. I grabbed a lot of notebooks, but... It was hard for me to look through them, and what's dated is at least a month old. I'm not sure about the rest."

Toward the bottom of the box, I see a familiar gilt title. Suddenly frantic, I dig the book out from the bottom.

Not again, Priya whispers, her fingers tracing over the book in my hands.

On the back cover is a circle with an eye within an eye. I hold up the book, showing it to Ruth. "This book, do you know where she got it?"

Ruth blinks at me, confused. "No, I don't even remember putting that in there. It must've been tucked between some of the other books I found."

"You've never seen this book before or seen Emma with it?"

"I might have," Ruth says with a shrug. "It looks familiar, but I don't know that I ever really looked carefully. Do you mind?"

I pass the book to Ruth, reluctant to let it go. She frowns at the title, then flips through the pages idly.

"It looks like a basic book on circles. Somewhat rudimentary and a little out of date, but still a solid guide."

She stops and presses her lips together. For a long moment, I watch her read the book, her eyes wandering over the page carefully.

"Is this about… Are they talking about binding *Mediums*?"

I nod, then reach for the book. Ruth stares at the page a bit longer, then closes the book and passes it back to me.

"You're sure your apprentice wasn't familiar with any other Mediums in the area?"

"No, she wasn't very active in the community, outside of her time with her aunt and me." Ruth furrows her brow. "That book, why is it important?"

"I can't discuss that, unfortunately. Just…" I trail off, uncertain. "If you remember where she got it, or if you know of anyone else who may have a copy, please let me know immediately."

"Of course," Ruth says, looking shaken. "Do you think she wanted to Bind a Medium?"

"I don't know. If you think of anything else, please let me know," I say. "I'll call your assistant again if I have any other questions. Thank you for your time."

"Of course," Ruth says, standing.

I grab the box and join her, walking toward the elevator down to the lobby. Ruth hits the call button for me and waits, shifting her weight.

"It didn't make any sense at the time"—she touches her forehead—"but I remember her asking me if I knew anything about Medium history. It's not one of my strengths, honestly. I spend so much of my time looking forward, I tend to forget about the past. But…" She stares at the box like it might hold the answers to her questions.

"Do you think she was trying to find out about that book?" She looks at me, eyes full of confusion and grief.

"Maybe," I say.

The elevator doors open with a quiet ding, and I step inside. Ruth presses the button for the ground floor, then steps back into her office.

"Take care, Detective," she says as the doors shut.

"Yeah, I will," I say to my reflection in the shining steel doors. I look down at the book where it rests, its cover glinting in the bright lights inside the elevator.

They must *be connected*, Priya says. She hovers nearby but keeps moving. I sense her anxiety through our Bond and try to calm her. It doesn't seem to help, but then again, I'm just as agitated as she is.

I can understand a historian having an old book, I start, *and a college student, that makes sense to me. But why does a teenager, a high schooler, have a copy of an old text like this?*

Priya shakes her head, then floats toward me. *I don't know, Kim,* she says, shaking her head and resting her hands against the box. *But we need to find out more about this book, and fast.*

When I arrive at HQ, the parking lot is nearly empty, most of the other officers having left for the day. There's still a small gathering of cars in the parking lot, likely because the night shift is here to handle whatever duties are expected of them. Night is creeping in at the edge of the horizon, orange light shining through the streets where buildings fail to block it. The windows of the skyscrapers are like flames—they lick at the skyline, fighting against the quickening chill of night. The air has a bite that finds its way through my jacket. With the box of Murphy's things in hand, I can't pull my collar tighter, so I hunch my shoulders and push my way into the building, shivering.

Cross sits at his desk with a ridiculous quantity of Chinese food containers standing in neat rows. He's fishing for something out of one of the white paper boxes, a napkin tucked into his collar, and he jumps slightly when I drop the box of Murphy's things on my desk. He tilts his head toward the box and swallows.

"What's that?" he asks, frowning.

"Ruth Peterson had some of Murphy's stuff that she thought might be helpful."

I pull the book out and hand it to him, my fingers lingering for a second on the smooth leather cover, the embossed rune catching against them as he takes the book.

"Look familiar?"

"You sure this isn't actually a very common, well-known book?" He waves it at me, eyebrows raised. "Because it seems like we're finding copies of it everywhere."

"Pretty sure," I say, sitting down. "I can follow up with that, though. What'd you get?"

"General Tso's, some egg rolls, fried rice, a few other things. Just dig around, you'll find something you like."

"So generous," I say, grabbing a container and a pair of

chopsticks. I take a quick bite of chicken. It's spicy and sweet as it lingers on my tongue, and I close my eyes for a moment, enjoying the simple pleasure of good food.

"It's pretty good," I say after swallowing. "Remind me to get the menu from you later."

We eat together in companionable silence. I try not to think about the flash of attraction I felt earlier in the day, but I keep getting distracted by his fingers and the way they rest gently against his chopsticks. A shiver creeps up my spine as I slowly wonder what they'd feel like on the back of my neck, skimming over my skin, sliding through my hair.

Not the right time, place, or person, I chide myself. I shake my head and look up to catch Cross watching me, inscrutable.

"Penny for your thoughts?" he asks.

Not for a million dollars, I think. "Just wondering about this book," I say, setting my food down. I pick it up and flip to the back cover. "Why do they all have a copy?"

"More importantly," Cross says, leaning back, "why are they all dead?"

"Besides the ritual about binding Mediums, this is a pretty standard book." I point at it. "There's a lot of basic stuff in here. Nothing that you can't find in a hundred other books on circles. It's historically interesting," I add as an afterthought, "just to see how things have changed since the book was written, but other than the binding ritual, it's just an old book."

"So, the ritual's got to be the connection. Was there any sign that Murphy knew either of the other victims?"

"No," I say. "Ruth said Emma kept to herself, wasn't really active in the Medium community. And you need a lot of Mediums to complete the ritual."

I flip to the back of the book and find the page describing the setup.

"For the successful completion of the binding, one must have Mediums present who represent each of the Affinities, including the one being Bound. As the Bound Medium's powers will be tied to the natural world, those Binding him must possess the ability to sever all possible methods of contact with the afterlife. Without this, the Bound Medium may eventually break their binding. With all seven Affinities gathered, the dark powers of the afterlife can be successfully and thoroughly contained."

I pause, thinking. "Cross, what was Casey's Affinity? Do you know?"

"I may have it written down, hold on." He starts flipping through his notes, frowning.

"Reader," he says.

They've all been different, Priya says.

Cross looks up from his notes at the same moment.

"They all have different Affinities. Murphy was a Seer, Moore a Shaker, and now Casey, a Reader."

"But they don't know each other," I say, shaking my head. "How can you complete a ritual without knowing each other? From what this says, you all have to be in the same room, around a circle with the Medium you're binding in the center. There's no way they'd be able to do this without at least meeting once. And Murphy wasn't even a full Medium yet. She wouldn't have the skills or knowledge to do this."

Cross starts flipping through his notepad.

"They have to be connected," I say. "Even if it's just through this book, there's something going on here that links these cases."

"We're going to have a hell of a time explaining that to the Lieutenant," Cross says.

"But you agree," I press.

"Yeah," he says, sighing. "Yeah, I agree with you. I don't know what's going on, but these victims are all part of the same case. It's a hell of a whodunit, but that's what we've got." He runs his hand over his face, fingers digging into his temples.

"Look"—I put the book back in the box—"we're not going to figure anything else out tonight. Let's call it, get some rest, and work on tracking down Casey's information in the morning. Sound good?"

"Yeah," Cross says, gathering empty food containers and putting them back in the takeout bag. "Sleep sounds great right now."

After he throws away the trash, he takes the time to wipe his desk down with one of the napkins. He tosses it into his trash can, and when it goes in, he makes a quiet noise, like a tiny crowd cheering.

"He shoots, he scores," he says softly.

I huff out a laugh and shake my head. "You're a strange guy, Cross."

"Says the woman who talks to dead people," he says,

mouth quirked in a smile. He grabs his coat from where it hangs over the back of his chair. I shake my head, then start heading toward the front door.

"You know," he says, his voice quiet, "honestly? I'm glad you were put on this case, Phillips. I don't think I would've noticed the book without you. I definitely wouldn't have put the three together."

I scoff, trying to keep the moment light. "You're a good cop, you'd have figured it out." I push the front door open, the cold night air sinking through my jacket. I shiver, and Cross steps closer.

"Get yourself home," he says, placing his hand on my shoulder. It's warm and heavy, and I shiver again. "It's cold out."

"See you in the morning," I say, his hand sliding away, fingers lingering for a long-held breath. I watch, throat tight, as he walks away.

Wrong place, wrong time, wrong fucking person, I think as I set the box down on the top of my car.

Kim, Priya says, voice teasing.

Not now, I cut her off. *Please.*

The drive home is long and quiet, leaving me to wrestle with my own thoughts about the case and about Cross. I fall into bed, convinced I'll be tossing and turning until morning, but I find myself drifting, sliding, until I'm asleep.

When my eyes open, I'm standing in the abandoned building, the now-familiar lockers stretching into the distance. I groan and close my eyes. I'm still in the hallway when I open them again. I cuss, and it echoes, bouncing through the lockers and back at me.

"All right, where to this time?" I ask myself, turning around. The hallway only goes in two directions, toward the lobby—where I went the last time—and toward where the figure was in the first dream. Looking down the hallway now, I don't see anyone waiting, and I take a tentative step forward. The floor groans. I feel it start to give beneath my foot, and I back up quickly.

"Okay, not that way," I say. I turn and head toward the lobby, deciding to turn right when I find another hallway. It takes me to a set of chained doors leading outside. The glass is broken, but when I press my hand against the open air, my palm meets resistance.

"Not getting out this way," I murmur. I nearly turn to leave, then pause. I slide into Second-Sight, letting it fall over the world in a blue-lit glow.

All around me are runes and sigils. Carved into the walls, the floor, the ceiling, they pulse in time with my breaths, a rising and falling light that casts the hallway into stark detail. I recognize most of them, familiar after years as a Medium. But, as I head back to the main hallway, I recognize fewer of them. I let my fingers trail over the walls as I walk by, the runes flashing as I come into contact with them. They snap against my fingers, tiny pricks of lightning that sizzle up my arm and into my chest.

Suddenly, a familiar symbol flashes beneath my fingers and I stop. It's a circle, with an eye within an eye. When I press my finger against it again, it starts to glow a dull blue, solid and steady, but dim.

"What are you?" I ask, leaning closer. The central eye blinks at me, and I fall back, startled. Slowly, it pushes its way forward, the light growing. The rune is a shining, bright blue, but the thing that comes out after it is dense shadow and darkness. It pushes away from the wall like a moving cloud, rolling in slow pulses as it flows toward me. I see flashes of light within the dense body, throwing the indistinct darkness into shifting curves of dim light. I take another step back, and something that looks like an arm reaches for me, light flashing up from its body and into a malformed hand. I stagger out of its reach, and its mouth gapes open, tearing the darkness in two. From deep within its throat, lightning flashes.

"Kim," it croaks, its voice sounding like broken rocks crashing together, like waves in a storm, like trees splintering. "*Burner.*"

I turn and run. I can hear it shuffling after me, like fabric dragging against rough stone. It's a tearing, ripping noise that dogs my steps. When I look back over my shoulder, it's reaching for me with both arms, the rune burning brightly from the center of its misshapen head, light roiling within the depths of its body. Its hand is cold and tight as it closes around my arm, painful and stinging where it presses into my skin. I open my mouth to scream and—

I wake up, gasping. I grab at my arm, trying to find anything wrong. I can still feel the phantom grip of the creature on my skin and I start to shake. Priya hovers nearby, watching silently. I turn on the light, then keep rubbing at my forearm, looking down at where my fingers have pressed red marks into my skin.

Another nightmare, Priya says, settling next to me.

Yes.

She nods, quiet.

I saw the rune on Emma's book. It turned into... something, I don't know. A spirit or creature. It was like a shadow or darkness...

Priya rests against me, cool and gentle. I close my eyes and let her presence wash over me. It's calming and I feel myself start to drift. I jerk awake, still sitting up, then lay down on the bed, rubbing the heel of my hands into my eyes, hard.

Was there anything else this time? Priya asks, turning the light off with a quiet click.

No, I say, rolling onto my side to look out the windows. *Just that.*

These need to stop, I Send, closing my eyes against the streetlight. *I need sleep.*

Priya rests next to me on the bed, and I feel a shield pop into existence around us.

I'll guard you tonight, she says. *And tomorrow, if necessary.*

I turn and look at her. Her hair is floating around her

head in slow waves, ebbing and flowing like the lake during a storm. Her whole body is glowing as she uses her energy to shield me. It slowly pours from her and settles around the bed in a brightly lit circle. I feel more at ease the longer she shields, and I drift off into the first solid night's sleep I've had in four days.

CHAPTER FOURTEEN

The next morning, Cross is waiting near our desks, a cup of coffee in each hand and a folder tucked under his arm. He passes me a cup without comment, followed by the folder, which is stamped "CONFIDENTIAL" in a deep red. I raise an eyebrow, and he gestures toward it.

"You're going to want to look at that," he says, sitting on the edge of his desk.

I take a careful sip of my coffee, then open the folder. There's a copy of a dental X-ray, Casey's name in block print in the upper right corner, along with a preliminary report from the medical examiner's office.

"The body was Casey's, just like you thought. Abramo rushed the identification for us and was able to get her dental records confirmed earlier this morning."

"Great," I say, sighing. "That makes three dead Mediums in less than a week."

"There's more," he says. "Look at the report. Abramo still has to do a full autopsy, so this is all preliminary, but judging by the wound patterns and the angle of the cuts, he thinks it might have been self-inflicted."

"What?" I ask, shocked. I set my coffee down and skim

the report.

"He'll have to do a more thorough wound analysis to find out for sure, but he seems pretty convinced that Casey did this to herself. The cuts on her face were deep and even, and, from what he can tell from her abdomen, the blade came in at a horizontal angle, rather than vertical. He said that's what you see in suicides, not homicides."

"Jesus," I say, sitting down. "It looked like she'd hit bone at least once, and on her face… He's saying it was *self*-inflicted?"

"Yeah," Cross says, shaking his head. "I don't want to think about it. In the meantime, we've got work we can do while we wait for the final report. I called the Field Museum earlier and set up an appointment. We've got an interview with Casey's boss, a Dr. Nicholas Reed, in a half hour. C'mon." He stands and grabs his keys from his desk. "I'm driving."

Morning traffic in Chicago is awful, especially on the expressways. It's normally a ten-minute drive from the district HQ to the museum campus, just a quick jaunt down the Dan Ryan to Lake Shore, but today, it's a slow crawl. We're bumper-to-bumper, the road clogged with locals and tourists alike. Honking horns fill the air and cover the quiet chatter of early morning NPR. There's a report about Ruth Peterson and the recent death of her mentee. We inch along the shoreline, Lake Michigan a shining emptiness on the horizon, while *Morning Edition* finishes up and goes into a commercial for an upcoming pledge drive.

We eventually get to the campus, a huge spread of grass

and trees nestled in between the lake and the city, and grab parking beneath Soldier Field. Cross and I walk out toward the Field Museum, a massive white stone building that takes up the entire length of the block. It's classic in design, built at the end of the 1890s as part of the Chicago World's Fair, with towering Greek columns flanking the wide front entryway. Next to the entrance, there are exhibit banners hanging from the facade, waving gently in an errant breeze off the lake.

The huge doors open into a vast main hall, a bank of ticket kiosks separating the waiting crowds from the exhibits. Smiling young men and women exchange money for tickets and maps, pointing visitors toward the mounted elephants and the T. rex skeleton that are the main attractions in the hall.

Cross and I walk up to the ticket counter. A fresh-faced young woman smiles broadly at us.

"Welcome to the Field Museum!" she says, reaching for two of the programs sitting on the counter. "Here are some maps for you folks. We have some very exciting special exhibits right now."

"Detective Cross and Detective Phillips," Cross says, interrupting. He pulls his badge out and lays it down on the counter. "We have an appointment to meet with Dr. Reed?"

"Oh, I'm sorry," she says, flustered. "You'll want to go to Information." She pulls the programs back slowly. "It's located next to the elephants, right in front of Sue."

Cross grabs his badge and we walk through the slow-moving crowd toward the half circle of the information desk. There's a pair of confused parents, their young children tugging them in different directions, trying to ask after the special exhibits. Cross and I wait, watching the volunteer—an older woman wearing glasses on a thin gold chain and a bright red shirt, the museum's logo emblazoned on the chest—direct them toward the stairs with a smile. She turns to us, still smiling.

"How can I help you folks?"

"My name is Detective Phillips. This is my partner, Detective Cross. We're here to see Dr. Reed."

"Dr. Reed. The one in anthropology or ornithology?"

"Anthropology, ma'am," Cross says.

"Let me call him, hold on just a moment." She picks up a white phone, then quickly dials an extension. Cross waits patiently while I let my eyes wander. There's Sue, the T. rex skeleton that takes up the back of the hall, the elephants, and the milling crowd. I drop into Second-Sight, and the permanent exhibit on early Mediums flares into blue-white light, the artifacts shining bright with ancient power, even after all this time. I turn when I hear the phone hang up, tearing my eyes away from the distant relics.

"He's on his way," she says. "He'll meet you by the back stairs, just past the ticket booths at the north entrance."

"Thank you," I say, heading toward the back of the building. Cross and I shoulder our way through the thick crowd around Sue, then stand idly by the back stairs, waiting. A few minutes later, an older man wearing a lab coat comes walking toward us, his strides purposeful and hurried.

"Detectives?" he asks, pushing his wireframe glasses up the patrician slope of his nose. "I'm Dr. Reed." He reaches out to shake our hands. "Please, if you can follow me."

We quickly step out of the publicly accessible area and into the depths of the museum. Dark wooden shelves, stuffed with specimens and artifacts, fill the back rooms. I catch glimpses of butterflies, desiccated skins, and broken pots. Dr. Reed goes past all of them with a nonchalance born of long familiarity. We reach a small office and he ushers us in, shutting the heavy door behind us.

The room is bordered with overflowing bookshelves. Books butt up against magazines. Papers stick haphazardly from between the pages, some nearly falling off the shelves. There are a few small artifacts here and there: a vase, a carving of some vague creature, a stone knife. Somehow, the clutter makes the place homey and inviting, rather than disorganized. Cross pauses for a moment in the doorway and steps inside carefully. I can tell that the mess bothers him and watch as he stuffs his hands into his pockets to stop himself from straightening something. Dr. Reed sits behind a large desk, the top littered with more paper and a computer monitor, and gestures toward the two chairs sitting in front of it.

"Please, sit down. I've already heard the terrible news about Stephanie. One of her neighbors called yesterday." He shakes his head and leans back in his chair. "I was hoping that my concern was premature, but.."

"What can you tell us about her?" Cross asks, taking his notepad out as he sits.

"Such a bright young woman," Dr. Reed says, sighing. "Very dedicated to her job. We hired her about a year and a half ago as part of a new team we were putting together here. We'd received a large number of new artifacts, specifically relating to Medium history in the Midwest. Turn-of-the-century stuff, very exciting. Stephanie was a fully trained Reader, as well as a graduate from Stanford's Medium History department, so it seemed a perfect fit."

"How'd she do?" I ask.

"Oh, she was great. She could gather such detailed information from the artifacts, it was incredible. We learned a lot about the early days, back when Mediums were first being widely recognized. We're planning an exhibit for next year using the team's data."

"Were there any items she was particularly interested in?" Cross asks. "Anything that held her attention?"

"Not out of that collection, no," Reed says with a frown. "There was something, a knife, that she kept coming back to. It had been donated to the museum, oh, about thirty-five, forty years ago. Very ornate, well crafted. I could understand the fascination."

Cross pulls a photo out of his pocket. As he slides it across the desk, I catch a glimpse of the murder weapon, its blade still coated in red.

"Was this the knife?"

Dr. Reed picks the photo up and goes a little pale. "Yes," he says, looking closely at the photo. "That's the one. I wasn't aware that she'd taken it from the museum's collection."

"We'll make sure it gets returned once the case is

closed," I say, uncertain if I'll be able to keep my promise.

"There will be an item number on the knife that can be used to identify it," Dr. Reed adds.

"We'll let the techs know to look for it. What else can you tell us about the knife?"

"Like I said before, it was donated to the museum about forty years ago. I think Stephanie was particularly interested in it because she couldn't Read anything from it."

"Really?" I ask, leaning forward. "She wasn't able to get any impressions from the knife?"

"No, and that was strange. She'd Read other items in the collection without any problems, but not the knife. Considering its age and the quality, I would have thought she'd be able to get a lot of information from it."

"It being a Medium's knife wouldn't have caused issues?" Cross asks, frowning.

"You'll have to forgive me if I don't get the details exactly right," Dr. Reed says, head bowed slightly, "but my understanding is that the longer someone owns something or the more important it is to them, the stronger the impression left. The ceremonial knives used by Mediums are extremely valuable to their owners. Therefore, the impressions left on them tend to be stronger than most other artifacts. This knife was very well crafted and had been with the family for generations before it was donated. I'd imagine it would have held great sentimental, as well as monetary, value to the family."

"How old was the knife?" I ask.

"From the silversmith's marks, it was made around the turn of the century, early 1900s. Ceremonial Medium's knife, very traditional design. Stephanie thought the runes and sigils on the blade indicated that it had been made for a Passenger, but there was a lot of debate about that point within the group."

"So, it was a pretty unique item," Cross says, taking the photo back.

"Oh, somewhat," Dr. Reed continues. "There are plenty of knives like this in the Medium collection here, with examples for every Affinity. Passengers are the rarest, so we have fewer artifacts relating specifically to them, though we still have quite a few." His shoulders straighten a little, his chest puffing out slightly. "We've one of the largest collections of Passenger-related items in the United States, actually."

When Cross and I are equally unimpressed, Reed coughs quietly and continues. "Now, if we could identify the original owner or find some more information about the item's history, that would make it more meaningful."

"If it was donated," I start, "wouldn't the donor have provided you with background on the knife?"

"If I remember correctly, it was donated as part of an estate settlement. I'll have to verify that, but I don't believe there were any living relatives who could provide any further details about the knife."

"And Stephanie, how was she?" Cross asks, flipping to a fresh page in his notepad.

"She seemed fine. I last saw her on Tuesday. She was working on completing our exhibit proposal." He looks at me again, eyebrows slightly raised.

"We're looking to get some additional grant money from the federal government, try to bring in some items from other museums for the show next year. She was working on getting the proposal finalized. I can take you to Stephanie's desk if that would help. Her things are still there. No one's touched them since she came to work last."

"That would be great," Cross says, standing. I join him, and we wait for Dr. Reed to walk us back into the main room. Around the corner from his office, nestled in between cases of artifacts, is a small desk. A computer almost entirely covers the desktop, and what little space remains has notebooks and what look to be old books piled on it.

"I'll get with our IT staff and see if we can get you into her computer," he says, gesturing toward the desk, "but in the meantime, you're welcome to look through anything else. Let me know if you have any questions."

"Thank you for your cooperation," Cross says as he picks up a notebook and starts flipping through it. "We'll find you if anything comes up."

"Before you go," I say suddenly, "how much do you know about a book called *On the Summoning and Capturing of Spirits through the Use of Inscribed Circles*?"

Dr. Reed frowns. "Doesn't sound familiar. Do you know when it was published?"

"The 1800s originally," I say, trying to remember. "I think the copy we've seen was from the 1900s though."

"My focus is more on ceremonial items, rather than

written works. I can try to look it up for you if you'd like or ask around the department."

"That would be great," Cross says. "Thank you."

Dr. Reed nods. "If you need me, I'll be in my office." He turns back the way we came.

"Find anything interesting?" I ask, pivoting toward the desk. I pick up one of the books. The canvas cover is discolored, turned a faded blue. *Field Museum of Natural History Medium Artifact Catalogue 1976* is printed in block letters on the front, any gilt or ornamentation long since worn away. Looking through the pile, the catalogues go back through the rest of the seventies.

"Not really," Cross says, turning a page in the notebook.

"Seems like she was looking for something," I say, opening the catalogue to flip idly through the pages. Each page contains information about an artifact, including a unique number, a short description, and a detailed history of the artifact. Some pages have pictures, but most don't.

"Probably the knife." Cross continues flipping through the notebook. "Most of her notes relate to finding good artifacts for the exhibit, but there's some stuff in the margins that keeps bringing it up."

The notebooks are spiral bound with college-ruled paper. I pick one up and open to a random page. There are neat notes covering the paper, with short scribbles in the margins:

Silversmith marks similar to British style, showing initials in rectangular punch. British silversmith, who moved to America? May help place owner.

Cross is right. Most of the notes pertain to the exhibit, but the knife keeps coming up again and again:

Sigils and runes from northeastern school, turn of century. Disagree with Robert about localization; I do not see any signs that it was farther south on the Atlantic than Massachusetts.

"She seemed obsessed with it," I murmur, turning page after page containing references to the knife.

Family heirloom potentially? Affinities follow bloodlines, perhaps ancestor commissioned and passed down to newer generations. Where did it come from?

"Any sign she found out when it was added to the collection?" Cross asks.

I shake my head and keep turning pages. There's more information in the main body of the page, relating to the other artifacts she was investigating. There are item numbers and Stephanie's notes.

"Didn't you go to school for this stuff?" Cross asks, still flipping through the notebook.

"Not really," I say, setting my notebook on the desk and picking up another. "I took a couple of classes on Medium history, but nothing this in-depth. Never got to handle any artifacts or anything, just books and papers."

"But you know about the history, right?"

I shrug. "A little. You got a question in mind?"

"What's the big deal about the 1900s? I mean, there's that standing exhibit downstairs, but that's like prehistoric stuff and shit. Why the big deal about the turn of the century?"

"Not that much, other than there was a big change in

how most Mundane people saw Mediums. They started being more commonly accepted, got the vote, were finally allowed to hold public office. Didn't you cover any of this when you were in high school?"

"Yeah," he says, mouth quirked up in a slightly self-effacing grin. "I didn't do that well in history."

"Apparently." I look back down at the notebook. As I go farther and farther in, the references to the knife increase. I frown, then flip to the front of the notebook. There are fewer side notes.

"What item number are you on?" I ask, looking up at Cross.

"What, in her notes?"

"Yeah." I hold mine up. "It looks like she talks more and more about the knife as time goes on. Maybe if we go backward, we can figure out when she found it, what catalogue it'll be in?"

Cross nods and flips to the front of his notebook.

"Number J1276. What've you got?"

"M9158."

We both set down our notebooks and pick up new ones. We trade numbers back and forth, getting closer and closer to the start of the sequence. The references to the knife slowly decrease.

"I think I've got it," Cross says. "There's a really long paragraph about a knife. H8902?"

I grab a catalogue, then another, trying to place the number.

"This would be a lot easier with a computer," I sigh,

grabbing another book and flipping through the pages. "I've at least found the Hs. See if there's anything else useful while I dig through this."

"Only if you're interested in midcentury chalk," Cross says, sighing.

I finally find the right catalogue, dated for 1977. About halfway through the book, I find H8902.

Silver ceremonial Medium's knife. 6" in length, which is significantly longer than most knives of the sort from this time. Ornately carved with sigils and runes indicative of a Passenger, but could also be for a Reader or Seer. The syntax is not clear. Based on the tool marks and style, the knife was originally created in the late 1800s to early 1900s. Unknown silversmith's makers mark. Likely a custom commission, made for the family. Donated to the museum as part of a bequeathal from Baker household. No living relatives and no additional documentation on the knife found.

"It was donated by someone named Baker," I say, "but other than that, there's not a whole lot. There's no picture, so we're going to have to depend on that item number, but it sounds right."

"Let's see if Dr. Reed knows anything more about this family, then let's verify we're looking at the right knife. Grab her notes, they might be helpful, too."

I nod, and we walk back toward the doctor's office, the catalogue and Stephanie's notes tucked under my arm. Dr. Reed looks up from his computer screen as Cross knocks.

"Did you find anything?" he asks, scooting his chair back slightly.

"A bit," Cross says, crossing his arms. "What can you tell us about the donation that the knife was part of?"

"Not much, I'm afraid." Dr. Reed frowns. "It wasn't very large, just a few minor items. The knife was the most interesting piece, honestly."

"And you don't know anything about the family? The catalogue said the name was Baker."

"It's a fairly common name. I'm not sure I'd be able to find anything with just that."

He pauses, furrows his brow, and turns to his computer. He quickly types something in and hits enter with a purposeful motion, before leaning back.

"That being said, I know someone who might be able to help you. His name is Brent Hewitt. He was a medical doctor but retired a few years ago. He's become a local historian, specializing in Mediums in Chicago, and he does a little genealogy work on the side, too. He might be able to tell you more about Mediums in the city who could have donated the items. Here."

He grabs a Post-it Note from his desk and scribbles a name and number on the paper.

"His phone number. He should be able to point you in the right direction at least."

"Thank you for your help, Doctor," Cross says, taking the note. "If anything else comes up, we'll give you a call."

"Thank you," he says, rising from his chair. "Let me see you out."

He leads us out of the labyrinthian corridors of the museum, dropping us off at the base of the stairs where we first met him. The museum is even more crowded than when we arrived, so Cross and I leave through the back and walk around the exterior of the building. The sky is cloudless and blue, with a slight breeze off the lake. Cross slides his hands into his jacket pockets and sighs.

"Another lead," he says, "but it feels like a dead end."

"There's no connection between the victims other than that damn book, and the way things are going, I wouldn't be surprised if two of the deaths are ruled suicides," I say, grimacing.

"If Abramo comes back with Casey's autopsy and says she did it to herself, definitively, we're going to have a hell of a time proving it otherwise. From her notes, she was obsessed with that knife. Who's to say it didn't take a darker turn?"

"Yeah," I simply say. We fall into an awkward, waiting silence. There's an answer to be found, something that makes the pieces of this puzzle fit together, but I'll be damned if I know where.

CHAPTER FIFTEEN

A bramo's report comes in the next morning.
Cause of death: suicide by self-inflicted facial and thoracic knife wounds leading to exsanguination.

I curse and throw the report onto my desk. Cross isn't in yet, so I'm forced to glare at his empty chair instead.

It's not suicide, Priya says, floating to sit in Cross's chair. *You know that.*

I know I know that. I sigh. *But it's going to be a lot harder to convince anyone else of that when the medical examiner of Chicago is saying it's a suicide.*

I lean back in my chair and press the heels of my hands into my eyes. It stings, and the darkness behind my eyelids lights up with bright red pinpricks. They fade slowly as I lessen the pressure, the pain receding.

And to be honest, there's nothing besides my gut telling me that Abramo is wrong. We're missing something, Priya, I just don't know what.

Why don't you try Reading the knife? she asks, flowing through Cross's desk to sit on mine.

Burner, remember?

Fully trained Medium, remember? We've got the knife. Let's scribe a circle and see if we can get anything from it.

I pause, then sit up, suddenly excited.

That's not a bad idea, I say. I pull open my desk and find the copy of *On the Summoning and Capturing of Spirits through the Use of Inscribed Circles* from the box of Emma Murphy's stuff. The first few chapters have information on scribing beginner-level circles, including the basics for a general Reading. It's been awhile since I've tried to do any serious Reading with circles, and the reference should help get the general outline down. With a few tweaks to account for the knife's inherent power and all the blood still on the blade, I might be able to get something useful from it.

If whatever was blocking Casey doesn't block me as well.

I'm diagramming circles in my notebook, writing sigils and runes only to erase and replace them with others when I feel a presence over my shoulder. I turn slightly, and Cross is there, body leaning slightly over mine, brow furrowed. His hand is on the arm of my chair, supporting his body as he moves in closer, his other arm lightly resting across the back of my chair. I can see small flecks of gold mixed in with the green of his eyes that I've never noticed before. He blinks, and I jerk back slightly.

"What're you working on?" he asks, subtly shifting his body away from mine. There may be a hint of a blush on his cheeks, but I turn back to the paper and clear my throat instead of trying to find out for certain.

"Priya suggested I try to Read the knife."

He frowns, looking confused and glancing down at my paper, then back at me.

"Do you know another Reader in Chicago? Someone

who might have better luck than Casey did?"

"No," I say, "but what I *can* do is scribe a circle and see if we get anything that way."

Comprehension lights in his eyes. "Gotcha. Like you did at the Murphy scene."

"Exactly, just around the knife instead of the general area." I frown and erase a rune for containment and replace it with two for control and confinement. With a sigh, I set the pencil down.

"It may not work, though. Whatever was stopping Casey from getting a clear Reading may stop me. She had the Affinity, I don't. Circles are inherently weaker than Mediums, so it's likely I won't get any further than she did. Not to mention all the blood on the knife and the fact that it's a Medium's blood and a Medium's knife… There's just a lot that could go wrong. I need to make sure I get the circle right in case anything turns south."

"Blood makes a difference?"

"Yes. Remember how I powered that circle with blood? It carries a Medium's power. We channel it most of the time, using the inherent power within our bodies to do things, but when it comes to acting on the external world, you generally have to use blood. So, circles are powered by a drop of blood, ceremonial knives are quenched with oil and some of a Medium's blood, and some protections can be strengthened by blood."

"So, all of Casey's blood on the knife"—Cross nods—"it's power."

"It's uncontrolled power." I stress the word. "Once the blood leaves our bodies, there's still power there, but it's not under our direct control anymore. That's why you have to be careful about how much blood you use in a circle. If there's too much, it gets unpredictable and dangerous."

"I'm following you." Cross pauses, looking at the circle in my notebook. "What can I do to help?"

"I need a space that has contact with the ground, either concrete or somewhere contained but outdoors. The circle will work better if I can draw it directly on the ground. There's more energy that way, but I don't think that's gonna happen in the middle of Chicago. Otherwise, we'll need to run out and get a large piece of stone, preferably something locally sourced."

"I'll see what I can find."

"Thanks. In the meantime, I'll finish this and get the knife. I should be done in thirty. Meet up here, then we'll head out?"

"Yeah," he says, nodding again. "Sounds good. I'm gonna give that Hewitt guy a call, too. Set up a meeting."

"Great." I frown down at my notes. "I'll be here."

He heads out of the main floor toward the back entrance, and Priya and I set to work. It takes us most of the thirty minutes to figure everything out. There's more than one argument over the specific meaning of the runes we use—scribing circles is all about subtlety and precision—but in the end, Priya and I agree on the finished design.

Looks good, she says. *We might actually get something from this.*

Then let's get started.

I text Cross, and he tells me to meet him in the back. There's a loading bay for deliveries and perps, and off to the side, a small, unused storage room.

"Best I could find," he says, shrugging.

I can tell that Cross has cleaned up the room a bit, his habitual fastidiousness coming into play. There's furniture pushed back against the walls, broken desks and chairs moved to the side to be thrown out and forgotten. The center of the room, though, is empty of clutter. The concrete floor is smooth and cool against my fingers as I bend down to examine it. I reach out with my senses and can feel a low thrum of power coming up from the ground.

"It'll work," I say, pulling out my notes and my chalk. "Close the door and make yourself comfortable. This is gonna take a while."

I start scribing the circle. First come the main lines, a central path for the power to flow through. At the cardinal points, I write out runes of seeking, searching, finding. They're linked with sigils of confinement, of binding, and of communication. I continue to scribe, the chalk scraping against the concrete as I tie more and more of the symbols together, looping them back into the central circle. By the time I'm done, the chalk is nearly gone and white dust coats my fingers. I lean back, muscles cramping, and nod.

"The knife."

Cross hands me a paper evidence bag, and I pull a latex glove from my back pocket. It slides on easily, snapping in the tense silence of the room. I reach into the evidence bag and pull the knife from it. Casey's blood is deep brown, almost purple, against the metal. I set it in the center of the circle carefully. As the metal hits the floor, it rings dully. I sigh, stand, and step back.

"Stay as close to the door as you can," I tell Cross. "I don't know what's going to happen here. Probably nothing, but if something starts, I need you to be able to get out of here and get help as quickly as possible."

"It didn't seem that difficult when you did it at the Murphy crime scene," he says, looking concerned.

"There wasn't as much blood there. Just… Be ready."

Priya, I Send, moving toward the edge of the circle.

She appears beside me, glowing softly in Second-Sight. I watch as she slowly pulls power to her, her body filling with light until it's streaming off her. Her hair whips around her face and head in unseen winds, and when she turns to look at me, her eyes are pure white.

Ready.

I pull my knife from my boot and press it against the tip of my finger. I feel the quick sting of pain for a moment, then watch as blood slowly wells on my skin. I take a deep breath, gather energy in the pit of my stomach and press my thumb against the edge of the circle.

It bursts into light, the power of it pushing against me. I can feel the circle straining, but it slowly settles. In the center, the knife is glowing. Blood blocks the light in irregular patches, dark shadows holding it back. The glow from the knife starts to trickle down the sides of it like water, pooling on the floor around it. The light forms a still, bright circle, the edges of it firm and solid, holding. I stand and take a careful step forward, the toe of my boot resting delicately in the blank spaces of the circle, the chalk lines undisturbed. In the pool of light, I can see images starting to form.

There is a circle of people, their heads hooded, faces hidden. The image shifts, and it's a young girl weeping, body hunched, a terrified look on her face. Then a house, the door broken off its hinges, banging slowly in the wind. A face that's almost familiar. Then blood. Blood everywhere, filling everything. The pool of light turns red and flows out of the circle in slow, careful streams. The knife starts to spin, scraping against the floor with a dull, painful keen that makes me clutch at my ears, the metal of my own knife, forgotten in my hand, cold against my face. I take a step back, leaving the circle, and watch as the knife continues to spin, picks up speed, and comes to rest on the tip of the blade, pirouetting on its point.

"Cross," I shout, hands still pressed against my ears, "get out of here!"

"What's happening?"

I can barely hear him over the screeching, tearing sound of the knife.

"Something's trying to break through," I shout back. "You need to go! Priya and I can protect ourselves, but you can't."

"Phillips, I—"

"Go!" I pull power toward me and push, hand held out in front of me. It's not much, but the blast hits Cross in the center of his chest and forces him back to the door. Our eyes meet—his filled with some unrecognizable emotion, somewhere between anger and fear—and he nods. He fumbles for the doorknob, then falls out of the room, the door slamming behind him hard.

Priya flashes in front of me, shedding light and power. I pull it toward me and use her Healing to block my ears. The room falls into a muffled silence, but I can still feel the pain of the sound, even though I can no longer hear it. I feel the spirit pressing against the edges of the circle, looking for a place to break through. There's a maliciousness to it, a sense of purpose and intelligence that I have never encountered before. It's patient and unrelenting.

It's going to find a way out, I say, letting my hands fall to my sides. I grip my knife, feel its answering call.

The circle is containing it for now, Priya says, *but I don't know how long it will hold. Do you think you can Burn it?*

Maybe, I say, flipping my knife in a quick, practiced movement so that the blade rests against my forearm, the haft resting against the bones of my wrist. *We're going to have to be quick.*

Understood.

I hear a sharp crack and watch as Casey's knife falls to the ground. From the center of the circle, a shape starts to rise. Its body is the same color as the pooled red light. Hunched shoulders flow into loose limbs that brush against the surface of the red pool. Light drips from it like water, falling in small splashes on the floor.

Kim, it says, its voice like a whispered breath against my ear. Even using Healing to muffle the sound, it's clear.

We've got to Burn it, Priya shouts, her voice distant and

indistinct. I nod slowly, starting to crouch. A sheet of light bursts from my outstretched hand and wraps around the creature. I can feel it struggling, and I break into a sweat as I fight to contain it. Something stretches and gives, and I watch through blurred eyes as one of the creature's arms reaches through the light. Pain wrenches through my gut, and the binding disappears in a bright flash. The power drains from my body in a rush, and I fight to stay standing. The creature turns its head toward me, and the face splits into an open, grinning maw.

I pull more power to me, grounding myself with the concrete beneath my feet. Again, I press my knife to my skin, feel my flesh part like an exhalation against the cool blade. Blood flows freely, running down my arm. I run my fingers through it and drop to the ground to hastily sketch runes. They flash into light and the circle brightens in response. The creature moves toward me, then flinches back from the bloody marks on the ground as I scramble back. It tilts its head, eyeing them slowly with empty sockets that ooze and shift in its formless face.

What have we here?

It reaches an arm out. A too-long finger forms, stretches, and rests lightly against my blood on the floor. I smell something like burning hair, and it laughs, almost childlike, delighted.

That's clever, it says, leaning closer. *Very risky, but very clever.*

I press my hand onto my bloody forearm and hiss at the sting. I pull power again, this time directly from my own life force. Blood can be a conduit, a way to transfer power, but it can also be a fuel. Like gas, blood can burn.

I'm suddenly filled with power. I gasp and wisps of energy flow out from my mouth like fog. A manic glee traces its way up my spine. The power races through me, overwhelming and welcoming. I'm filled with purpose, with direction, with the urge to destroy the dark thing before me. *This is what you were born to do*, it whispers, twisting itself within my bones. My mouth breaks into a grin I can't control. The creature in the circle looks at me, then takes a hesitant step back.

You will kill yourself, it says, still slowly retreating.

But I'll Burn you, I Send, twisting my knife so it no longer rests against my arm. *I'll stop you first.*

I step into the circle, the power zinging up my legs whenever I step on a chalk line. I absorb it, sucking the light into my body. The creature roars and lunges toward me. With a shout, I duck under its grasping arms and plunge my knife and bloody arm into the soft flesh of its body. It presses against me, so cold it stings. Its body wraps around mine, muffling everything. Darkness overwhelms me, my body and the power contained within the only source of light. I can feel the spirit trying to break through, to take me over, tiny pinpricks of pain where it touches my skin. The light attacks it, cutting the seeking tendrils away. I push outward, forcing the power from my body down my arm, along the knife, and into the point that presses hard against the creature's skin. There's a long beat, a moment that stretches and contracts. I can hear my heartbeat singing in my ears, can hear the creature open its mouth to speak.

The body explodes around my arm. There's a scream—mine or the creature's, I don't know—and it falls to the ground. It writhes, twisting and scrabbling to hold the growing wound together. Its fingers bite into its flesh, but the red skin continues to part and tear. Tatters of its body fall to the ground, lying flat and steaming on the floor. It slows, twitches, then stops entirely, going limp. The remains slowly disappear, melting into the concrete, leaving small smoking puddles that also fade into nothing. I stand above the last bit of red, triumphant and filled with the echo of power, steam wreathing my feet.

I hear Priya screaming, hear Cross banging at the door, hear my head crack against the ground as I collapse, the world falling into darkness.

CHAPTER SIXTEEN

I come to on my side, my body rolled into the recovery position. My left leg is bent at the knee, stopping my body from falling forward, my arm propping up my torso. Cross kneels nearby, eyeing the door worriedly. The back of my head throbs with a sharp pain, and I groan, closing my eyes to slits. I reach my free hand up and touch the center of the pain, finding a lump. My fingers come away sticky with blood.

"She's awake!" Cross shouts, leaning down toward me. "Phillips, are you okay? What hurts?"

"My head," I say, letting my eyes close all the way, "and my shoulder."

I open my eyes to find him looking at me, brow furrowed and mouth turned down.

"You think you can get up?"

"With some help, probably," I say, rolling onto my front. It makes the room twist and turn, my gut clenching. I press my forehead to the cold concrete, arms pushed against my sides, palms flat on the floor near my head. I take a deep breath and push up. Cross's hands wrap under my arms, the deep cut on my right arm throbbing painfully. He starts pulling. I'm grateful for his extra strength as the room continues to twist and rock like a boat in an unseen sea. I lean against his chest heavily, resting my head on his shoulder. After a slow, quiet moment, his hand rests gently on my back, rubbing slow circles into the space between my shoulder blades. I sigh and he reaches another hand up to press against my hair, pulling my head into the crook between his neck and shoulder.

When his fingers brush against the place where my head hit the concrete, I wince.

"You gave yourself a pretty good bump there, Phillips," he says, fingers gentle on my scalp.

"Yeah," I say, eyes still closed, "clumsy of me. I pulled too much, nearly drained myself completely."

His fingers still, stop. I pull away and meet his eyes, my lids heavy with exhaustion.

"You've gotta be more careful," he says, voice quiet and serious.

My eyes lock with his. I lose track of time for a moment, either because of the comfort and concern I find in his gaze or the way the light plays off the gold and green of his eyes.

Kim, the Lieutenant is coming, Priya Sends, and I take a shaky step back. *There are a lot of people coming, actually.* Cross's hands linger, caress as they fall from my body.

"People are coming," I say as a way of apology or explanation, I can't tell.

He nods, then looks at the blood on his hand and sighs.

"We need to get you to an EMT, get you cleaned up." He turns toward the door.

I wince, my head throbbing.

Lieutenant Walker comes striding into the room, face pale and furious.

"Detective," she says, "what the hell were you trying to pull? The whole building was shaking. We nearly had to evacuate."

"I'm sorry, Lieu," I say. "We were trying to get more information on the weapon from the Casey case and it got out of hand."

Cross catches my eye as I fumble with the words. He raises an eyebrow, but I shake my head. He frowns.

"We need to get you to Provident," she says, turning to leave. There's a crowd of worried faces staring at me. I start to take a step back toward Cross, yet catch myself and stop.

"No, ma'am," I say, my voice weaker than I'd like it to be. "I just overextended myself. If there's an EMT on-site, that'll be enough."

"What happened?"

"Something tried to come through," I say. "The blood on the blade, it… I should've known better."

"Damn right you should have," she says, hands shaking and clenched. "You've been at this long enough to know the precautions you need to take. You put your life and your partner's life at risk, not to mention the rest of headquarters."

"There was a circle—"

"And if that failed? What would the officers and administrators in the building have done if a dark spirit had been released? What about the civilians? You're not the first Burner in this department and you're not the first Medium to overstep their bounds. I don't want you taking any more risks like this, do you understand me? Especially not over a goddamn suicide."

"Yes, ma'am," I say, shaken. I start to shiver and cross my arms, holding them tight to my body. Blood pumps sluggishly over my fingers, warm and sticky.

"Any more incidents like this and I'm putting you on leave," she says through clenched teeth. "I can't have my detectives getting hurt or putting other people at risk."

"Yes, ma'am," I say. "Is there an EMT I can see? I hit my head pretty good."

"You're lucky I'm not shipping you off to the hospital." She steps back into the hallway to let Cross and me through. "An EMT should be here in a few minutes. You can wait for him, and then you can get the hell out of my building."

The crowd that gathered starts to disperse, people shuffling their way back toward their desks. I can feel more than one set of eyes watching as Cross and I leave the storeroom.

"Cross, you keep an eye on her. Make sure she's seen to and that she doesn't have a concussion. And after she gets checked out"—she points at me—"I want a full report. What you two were doing, why, and what happened."

"Yes, Lieutenant," Cross says as subdued as I am.

"Also," she says, voice still angry, "someone called for you, a Hewitt? He said he'd be coming in this afternoon to talk to you. I didn't recognize the name. What case is he from?"

"He knew Casey," Cross says, lying. "We're just trying to understand her state of mind, make sure we've got the right COD."

"Don't spend any more time on this than you have to. The ME said it was suicide."

"Yes, Lieutenant."

"Get her to the EMT, then get her home. She's done for the day."

Frowning, Lieutenant Walker sighs and heads back toward her office.

"I mean it, Phillips!" she yells back, waving her finger at me again. "I want you out of here as soon as you get cleared."

More than a few heads turn as Cross helps me back to my desk, where I fall limp and exhausted. No one approaches, thankfully, but I can feel the people watching me. The room spins, and I hold on to the edge of my desk, my fingers pale and shaking. My arm is still bleeding, and Cross presses a napkin against the cut, stemming the flow.

"I'm going to wait for the EMT, make sure he gets to you right away. Stay put."

"I'm not going anywhere," I say, leaning back and holding the napkin hard against the cut. I close my eyes, letting my head fall onto the back of the chair. I can sense Priya nearby, just as worn out as I am. She's a gentle touch, but not much else.

A few minutes later, Cross startles me out of my doze, laying his hand lightly but unexpectedly on my shoulder.

"Hey, the EMT's here," he says, pulling his hand away as I blink myself awake.

"Detective Phillips?" The EMT is a young guy, hair dark and cut short. "I need to look at that arm." He gestures to where my hand is still pressing the soaked napkin against my skin. I pull my hand away. The cheap paper sticks, clinging to my skin where the blood has started to dry. With careful movements, he pulls it away. It stings, but it's distant, muffled.

The cut on my arm is straight and clean but deeper than I expected. If I weren't so damn tired, I'd be nauseated. Instead, I watch with detachment as the EMT slowly cleans the wound, injects me with some numbing agent, and puts slow, careful stitches in a straight, even line up my arm. Cross sits quietly at his desk the whole time, wincing as the needle goes in and out of my skin.

"You're going to want to see a doctor to have those removed in a few weeks," the EMT says, wiping up the traces of blood still on my arm. He starts placing non-stick pads over the stitches and wraps my arm in bandages. "And make sure you don't do too much. You pull those out, it's going to be harder to stitch up cleanly."

"Gotcha," I say, closing my hand into a fist and feeling the stitches pull slightly.

"If you keep it clean and dry and take it easy, you should be fine. If you get any swelling or redness, go see a doc. Now, let me get a look at that head of yours."

It stings when he presses his fingers against my scalp, and I wince, leaning away from the pressure.

"Sorry," he murmurs, moving my hair aside. "Doesn't look like you broke the skin too bad. No stitches, but you're going to want to be careful washing your hair for a couple of days."

He presses harder against my scalp, and I suck in a breath between clenched teeth.

"Nothing broken, but it'll be sore for a while. Advil, as needed, should take care of most of the pain, but if it gets bad, you can take Tylenol in between. Ice'll help, too. Can you follow my finger?"

I let my eyes trail his finger as he moves it back and forth before my face, then up and down. He hums softly and pulls a penlight from his pocket. "I don't think you've got a concussion," he says, shining the light in my eyes, "but if your headache gets worse, you start feeling nauseous or vomit, see stars, anything like that? You need to get to an ER."

I thank him, and he stands up from where he's kneeling in front of me, patting my knee reassuringly.

"Take it easy, Detective." He smiles. "You'll be feeling better in no time."

He walks off, his medical bag in hand. Sighing, I lean back in the chair.

"So," Cross says, clearing his throat, "did you get anything out of that besides a new scar and a knock to the head?"

"Maybe," I say, eyes closed. "There were a couple

visions before that thing tried to get through. Some people in a circle, a house. I think maybe Murphy or someone else, I'm not sure. And there was a face… I couldn't place it, but it seemed familiar."

Cross hums, and I hear his chair creak as he shifts his body.

"No signs of Casey, though?"

"No," I say, frowning. "No, I didn't see anything about her."

Silence falls between us, heavy and still. I can hear him breathing, hear him moving in his seat, leaning forward onto his desk.

"Hewitt is going to be here soon," Cross says. "There's a cot in the back you can lie down on if you need a rest, or I can get one of the other officers to take you home."

"No," I say, shaking my head. A sharp lance of pain shoots through my head and makes me clench my teeth. "No, I need to be here for this."

"I'm pretty sure Walker would have something to say about that. You sure you can handle it?"

"Yeah, I think so, if we make it quick."

"You get too tired, you let me know, okay?" He reaches across and lays a hand on my desk. "I'm here to help."

I want to reach forward and place my hand on his. I want to feel the careful rise and fall of his strong bones, want to feel the rasp of his skin against mine. My hand starts to lift from the armrest and settles again.

"Thank you," I say instead, throat tight. "For that. And

for back there. Sorry about the—" I hold my hands in front of me, miming the push I'd given him.

"It's all right," he says, leaning back. His hand trails over the surface of the desk, slow and reluctant, then settles in his lap. "I understand why you did it. Hopefully something will pan out with Hewitt."

"Yeah." I rub at the numb skin around my stitches. "I can't imagine it'd go any worse."

CHAPTER SEVENTEEN

C ross and I wait. I do my best to keep my eyes open, fighting against the urge to sleep. I feel empty, drained, like weight is missing from my bones. When I reach for my power, it answers slowly, muted. Pulling on it causes my head to throb, and I stop, waiting for the pain to fade. I start to doze, my chin dropping to my chest as I run my fingers slowly up and down the bandages on my arm, counting the wraps slowly while waiting for Hewitt to show up. I lose track of time, drifting toward sleep in a haze of dull aches and pains.

I dream for a moment. Flashes of a dark, open mouth reaching for me, of a half-forgotten face. I feel myself sinking deeper into the dream, start to catch a glimpse of an abandoned building, the doors familiar and frightening. My body drifts slowly, inexorably, toward them. I turn to fight the pull, to run, and—

Cross clears his throat, and I jerk awake suddenly, my fingers still resting against my arm. He inclines his head toward the door, and I turn around in my chair, the metal bearings squeaking, my heart racing. I fight down the panic and take in the man heading toward us.

Escorted by a uniformed officer, he's unassuming, his

hair short and a shocking white against his dark skin. He's older, but his chest is broad, his steps purposeful and strong. He's wearing a faded blue button-up shirt and khakis with a pair of thin silver glasses hanging from a chain around his neck. He holds a manila folder loosely in his wrinkled hands, and he smiles when he sees Cross start to stand.

"No need to get up, Detective," he says, waving a hand toward Cross. "Not on my account, at least."

"Mr. Hewitt?" Cross asks, rising to his feet anyway. The man rolls his eyes but keeps smiling.

"Mr. Hewitt is my father," he says, still smiling and reaching out to shake Cross's hand. "Please, call me Brent."

"Brent," Cross says, gesturing toward his desk, "have a seat."

"Thank you." He lowers himself into the spare chair next to Cross's desk and sets the manila folder down. When he looks at me, he frowns.

"What happened here?" He reaches for my arm. Still wrestling with the panic of the half dream, I pull it back, flinching before he touches me. "My apologies," he says, his hand hanging awkwardly in empty space. "Too many years in the medical profession, I'm afraid. Do you mind?"

"No," I say, laying my arm on the table and feeling embarrassed. He reaches for my arm again and sets gentle fingers against my skin. He leans in, clucking his tongue quietly, and closes his eyes. I feel a buzzing in my arm, then a slow burn. I drop into Second-Sight and see blue lines racing underneath the bandages and around the cut, stitching the skin together. The redness around the edges starts to fade, the skin slowly coming back together. It immediately starts itching.

"You're a Healer," I say. I grab his hand, stilling him. The blue light fades, and he opens his eyes, meeting mine. A young man materializes over his shoulder, eyes gray and watchful, and lays a hand on Hewitt's shoulder. His partner.

"Yes," Hewitt says, "I am. Retired now, but it's hard not to help where I can. And that's a pretty nasty gash, Detective."

There's something in his eyes, something quiet and judging. Healers can feel more than just physical injuries, and I get the sense he knows exactly how badly hurt I am.

"It's all right," I say, pulling my arm away and leaning back. "It's nothing."

He frowns but turns back to the manila folder.

"Dr. Reed recommended we talk to you. Do you mind if I record this?" Cross says, pulling out a handheld recorder.

Hewitt shakes his head. "No, that's fine. I expected you'd need to do that when we first talked."

"You're an expert on local Medium history?" Cross starts.

"That's right," Hewitt says, opening his folder. "It started as a hobby, but now that I'm no longer working, it's become a passion of mine."

"Were you able to find anything relating to the collection?"

"I gathered as much as I could from what you told me over the phone, Detective Cross, but I'm afraid the 1970s are a bit more modern than my usual area of expertise. Here," he says, spreading out a series of loose-leaf pages. Each one has a newspaper clipping attached, some with photos. I pull a few pages closer, flipping through them quickly.

"These are all of the big news stories I could find relating to Mediums during that time. There were a few famous names like McKenna and McCormick, but I didn't see any major families past that."

"Anyone named Baker?" I ask, searching for the name in the few news articles I have spread before me.

"No, not that I could find," he says, shaking his head. "But, again, I'm not as familiar with Medium families from this century, and Baker is a pretty common name."

I sigh, passing the papers to Cross.

"What about any specific Affinities?" Cross asks, taking the papers from my outstretched hand.

"Lots of Burners," Hewitt says, "and a few Readers and Healers, nothing that exciting. And nothing about an estate being gifted to the museum."

I sigh again, rubbing a hand over my face. There's a tense moment, the stillness interrupted slightly by the noise of other officers moving around the squad room and Cross shuffling through Hewitt's notes.

"I'm sorry," Hewitt says, sighing. "It's like finding a needle in a haystack, I'm afraid. There were more Mediums in Chicago fifty years ago, but then the population started to drop, we started becoming less common, and, outside of a few major families and major stories, the papers stopped reporting on us."

His mouth is downturned, his eyes lingering on the pages on the desk. "On top of that, most of my research relates to the turn of the nineteenth century, rather than the twentieth. I'm out of my element, I'm afraid."

"What can you tell us about the Moores?" I ask impulsively. Cross raises an eyebrow as Hewitt perks up.

"The Moores? They were some of the strongest Shakers in the area during the late 1800s. They've since relocated, most of the family settling in the West, but there are still a few living around here." He pauses and raises his brows. "There was something in the news recently... about a suicide. A boy with the last name Moore."

"Were they still active in the community during the midcentury?" I ask, ignoring his paling face.

"Just Caroline," he says, "but she left in the late fifties. What would that have to do with a donation to the museum? Is this connected to that boy?"

"Mr. Hewitt," Cross says, leaning forward, "my partner and I appreciate your expertise—"

"Have you ever heard of a book called *On the Summoning and Capturing of Spirits through the Use of Inscribed Circles*?" I cut in.

Cross falls silent, eyes filled with anger. Hewitt's eyes are wide, and he hurriedly starts to gather his papers together, stuffing them haphazardly back into the manila folder.

"I think we're done here," he says, starting to stand.

I grab his arm, tight, and wince as the stitches pull. "Sit down," I say, voice hard. He eyes me warily, then slides back into the seat.

"What do you know about the book?" I ask, slowly releasing his arm. He rubs at the imprints my fingers leave behind, frowning.

"I know you shouldn't know about it. I've only heard of it because of my research," he says. "All copies of it were supposed to be destroyed decades ago, along with all record of it. I know that the people who *do* know about it are afraid of it, of what it means. And I know *you* shouldn't be talking about it after nearly killing yourself with a Burning."

Cross looks at Hewitt, then back at me. "What's he talking about, Phillips?"

"Don't worry about it," I say, brushing him off with a twinge of guilt. "Why was it destroyed? Why were people afraid of it?"

Hewitt looks like he's not going to say anything, his mouth a tight line, hands clenched in his lap. I reach down, open a desk drawer, and pull Emma's copy of the book out, tossing it onto the desk, front cover down. He jumps at the heavy thunk it makes, then reaches hesitantly for the book. He flips it over, reads the title, and blanches. Dropping the book, he shakes his head back and forth.

"No," he says, backing up slightly. "You shouldn't have that. You don't know what you're getting involved in."

"Then *tell me*," I say, leaning forward. "What's in this book that's so dangerous?"

Hewitt presses his lips together tightly, gaze hard and

unwavering as it meets mine. I'm exhausted, but I call on years of experience in interviews and interrogations to shift my face into my most intimidating expression. It must work, because Hewitt glances away, slumping in his chair.

"It's the binding," he says, sighing. "The last chapter."

"And that's a good enough reason to destroy it?" Cross asks.

"Yes," Hewitt says, insistent. "Absolutely. You have to understand, it's not like binding a Turned spirit. That's part of the natural process, a way to help someone into the afterlife when they're unable to do it themselves. This binding, it cuts a Medium off from the afterlife entirely. It seals their powers away and keeps them from passing on when they die. It guarantees that there will be a powerful, dangerous ghost left behind, one that *will* Turn. There's no other alternative."

I lean back, stunned.

"Can't a Burner just get rid of it?" Cross asks, confused.

"Yes and no," I say, looking at the book on the desk. "When you die, if you leave a ghost, it will take after you. Same mannerisms, same thought patterns, same strengths and weaknesses. Generally, the ghosts who Turn don't have a lot of knowledge about the afterlife. That's part of what makes them Turn, the fear and disorientation."

"A Medium wouldn't have that," Hewitt says, breaking in. "We spend our lives interacting with the dead. We're bound for life with a ghost partner. When we die, we die with a full knowledge of what waits."

"So, Mediums don't Turn?"

"Not like Mundane people do," Hewitt continues. "No. If a Medium Turns, they become stronger than they ever were in life, but without any sanity to control it."

"Oh."

"Yeah," I say, running a hand over my face.

"That's why the book had to be destroyed," Hewitt continues, glancing back at the copy on my desk. "It put too many people at risk. When it was written, the community wasn't as cohesive as it is now. There was a lot of infighting, different families scrambling for power. It's why there are so few Passengers now. Most of those bloodlines were eradicated in the 1700s."

"So, Mediums would use this binding as a weapon? To stop their enemies?" Cross asks.

"Yes," Hewitt says, "or at least that's what they'd say. Sometimes it was just done out of spite, and then they wouldn't tell anyone where the binding occurred. After death, the Medium's ghost would naturally go to where they were bound, rather than staying at the place of their death or following their body. And if you don't know where the binding happened, the ghost can't be freed before they become dangerous. When the first public congregation of Mediums happened in 1902, there was a vote to ban the binding and destroy any record of it. They burned hundreds of copies of that book. I don't, or rather *didn't*, know any still existed, not even in the Library of Congress."

And we have three copies, I think, body cold.

"What are you going to do with it?" Hewitt asks.

"It'll get filed in evidence," Cross says, "and then it'll

get put into storage until we're able to close the case."

"Keep it under lock and key," Hewitt says, drawing his brows together, "and don't let anyone know you have it. There are people who would kill for that book."

And that could be our motive here, I think, taking the book back. I let my fingers rest on the rough-cut pages and start to open to the back. To the binding.

"Detective Phillips!"

I turn to see Lieutenant Walker bearing down on me, her expression cold.

"Grab your things and get out of here," she says, pointing toward the door. "You were supposed to be gone an hour ago. If I see you again in the next twenty-four hours, you'll be put on administrative leave, and I'll be taking your gun and badge. Am I clear?"

"Yes, ma'am," I say, standing quickly. "Cross, keep me posted. And don't go anywhere, Mr. Hewitt, I still have—"

"Out!" she shouts, and I grab my coat, tugging it on quickly and heading toward the door. I'm light-headed when I sit down behind the wheel of my car, but it passes. I can see Hewitt's shocked face through the glass doors. Our eyes meet for a moment, and he nods. There's some message he's trying to send, but all I can do is return the gesture, uncertain, Emma's book sitting forgotten on my desk.

CHAPTER EIGHTEEN

With little else to do and my energy fading, I drive home. The walk up the stairs to the fifth floor takes a long time, my head aching and my body weary. I lean heavily on the railing and pause about halfway up to let the gray around the edges of my vision fade. My door is heavy and slow to open, and I lock it behind me before sinking down onto the welcome mat. I catch my breath, eyes closed, head tipped back against the door. After a few long minutes, I get back to my feet. Hand pressed against the door in support, legs weak and trembling, I struggle to stand and make my way to the bedroom. I carefully undress before I slide between my sheets. The bed is warm and inviting, the pillow cool against my face. I burrow in, falling asleep almost immediately, the lights still on.

My dreams are peaceful, thankfully, and I wake up feeling rested, if not fully recovered. I stretch, groaning as my muscles twinge, the cut on my arm pulling painfully. I check the stitches, but they're holding. The areas where Hewitt used his power look days old, rather than hours. There's a deep-seated throbbing in my side, and I stretch again, trying to work it out. When the ache refuses to go away, I sigh and fall into Second-Sight, the room around me snapping into blue-lit view.

I reach out with my power tentatively. There's no pain, and I can already feel my spiritual reserves recovering. Priya is a solid presence nearby, and she responds to my gentle touch with a soft brush against the back of my head. There's a slight tingle and the last edges of my headache fade.

Welcome back, she says. She frowns slightly as she settles next to me on the bed. *Are you okay?*

Yeah, I think I'll be all right.

No more of this, she says, her fingers breezing over the stitches. *It was reckless and you know it.*

I didn't have a choice, I say, shaking my head. *Was I supposed to let it out?*

There are plenty of other options before you Burn yourself through.

But none that would have worked.

She frowns and rolls her eyes. *You always have had a flair for the dramatic*, she says, coming to rest beside me on the bed. She leans into me, a coldness against my side. *Just be more careful, okay? You should've seen Cross when he found you.*

What happened?

Went white as a sheet and kept yelling your name, she says, floating toward the door. *There was a lot of blood, and I think he was concerned that you'd bled out. He propped you up, got pressure on your arm, and waited for help. I never imagined I'd see him shaken, but finding you on the ground... Well, he was pretty upset.*

I frown, rubbing my fingers over my bandages again,

wondering what was going through his head when he found me covered in blood and unconscious. I think of the way he held me afterward, of his hands in my hair, the warmth of his body against mine, and I shiver.

I'll be more careful, I say, throwing my legs over the side of the bed. *I promise.*

Priya tilts her head in acknowledgment and fades out of sight.

I take a long shower and clean off the blood and sweat still clinging to my body. I wash my hair one-handed, keeping my injured arm out of the water. The stitches itch in the humid air, and the wound on the back of my head stings as I rinse out the shampoo. I shut off the water and step out into the steam-filled bathroom. Wiping the mirror clean, I look myself over. My hair is tangled, blond strands clumped together from sleep and rushed washing. There are healing cuts on my face and shoulders, dark bags underneath my blue eyes. I pull a brush through, wash my face carefully, and wrap myself in a heavy towel. I bandage my arm quickly and head into my bedroom to get dressed.

Throwing on an old T-shirt, the fabric soft and faded from years of wear, and a pair of CPD sweatpants, I wrap an old cardigan around my shoulders to hold off the slight chill in the air. I settle on the couch, my bare feet tucked under my legs, and turn on the TV, trying to relax. I can't find anything worth watching and leave the TV tuned to an old episode of *The Big Bang Theory.* I use my phone to read a few news stories and play a level or two of Candy Crush before tossing it down, still bored and restless.

I lean back into the couch cushions, staring at the

ceiling.

How did Hewitt know so much about the book? I wonder, eyes softly focused on a crack running through the center of the ceiling. *If he had been studying Mediums at the turn of the century, if all record of the book was supposed to be wiped, he wouldn't have been able to find out about it. And if he was able to find information about the book, why wasn't he able to find a Passenger named Baker? The Affinity alone should've made that easy.*

I pause, considering.

"How old do you think Hewitt is?" I ask aloud, sitting up and looking around the apartment. Priya pops into view and shrugs.

I don't know. Mid-sixties, maybe early seventies?

"That'd make him a generation younger than my grandma," I say, standing up and heading toward the spare bedroom. "If he grew up in Chicago, maybe she knew or worked with him."

My grandma used the second bedroom as a craft room when she lived in the apartment, but I converted it into an office after I moved in. I'm not a well-organized person, and the office shows it the most. A worn desk is tucked next to the window in the back corner. An old computer takes up most of the surface, the monitor one of the big, bulky kinds that went out of fashion after Y2K. The rest of the desktop is littered with papers, and there's an old rolling chair with a box on its seat parked in front. A few bookshelves around the edges of the room are mostly filled with haphazard, shifting piles of disorganized books. The rest of the room is littered with boxes, some open, some shut, most of them labeled with my rough scrawl, but there are a few tucked in the back with my grandma's careful script.

Besides the apartment, my grandma left me most of her things. I cleared out the place after her death, a process that was equal parts tedious and heartbreaking. She was always a well-organized woman, but a bit of a pack rat, and I had to go through a lifetime of keepsakes. Knickknacks, newspaper clippings, old letters, they all went into box after box as I made my way through the apartment. Most of it was thrown out to make space for my things, but I kept her diaries. I was able to give up a lot of her things, but not those. Hardback books that she'd written in her entire life filled three paper boxes, a surprisingly small amount of space to fit an entire lifetime.

The diaries are tucked in the corner, one of the only piles that's carefully stacked. I open the first box, then start thumbing through the books. The years are written on the spines in white paint pen, each number precise and beautiful. I let my fingers rest on the worn covers for a moment, wondering if I can still feel anything of her presence. Priya knocks me from my reverie, drawing me back to the present.

Do you really think there's a chance she knew him?

I can feel her peering over my shoulder, watching my fingers as they move from spine to spine.

I think it's more likely than not, I say, moving the top box to the floor. I take out the first layer of diaries from the next box, the dates still too recent for what I'm looking for. Underneath, I find a dozen diaries from the seventies.

I pull them all out, put the rest away. The lid slides on easily, and I push the stack of boxes back. It takes me a moment to balance all the books in my arms, my stitches stinging, and I make my way back into the living room.

After I set the books down on the couch, I push the coffee table back, clearing a wide space on the floor. I spread the diaries out on the floor and coffee table, then settle down in front of the couch, legs folded in front of me. I grab the first diary and start reading:

January 1, 1971
Warmer than usual. Some rain, no snow. Received letter from Laura today. She and the kids are doing well.

My grandma's writing sprawls across the page, the letters beautiful and flowing. I start to skim, waiting for something to jump out at me. Names, dates, events, something that might point me in the right direction. It takes me most of the morning, but I get through the first half of the decade and find nothing past old memories and her familiar writing and thoughts.

I take a break for lunch, my stomach growling. I put a bowl of soup in the microwave, then wait for it to heat up, hip leaning against the counter, spoon resting against my lower lip.

How's the search going? Priya asks, body halfway through the countertop.

Not great, I say. *Nothing so far about a Brent Hewitt. Caroline Moore's come up a time or two, but that's not terribly surprising.*

Grandma liked to keep up with the major Mediums in the area.

Priya frowns, then settles next to me. She pulls her legs up onto the counter, crosses her legs at the ankles, and leans forward. If it weren't for the inch between her and the counter, she'd look like any person just relaxing with a friend.

It's a bit of a needle in a haystack, she says. *While Sadie may have known Hewitt when he was a boy, she may not have remembered him or made note of it. She worked with a lot of young people, didn't she?*

Yeah, she did. Not many Healers, though. If she had worked with him, I think she would've written about it.

I run my fingers over the healing skin around the stitches in my arm.

He was pretty strong, I add. *Had a delicate touch.*

The microwave beeps and I step forward, carefully holding the hot bowl between my fingers. I set it on my small dinner table and sit down to eat. Steam curls up from the bowl, and I burn the roof of my mouth on the first sip.

That's no guarantee she would've written about him, Priya continues, still sitting on the counter. *Anything about a Baker?*

I shake my head and take a more careful sip.

No, no Baker. No Passengers either. I may need to follow up with Dr. Reed to see what Affinity the rest of his team thought the knife was. I think he said that Casey was the only one who thought it belonged to a Passenger.

You may have to wait until Monday to call him, Priya says. *The museum's open, but I'd be surprised if he was there today, especially after losing a colleague. And Lieutenant Walker wouldn't like for you to be doing anything related to that case right now, I don't think.*

She'd kill me, I say, finishing the last of my soup. *No, I'll follow up with him later. And I still have another five years to get through. No point in giving up yet.*

I leave the bowl in the sink, rinsing it quickly before resting it on top of other dishes waiting to be run through the small dishwasher. Priya joins me in the living room, disappearing as I get comfortable on the floor again. I push the diaries I've already read under the coffee table with my foot, then pull the remaining ones closer and start reading.

The first one I check, 1976, is a bust, and 1977 is looking to be more of the same when I find a huge section of pages missing. There are still bits of paper stuck in the binding, a few letters here or there peeking from the edges, but otherwise, there are about twenty pages gone from the middle of the diary. I frown as I look at the last entry before the missing piece.

June 14, 1977

The rain has finally broken, though it's still hot and now very humid. I had some troubling news this morning, and I've struggled to write it down. According to the paper, Baker is gone. Old age, it says, nothing traumatic or frightening, but I cannot stop thinking about him. All alone in that house, family and friends long since gone. It's been so many years since I've seen him, and I promised myself I wouldn't think about what happened then, but I find myself going back more and more. When someone has that big of a role in your life, in directing you toward your future path, it's hard to forget.

He'd always been a handsome man, with striking eyes and a wide, open smile. That's what I always remember first, his smile. So bright it would light up the room, his laughter always ringing out. It changed toward the end. It became something that I feared, something that always left me chilled and shaking inside. I hated that. I think it influenced me more than I should have let it, and Caroline was so convincing.

In the end, I did what I had to do to keep myself safe, but I remember his smile, and

"Shit," I say, leaning back against the couch. The next entry is weeks later, and there's no mention of Baker or what my grandma was thinking.

What is it? Priya asks, floating to rest on the couch. She looks over my shoulder, then raises a slender eyebrow as she reads.

Shit.

"She never tore pages out," I say, running my finger over the rough edges. "What did she write? Do you think this could be the same Baker as the one who donated the knife?"

The dates match up, Priya says, frowning, *but a handsome man with a smile she never forgot? Sounds like he could have been a boyfriend or lover, rather than an acquaintance.*

"Maybe. There's no other mention of him, though. I can work with the date, check it against death records and see if anything comes up."

I sigh and put the diary on the table.

"I'm going to have to go through her older diaries, too," I say, standing up. I grab the diaries, piling them in my arms, and head back toward the office. "If he was a boyfriend, she may have written about him before."

I set them down in their box haphazardly, then open the last box of diaries. They start in the mid-fifties, and I start pulling out books.

"She married Grandpa after the war, so if she was seeing someone, it would've been before then. The late thirties would probably be the best place to start, and I know she was keeping diaries then. They're just at the bottom of the—"

I stop. The book under my fingers doesn't feel the same as the rest, and now that I'm focusing, it's not the same type as the rest of the diaries. It's a wider binding, the edges embossed, the cover made of leather instead of canvas, and there's no date on the spine. I pull it from the box, turn it to see the front cover, and drop it like a hot coal.

The title is in faded gilt, the letters pressed into the cover:

On the Summoning and Capturing of Spirits through the Use of Inscribed Circles.

CHAPTER NINETEEN

"What the hell?"

I take a step back. Priya appears next to me and flares her power. Her hair whips around her face from an intangible wind, her eyes flashing white.

Where did that come from? she asks, placing herself between me and the book like it might attack.

"It was in with her diaries," I say, voice shaking, and I step through Priya to pick up the book. There's a symbol embossed on the back, a circle bisected by a cross with one arm longer than the rest. Like the other symbols, I've never seen it before. But something about this one feels familiar, and I let my fingers rest against it for a moment before shaking off the sensation. The rune is in the same place as the ones on Moore, Hewitt, and Casey's copies, the symbol itself the only difference. My grandma's name is written in her neat, careful handwriting inside the front cover. I shiver and close the book.

"It's her copy."

I head into the living room and throw the book onto the coffee table, then sit down on the couch and pull my feet up, wrapping my arms around my knees. I stare at it for a moment, its gilt cover familiar and terrifying.

"She knew Moore," I say slowly. "Caroline, that is. She mentioned her before, and she says something about Caroline in that missing entry. Caroline was so convincing…"

I stop and hug myself tighter. It's so simple, but I can't make myself say it.

She Bound someone, Priya says, still pulsing with restrained power. *She and Caroline.*

"If I had to guess," I say, finally grabbing the book and opening it to the last chapter, "the other Mediums were related to Murphy and Casey. That's why they had the books."

That's why I have a book, I think to myself, my hands shaking as I open to the ceremony.

And Baker? Do you think that's who they Bound?

"Hewitt said that Mediums regularly hunted down Passengers, and if Casey was right about the knife, that was his Affinity."

We have a Seer, Reader, Shaker, and now, potentially, a Burner involved. If Baker was the victim and he was a Passenger, that leaves a Healer and Speaker.

"Why would she do it?"

The silence that follows swallows me up. My throat is tight, mind racing as I try to understand.

My grandma was the only person I could depend on when I was younger. She knew what it was to be a Medium, what it meant when I spoke to people others couldn't see. When my parents failed to understand, when they were unable to cope with my powers, Grandma Sadie was always there. Warm, comforting, understanding, kind. She raised me as much as my parents, as much as Taka. She was a constant source of support. She left everything to me, gave me a home in every sense of the word. I shake my head, still disbelieving.

"How terrible could he have been for her to do this?"

More importantly, Priya says, resting her hands over mine, *what do we do now that you're linked to this?*

"What do you mean?"

Every victim had a copy of the book, Priya says, pressing. *And now you have one, along with possible evidence that your grandmother was involved in a binding with one of the victims' ancestors.*

"You think whoever is committing these murders," I say, slowly, "might be after me, too."

Priya doesn't say anything, waiting.

"The binding, that's the motive. Whoever is doing this, they're coming after the families of those involved, getting revenge for whoever this Baker person was."

He might be a Passenger, too, Priya says, her face drawn tight with worry. *If the victims were related to the Mediums who did the binding, it makes sense that the person killing them would be related to the person they Bound.*

"It would explain what happened with Moore," I say. "Passengers can take control of someone, make them do things they don't want to."

And stay with a body after a person passes.

"God," I say, shaking my head. "He could have killed

every one of these people without having to even be there. With Murphy, he could've taken over one of those homeless men. Hell, if it had been Richardson, it would have been easy, especially if he has the Sight. And Casey... If he possessed her, it would explain why the wounds looked like they were self-inflicted. Shit. I've got to call Cross."

I set the book down and fumble for my phone. It rings a few times, and when Cross finally answers, loud voices and clinking glasses nearly drown out his voice.

"What is it, Phillips?" he asks, sounding tired.

"We need to talk to Hewitt again," I say, heading toward my bedroom. "As soon as possible. I think I've figured out what's happening with the Mediums, with that book. It's a little crazy, but—"

"Hewitt's dead," Cross says, cutting me off.

"What?"

"Last night," Cross says, the background noise fading. "He passed away from natural causes. Heart attack according to the EMTs who responded to the 9-1-1 call. He still had my business card on him, so they called me. But what'd you say about the case? Lieutenant Walker told you to rest. You're not supposed to be working on it."

"Nothing, don't worry about the case," I say, still reeling. "Hewitt's dead?"

"Yeah," Cross says slowly. "Are you okay? You sound a little—"

I hang up, set the phone down, and grab my knife from my bedside table. I head toward the office and pull open a desk drawer filled with chalk. Grabbing a handful, I take it with me into the living room.

I spend the rest of the evening carving sigils and runes into the door and window frames, scribing circles of protection around the apartment in huge swaths of white. The wards flare to life as I press my blood into the marks, each one disappearing from normal sight and coming to life in a blue-cast haze. My phone rings a few times, but I barely notice it, wrapped up in the feeling of panic and the rush of power as it leaves my body. Each time I press a bloody finger to a circle, it leaves me light-headed, my vision graying at the edges, but I don't stop. I start sketching on my own skin, blood smearing in wide swathes across my body. They flare to life, then disappear, my body swept up in cold waves of power. Priya hovers, watching my frenzied activity with quiet anxiety and fear.

By the end of it, every surface of the apartment is covered in runes, sigils, and circles, sealed against other Mediums, ghosts, anything I can think of that might cause me harm. I take a few exhausted steps toward my bedroom, but give up and fall onto the couch, dropping quickly into troubled sleep. I swear I hear fists pounding against the door, against the windows, the wind whipping outside like angry, frustrated screams.

CHAPTER TWENTY

I wake up on the couch early the next morning, body screaming from the fight the day before and the awkward position I fell asleep in. I groan, then head to my bedroom to get dressed. As I slide my Glock into its holster, coffee cup sitting on the table by the front door, Priya stops me.

Where are you going? she asks, keeping herself between me and the door.

"You know that never works," I say, reaching through her to turn the knob. She floats toward my coffee, frowning.

I'll take the heat from it, she threatens, her hand reaching toward the steaming cup. I can see the tendrils curl around her hand and disappear.

"That's low," I say, quickly grabbing the cup and taking a step back. "We're going to Hewitt's."

He's dead, Kim.

"I know." I take a careful sip of the coffee. "But he knew about the book, about the ritual. He's got to have notes or something about it in his apartment. Without more information about the binding, we're going to be flying blind. There are at least two more potential victims out there, and we have no idea who they might be. I can't let their blood be on my hands."

Priya frowns, but nods.

And what are we going to do once we get there?

"We'll figure that out once we get there," I say, grinning. She rolls her eyes, but moves out of my way, leaving my coffee warm in my hand.

I'm able to pull up Hewitt's address through a quick Google search. He ran a business out of his home looking up family genealogies, and the address is posted on his website. It takes about twenty minutes to get there, the early Sunday morning traffic light and free-flowing. I park down the street from his house, the front door broken from where EMS must have forced their way in, now wrapped in police tape. The sun is just starting to come up, and I can see a cruiser parked farther down the street, a dark uniformed figure sitting behind the steering wheel, newspaper in hand.

"Shit," I say, leaning back in my seat. "I'm not going to be able to go in, not with someone watching the place."

Is that usual? Priya asks.

"I bet Cross put someone on the detail until Hewitt's family fixes the door. It feels like something he'd do. We could try waiting him out?"

Priya gives me a look, and I sigh.

"Yeah, I don't think that'll work, either. And it's going to be too bright out for me to break in now."

We sit in silence for a few seconds, both of us watching the officer. Besides turning to the next page in his paper, he doesn't move.

"You're going to have to do it," I say, voice firm.

I'm not breaking into a dead man's home, Kim.

"It's not really breaking in," I hedge. "We're just looking for information to help our case."

Then why don't you go up to the officer, explain what's going on, and let yourself in? Or come back tonight?

"I'd need a warrant, I don't have anything close to probable cause, and my gut's telling me we can't waste any more time on this."

I turn and face her, pleading.

"All you have to do is go inside, flip through his papers, and see if there's anything relating to the book. It'll take you ten minutes, and then we'll be out of here."

Ten minutes, she says, face serious. *That's it. And you're calling Cross as soon as we're done and getting him up to speed.*

"Agreed. Do you need me to move closer, or can you reach it from here?"

I should be okay, but it'll be a stretch. If it starts to hurt, I'm stopping.

Priya fades, dropping her physical manifestation. I can feel her moving away through our bond, which starts to stretch as she gets farther away.

His wards have been tripped, she says. I drop fully into Second-Sight, and I can see the ghostly shape of sigils and runes around the door. When a Medium dies, their wards and circles will fade with time, but these look like they've been forced, some brighter than others, a few empty spaces hinting at sigils that have lost their power entirely.

Someone pushed their way in here, she says. *I can see the burn marks around the doorframe.*

Keep going, I Send, suddenly nervous. *And if anything happens, run.*

I feel her assent through the bond, though she doesn't Send anything. The minutes start to drag. I can feel the bond stretching. She's near the edge of how far she can go, my heart beating painfully as she pulls against the astral ties that keep us together. I can feel it taut between us, a psychic pain that leaves my nerves raw and singed, my chest and throat tight. Right when I think it might be tearing, she starts Sending me images in a sudden rush.

Sheets of paper scattered on a desk. Genealogies drawn out, the branches ending in Hewitt's own name. Then more pages, more family lines. Familiar names. A book, the title glinting in the early morning light, a symbol embossed on the back cover. And finally, a list of six names.

My chest is aching as Priya flies back toward me, her presence in the car like a huge, gasping breath as the bond snaps back.

"What'd you find?" I ask, breath coming fast. heart pounding.

He was working on his genealogy, she starts. *I think just for fun or for practice for his business, it wasn't clear from what I could see. I think he found something that belonged to his grandmother, a Comfort Bell, but that's how he learned about the binding. She was one of the Binders. He tracked down the book, started making connections. He's got Murphy's family tree in there. Same with Moore's, Casey's, yours. And a list of names. It looks like it's the rest of the people who did the binding.*

"He must have found something about the binding while looking into his ancestry. So he knew who I was," I say, frowning. "He knew about the book because he had his own copy. And when he came into the station, he knew I was connected to the binding and didn't say anything."

That's what it looks like.

"Was there anything else? Any other genealogies?"

No, the last one wasn't there or he hadn't started it yet. Just the binder's name: Robert Barrett.

"I bet Hewitt didn't die from a heart attack," I say, my intuition hinting at the truth. "I bet whoever is doing this came for a little visit last night and took care of him. That makes four victims, and judging by this, our guy is getting a hell of a lot better at making it look like an accident. I wonder if Hewitt even made the 9-1-1 call or if that was the murderer making the call for him." I shake my head, worried and just a little scared.

"Casey must have been a fluke," I say. "Something about the knife set him off, made him lose control."

I run a hand down my face and sink deeper into the seat.

"We need to call Cross."

Priya bobs her head, but doesn't say anything. I start the car and pull away, Hewitt's empty house with its broken wards fading behind us, my phone cold against my face as I wait for Cross to pick up.

CHAPTER TWENTY-ONE

C ross picks up after a few rings, his voice gruff and sleep-roughened. I glance at the clock and wince slightly at the hour.

"Cross," he says, his name slipping out on a groan. "What is it?"

"It's Phillips. I need to talk to you about the case."

"Yeah," he sighs, "you said that last night before you hung up on me and then refused to answer your damn phone."

I feel a twinge of guilt, but press on.

"I can meet you at your place," I say, my tone cajoling. "I'll bring coffee."

There's a pause, and I can hear sheets rustling in the background. He must still be in bed, and I find myself distracted by the thought of him without clothes, body warm and flushed from sleep, wrapped only in skin and blankets.

"And breakfast," he says, shaking me from my wayward thoughts. "I'll text you the address."

"Okay," I say. "See you soon."

My phone chirps a few moments later with an address, then an order for an egg sandwich and coffee—two creams, no sugar.

I put Cross's address into my phone, then grab food from a small diner I find on the way. I walk up the steps of his apartment building, his coffee and sandwich in my hands. The building's newer than my apartment, the brick exterior neat and square, the mortar still bright white. There's a small awning over the front step and a bank of names on an intercom panel. I press the buzzer for Cross's apartment and the door clicks open without a word from the intercom.

The lobby isn't huge, but a small couch and chairs are placed next to the mailboxes. A battered bike is propped up by the door, a lock threaded through the wheels and frame. I don't see an elevator, just a set of carpeted stairs with black iron railings leading up. I peek back out the door, note Cross's floor and apartment number, and start climbing.

He's only on the third floor, but after the last few days, I'm breathing heavily by the time I reach his door. I knock, then wait. Tempted to take a quick sip of his coffee, I raise the cup to my lips when the door opens.

Cross leans in the doorframe, his shoulder pressed against the wall, head just peeking out. His dark hair is still rumpled from sleep, some of the longer strands falling onto his forehead in an artless sweep. He's shirtless, his chest taut with muscle, his stomach sculpted, a small trail of hair leading down toward the waistline of a worn pair of sweatpants. He coughs slightly, and I tear my eyes back up to his face. He's smirking a little, but pushes back from the doorway, waving me in. He plucks the coffee and sandwich from my hands as I walk past him. For a moment, I feel slightly lost, grasping at air as I look around the apartment.

It's spotlessly clean. A white couch is pushed against one wall, a contrasting throw blanket draped carefully over its back. There's a plush matching chair to the side, with two small tables bracketing it and the couch. A large entertainment center takes up the other wall, with neatly arranged movies on the shelves. As I move closer, I can see they're alphabetized. The coffee table is empty except for a remote control that's been placed exactly in the corner, just within reach of someone sitting or lying down on the couch. Cross shuts the door and flops onto the couch, setting his coffee and sandwich down.

"Take a seat," he says, gesturing toward the chair. I slip out of my coat, throw it over the back of the chair, then sit.

"So, what'd you want to tell me?" he asks, unwrapping the sandwich.

"You going to put on a shirt first?" I ask, eyebrow raised.

Cross grins. "Nope." He takes a bite of his sandwich. "Talk."

"All right," I say, glaring slightly. "I think I've started to figure this out, but I'm going to need you to hold off on any judgments until I lay it all out."

"I've got time," he says, waving me on.

"I went to Hewitt's house," I start. He frowns and I hold up a hand, stopping him. "I know, just bear with me. I wanted to see if he knew anything else about the book or had written anything down. After I stopped to think about it, it was a little strange that he knew so much about a book that was supposedly destroyed at the turn of the century. I went to his house this morning, Priya peeked inside, and she found a copy of that same book."

"Hewitt lied about having a copy of the book," Cross says, leaning back. "Explains why he knew so much about it."

"There's more to it than that. The book was with a bunch of genealogies going back to the late 1800s, four of them that just happened to end with our victims' names."

"And you suspect that Hewitt had something to do with the deaths."

I shake my head. "No, I think our victims are tied to the binding ceremony in that book, that they're all descended from a group of Mediums who Bound someone. There was a genealogy for Hewitt, too, and his ancestor was on the main list of six."

"Six names? This ceremony needs one of each Affinity, right? I thought there were seven," he says, frowning.

"I reviewed the ceremony, and it requires seven Mediums in *total*, including the person being Bound. So, leaving out the victim, we've got six. I think whoever is committing these murders is getting revenge for the person who was Bound originally. I think Hewitt's our latest victim, and that our murderer made his death look like natural causes."

"What about the 9-1-1 call?" Cross asks, clearly not buying my theory. "Why would Hewitt call about chest pains if he was being murdered? And why would our murderer bring the authorities into it, if he was in the process of killing Hewitt?"

"If I'm right, then our victims are all descended from this group of Mediums. So far, they're all unique in their Affinities: Seer, Shaker, Reader, and now a Healer. If I had to guess, their ancestors had the same Affinities. Those tend to travel in bloodlines, which is why you end up with families who all have a specific Affinity. I think our killer is descended from the Medium who was Bound, probably whoever that Baker guy was, and they likely share the same Affinity."

I pull out my notebook from where it's tucked into my jacket pocket and flip back through my notes.

"Look," I say, pointing to a line of scribbled text, "assuming Casey was right about the knife, Baker was a Passenger, which could make his descendant a Passenger, too. And if our killer is a Passenger, he'd be able to possess someone and make them do something against their will, like call 9-1-1 about a heart attack they're not having. Then he just makes the victim's heart stop, and the death is ruled as natural causes."

"Mediums can do that? Stop someone's heart?" Cross looks shocked, eyes wide.

"Among other things, though we don't do that stuff anymore," I say, pressing forward. "The point is, if Baker's descendant is coming after the families that Bound Baker, we've got a way to find the rest of his targets, stop him from hurting anyone else, and *catch him*."

Cross shakes his head, frowning.

"That's certainly a theory, but the notes from the

museum said Baker didn't have any living relatives. Why are you so sure that our murderer is related to him or this binding?"

"Because a revenge motive makes the most sense. None of our victims are connected. They didn't know each other, didn't run in the same circles. Some of them are multiple generations apart in age. The only thing tying them all together is that book, and the only noteworthy part of that book is the binding ceremony. There's a chance the museum staff weren't thorough when they looked for Baker's family. If they were just checking for direct descendants, they might have missed nieces, nephews, second cousins, whatever. As long as the bloodline is strong, the Affinity will reappear."

Cross frowns, considering, then finishes his sandwich. The apartment is achingly quiet as I watch him mull it all over.

"What does our murderer get out of this?" he finally asks, shaking his head. "Baker's long since dead. Same with the people who Bound him. What does killing their descendants do?"

I sigh. "That, I don't know. Revenge is the easiest explanation, but we don't need motive for a conviction. If we can lock down intent and opportunity, then we can get this guy. We just have to find him first."

"Opportunity is going to be kind of hard to prove if the guy is just jumping in and out of bodies," Cross says, eyebrow raised.

"Now that I know what to look for, I should be able to find signs of possession in the bodies. I'll need some time at the morgue with all of the victims, but if a Passenger was Riding any of them, there'll be evidence of it."

Cross takes a sip of his coffee, then nods.

"You said Hewitt had a list of the Mediums involved?"

"Yeah," I say. "He'd found five of the six binders, but nothing on Baker's descendant."

"So we've got four dead and two remaining, one unknown. What Affinities are left?"

"Assuming that Baker's descendant is a Passenger, a Speaker and a Burner."

Cross stands and stretches, grabbing the wrapper to his sandwich and his now-empty coffee cup.

"I'm going to be honest with you, Phillips," he says, frowning. "I don't know that I buy your theory. It seems like a whole lot of coincidence and not a lot of evidence. We've got four bodies, two of which don't look like murders. The circumstances around Murphy's death are weird, I'll give you that, but Richardson looks good for that. And as for whatever the hell happened to Casey"—he shakes his head and sighs—"I can't believe she did that to herself, but I trust Abramo. And there aren't any connections between the bodies except for that damn book. If it weren't for that, I'd think you were grasping at straws." He pauses, then shakes his head. "But my gut is telling me that it's tied up in all of these cases, and I know you're a solid detective with good instincts. I'm going out on a limb here, Phillips, but I think you might be right."

I nod, throat tight.

"Let me get dressed, and we'll go out and find the next

potential victim." Cross turns and starts walking toward the back of the apartment. "Which one did Hewitt identify before he died?"

"The Burner." I pause, then take a deep breath. "He found me."

"What the hell are you talking about?" Cross asks, freezing, his expression caught between disbelief and annoyance.

"My grandmother's name was on the list. Sadie Phillips."

"And your name was on the genealogy," he says, his tone flat.

I nod. "I found her copy of the book, too."

"What? When?"

"Yesterday, while I was going through her old diaries. I thought she might have known Hewitt, and I found it mixed in with some of her things. It had a different symbol on it, but it was in the same place as the symbols on the other books we've found."

"When were you going to tell me about this?"

"Today." I shrug.

"But not immediately."

"I wanted to ease you into it," I say, wincing. "I thought you might take it badly."

"What, that based on *your* theory of the case, you're a potential target for a killer with four bodies on him? Yes, I would imagine that your *partner* would take that badly."

"I've got protections in place," I say, starting to get defensive. "And I know what to look for. I'm better prepared than they were. I'll be fine."

"You'll be fine," he says, scoffing. "Moore had protections tattooed into his *skin*, and this guy still got him."

"But he didn't know that a Passenger was after him. I do."

"And that's enough to keep you safe? Damn it, Phillips, I just saw you nearly die two days ago. I can't see you like that again."

"I hit my head. I was fine."

"You threw me out of the room, there was some giant creature coming out of the floor, and everything smelled like blood. I didn't know if I was going to come back to find you or your corpse or some undead creature unleashed on the department. So pardon me if I question your ability to keep yourself safe."

A tense silence falls between us. Cross's body is stiff, his shoulders tight, face unflinching in anger. The silence builds until it's nearly unbearable, till all I can hear is my rapid heartbeat in my ears.

"I'm scared," I say, my voice breaking. "I don't know when this guy is going to come for me, and I'm terrified I won't be ready. But I can't do anything about it right now, except try to find his next victim—his *last* victim—and protect them. They have no idea what's coming, Cross. And this guy can come from anywhere. He's proven that already. If I don't find this person, if I don't stop him, then the next victim's blood is on my hands. And I can't have that."

Our eyes meet, his defiant and filled with anger and

fear, but I can sense something changing in the room, a shifting energy between us that suddenly seems to snap into place.

"Okay," he says, still mad. "But I'm not leaving you on your own until we stop him. You're right, we don't know when he's going to attack, but you're not going to face whatever he throws at you alone. Not again."

"That creature wasn't someth—" I start, but Cross cuts me off.

"I don't care. You've spent too much of this case trying to do things on your own. We're partners. I'm here to watch your back, and I've done a damn poor job of it so far. I may not be a Medium, and I may not know everything about your world, but I'm far from useless. So, until we close this case, I'm stuck on you like glue."

"Fine," I say, grabbing my jacket angrily. "Get dressed, and let's go."

He smirks and stomps off into the back of the apartment. I hear a door slam, and I shove my arms into my jacket sleeves, then jerk the collar up around my neck.

He's right, Kim, Priya says quietly. *You're in a lot of danger. He can help.*

I know, I say, stuffing my hands into my pockets. *But he's completely unprepared for this. It's not safe.*

He's a cop. I don't think he expects to be safe, she says.

I'm not going to let him get hurt because of me.

Then we'd better find this guy, and soon, Priya says, and I can hear the worry in her voice. *Whoever's killing these Mediums, he's escalating. I don't think he'll wait very long before he tries to kill you or the other descendant.*

We're going to have to figure out who that is, I say, looking up as I hear Cross's footsteps.

He stops in the middle of the apartment. He's wearing a T-shirt and jeans, a small workout bag slung over his shoulder, his gun at his hip, detective's shield glinting on a chain around his neck. His eyes are bright and focused, locked with mine. I stand straighter, shoulders pulling back almost against my will as I face down the challenge in his gaze. He nods, then heads toward the door and slides on a jacket.

"C'mon," he says, opening the door and waiting for me to leave. "We've got a murder to stop."

CHAPTER TWENTY-TWO

"So," Cross says as we walk into headquarters, "where do we start?"

"We don't have direct access to death records," I begin, heading toward my desk quickly. "They're not public record and we don't have enough to request them directly. But there might be some resources online that we can tap into."

"I might have an ancestry.com account," Cross says a little sarcastically, pulling out his chair and booting up his computer. "I had to do a research project when I was in college. It could still be active."

I roll my eyes. "I'll see if there's anything else available. We might be able to get historical birth or death records, and since we're looking for someone who's probably been dead awhile, it could be a start."

I grab a Post-it Note and carefully write down the last name from Hewitt's list before I pass it to Cross.

"Robert Barrett. If we're right about the killer's Affinity, we're looking for a Speaker. That should help narrow down the search."

Cross knits his brows, already focused on his computer screen. I pull up Google and start looking. A generic search for Robert Barrett pulls up a painter, still living in Utah. I add "illinois" and "chicago" to the search with similar success. Changing course, I start looking for online death certificates and find a hit with the Cook County Clerk's office. I'm about to finish registering when Cross speaks up.

"I think I might have something." He pushes away from his computer. "I've got a Robert Barrett, born and raised in Chicago, who served in the Korean War with the Seventh Infantry as a Speaker. He received a Purple Heart in 1950 and a Presidential Unit Citation in 1951, came back to the States in '52."

"You got all of that off ancestory.com?"

"And a little off Wikipedia," he says, mouth twitching into a half grin. "He went on to do some important work with the CIA during the Cold War. Died in '92."

"Is there anything about his family?"

"Not really. Married in '54, had a son and two daughters, but the son died in the Gulf War, and the daughters may have married. I'm not finding anything for either of them with a last name of Barrett."

"I'll start looking for marriage certificates. You want to give me the names?"

"Yeah," he says, scribbling them down. "Here you go. You want me to keep looking?"

I pause, then shake my head. "No, something in my gut is telling me this is the right guy. Caroline Moore would've involved herself with powerful Mediums, both in terms of their abilities and their social status. It makes sense that she'd work with a decorated military hero, especially one who can keep a secret."

I lean back in my chair, arms crossed, and continue. "We need to find out more about this Baker guy. See if you can pull anything up about him. If we can track him down, we'll be able to track down the killer. I want to cover both avenues, just in case we can't find our next victim."

Cross nods. "My thoughts exactly. I'll start tracking him down while you work on the marriage certificates. Good luck."

"I think you're going to need it more than me," I say, shaking my head. "I at least have first names to work with."

Thirty minutes later, I'm neck deep in marriage certificates and no closer to finding Barret's daughters. My phone, skittering across the surface of my desk as it rings, is a welcome interruption.

"Detective Phillips," I say, closing out of another dead-end tab.

"Detective, this is Officer Williams from the second district?"

"I remember," I say, leaning back. "How can I help you?"

"Ma'am, we've got another body. I think it's another Medium."

"Fuck," I say, the word slipping out of my mouth on a heavy breath. Cross looks away from his computer, frowning. He mouths *what is it?* and I shake my head.

"How do you know it's a Medium?" I ask, hoping he's

wrong.

"He had the designation on his driver's license, and a registration card for the Chicago Medium Society in his wallet. I'm real sorry, but you need to get down here. We've got the body cordoned off, but it looks like it's going to rain. We need detectives down here and you're the only Medium we know of on staff right now."

"I understand. Send me the address. Cross and I will be there as soon as possible."

I set the phone down—hard—on my desk.

"We're too late," Cross says, reading something from my expression. "There's another body."

"Yeah," I say, sighing. A heavy weight settles in the pit of my stomach. It's a mix of regret, of fear and shame of that fear, and of impending, seemingly unstoppable doom. I swallow, pushing it down until it's a cold, hard ball deep in the center of myself, and then I push further, until it almost disappears until I can look up and meet Cross's eyes without any of it showing in mine.

"Let's go."

The crime scene isn't far from headquarters, and Cross and I make it there quickly. Heavy clouds are forming in the sky, hinting at a late-autumn rainstorm that will likely last long into the night. Flashing red and blue lights come from an alleyway, the light glancing off the concrete buildings in the shadows lost between them, crime scene tape cutting yellow lines through the alley. Cross and I climb out of my car, the doors echoing loudly in the street when they close.

Officer Williams is standing next to a police car that's blocking the entrance to the alley and waves me over. Cross and I duck under the crime scene tape, then walk over to him.

"What did you find?" I ask when we reach him. He ducks his head to the side leads me down the alleyway.

"Not sure what's happened here, but I'm pretty sure you're going to want to see."

There's a second patrol car at the other end of the alley, its lights going as well. Another officer stands next to it, his hand resting on his gun, body tense and shifting anxiously. Williams hails him, and I can see his shoulders fall as the tension leaves him.

The alley is hardly anything to talk about. There are a few broken-down fire escapes leading to windows on the upper stories, with a few industrial doors leading into the back. Trash is piled up in small mounds against the bottom of the building, some of it sprawling into the center of the alley. A dumpster, one of its wheels broken, tilts crazily on the uneven asphalt, and the plastic lids that would normally hold in the trash and stink are missing.

As we get closer, I notice dark marks on the walls of the buildings. They're hard to see in the half light of the alley, the buildings blocking what little sun is making it through the cloud cover. I walk over, then run my finger through the residue. A dark smudge clings to my finger, and I rub it against my thumb, feeling the grittiness.

"It's ash," I say, turning to Cross and Williams, "or soot. There had to have been a fire here large enough to singe the buildings. Any signs of arson?"

"No. Besides the trash in the alley, that's the only thing that was here," Williams says, pointing to the dumpster.

"The body's in there?" Cross asks, moving forward.

"Yeah," Williams says, pulling a pair of gloves from his belt and passing them to Cross. "He's right on top. A guy found him this morning while taking out the trash."

Priya, I say, reaching out for her. *Do you see anything?*

I drop fully into Second-Sight and look around the alley. There's nothing worth noting until I notice that there's literally *nothing* to see. Generally, there's always something to be found in Second-Sight. A spirit, some remnant of supernatural activity, pooled energy, anything. Even a forgotten sigil or rune will show up usually, but the alley is empty. If there was any supernatural activity here, even months ago, it's been wiped completely clean.

"You've called the ME?" Cross asks, inspecting the body. "We won't be able to turn him until the techs get here."

"Yeah, they're on their way," Williams says.

"And there hasn't been any other activity in the alley?" I ask, moving toward the dumpster and the victim.

"The guy who found the body came out around eleven o'clock, and we were on scene by eleven ten, eleven fifteen at the latest. Then we blocked off the scene and called you. There've been a few people mingling, trying to figure out what's going on, but no one saw anything before the body was found. This isn't a heavily trafficked area."

The victim in the dumpster is a slight young man, hair a nondescript brown. He's got a light blue windbreaker on, jeans, and a pair of Chuck Taylors.

"You said he had ID? What's our vic's name?"

"Daniel Young," he starts, but all I can hear is a sudden loud buzzing in my ears.

Kim, Priya says, her voice shaking. *It's Daniel?*

"Oh shit," I say, taking a step back. "Cross, I know this guy."

"Wait, what?" He turns away as the team from the ME's office arrives at the other end of the alley, their white van bright in the dim light.

"Danny Young. Fuck." I turn and press my hands against my forehead, dragging my fingers through my hair and cursing again. I hear Cross telling Officer Williams to coordinate removal of the body, and then I hear his quick footsteps coming up behind me. I tilt my head back, looking at the dark, roiling clouds above and wish we'd been faster.

"You all right?" Cross asks, his hand gentle on my shoulder. I let it rest there for a moment, taking more comfort from the slight gesture than I should, and nod shakily.

"Yeah."

"How'd you know our vic?"

"We went to school together." I frown. "He was a few years ahead of me, but we took a couple of the same classes and became friends. Lost touch after school, but for a while there, we were pretty tight."

My throat tightens, and I cough, fighting against the shock and tears.

"He, uh, he moved out to the East Coast after school. Some kind of government job he couldn't talk about. I didn't even know he was in town. Damn it."

"Were you guys... involved?" Cross asks, tone carefully balanced between comforting and inquiring. It's a tone I'm familiar with, the kind you use when asking loved ones about their dead.

"No," and I'm surprised to find a laugh fighting to come to the surface. "No, we were just friends. There was a time or two where it seemed like it could be more, but it never happened."

"Do you think he's our descendant?"

"Maybe. I never met his folks, and I didn't think to ask if he had any other Mediums in his family. I knew he was a Speaker, but we didn't really talk shop, you know? Our Affinities were too dissimilar."

"We've got a name we can cross-reference now, at least," Cross says. "It should make it easier to find out if he's descended from Barrett."

"Yeah," I say, looking back toward the dumpster. Crime scene techs are investigating it and the surrounding area, and I can see Abramo looking at the body. I hear the clatter of a gurney and shiver. I turn my back to the dumpster, to Danny, and look toward my car.

"I'm going back to headquarters to find out if they're related," I say. "Can you manage the crime scene?"

"How about you go wait in the car, I'll get the crime scene, and then we head back to HQ together?" he asks, arms crossed.

"Cross," I say with a huff, "there's no time for this. I know you want to keep an eye on me, but I'll be fine at headquarters, and we have to get ahead of this guy. His timeline is escalating,"—I step closer and whisper harshly—"and whatever he wants from this, I'm all that's left."

"Yeah," Cross says, running his hand through his hair. "Just, be careful, okay? I'll get what we need and text you when I'm on my way back into headquarters. Let me know if you find anything?"

"I will," I say, taking a step toward the car. Cross quickly grabs my arm, and I jerk to a stop, his fingers warm and tight against my wrist.

"Phillips," he says, voice low and serious, "I'm not going to let this happen to you. We're going to find this guy before he can get to you. I promise."

I place my hand on top of his. He squeezes gently, then lets go, his fingers brushing against the thin skin covering my pulse as he pulls away.

"I'll see you back at HQ," I say. He nods and heads back toward the dumpster.

Watching him walk away, I feel shaken and uneasy. I can sense Priya nearby, quiet and grieving, her emotions echoing mine in a low thrum across our Bond, a feedback loop of sorrow.

We're going to have to be careful, I Send her, walking toward the car. *We're not going to be next.*

I feel a surge of agreement, of anger and resolution from her. I let it bolster me, twisting the mess of emotions into a razor-sharp cord of strength. Whoever this bastard is, he's not getting me.

Not without a fight.

CHAPTER TWENTY-THREE

I pull into the parking lot outside headquarters. The rain that had been threatening to fall earlier has turned into a torrential downpour. After running from the car to the front door. I'm soaked through. I duck under the awning over the entrance, then roll my shoulders, trying to shed the water. I push my way inside, rain still dripping from my hair and jacket, and head immediately to my desk.

Opening Facebook, I search for Danny's profile and find his mom. Her first name matches one of Barrett's daughters. A coldness spreads from my chest out to my fingers, my throat tight. From her page, I'm able to find her sister, a match for Barrett's other daughter. I swallow, then lean heavily into my chair, which groans loudly as it rocks back.

It's him, Priya says, voice tired and sad. *Danny's the last one.*

Not quite. I'm still here. And he'll be coming for me soon if his timeline is anything to go by.

We have to find him, Priya says. She floats closer to me, envelopes me in arms that feel like cool waves against my skin. I close out of the browser, then close my eyes, breathing slowly, body chilled from the rain and Priya.

Baker's the last piece to this whole mess, I say.

If we're able to find his descendant. We don't have a lot to go off of, just a last name and a probable date of death.

There has to be something.

What about the nightmares? Priya asks, still enveloping me in ethereal arms. *Do you think they could be connected?*

I haven't had one since we investigated the Casey crime scene. And there's nothing in them that points to the case. They're just dreams, Priya.

She sighs, clearly frustrated and worried. She drifts forward, faces me, and crosses her arms, half of her body hidden by my desk.

They started right after you Burnt Emma. What's to say they're not connected?

I pause, considering. The nightmares themselves are vague, indistinct memories that have faded with time and the exhaustion that comes with an investigation. I remember someone at the end of a long hallway, a sense of overwhelming fear. And a symbol: a circle, bisected by a cross with one arm longer than the others. I frown, then pull my notebook from my jacket pocket. When I flip to my notes about my grandmother's diary, there, tucked into the corner of the page, nearly forgotten, is the same symbol, copied from the back of her copy of the book. I stare at it for a long moment, wondering.

Priya continues. *And then there's the spirit that possessed Moore's body and the creature that attacked when you were trying to Read Casey's knife. The first could have been done by a Passenger, though he'd have to be extremely powerful. It addressed you directly, knew who you were.*

Yeah, it knew my name. But we just assumed it was a spirit.

If he were strong enough to possess a corpse, he could have been strong enough to set a trap for you with Casey's knife. Priya looks excited, floating around me so that I have to crane my neck to watch her. *He would have to know that you'd use it to try to gather information on him. Why leave it at the crime scene otherwise? If he knows who you are, he knows you're a homicide detective. He'd know you couldn't clean the blood from the knife, and he'd know that it would leave you vulnerable.*

But if it weren't for the knife, we wouldn't know about the Baker family connection. Why give himself away?

Maybe as bait? He told you to find him and this would help.

If the trap didn't kill me.

Priya pauses, and in the silence, I hear my phone vibrate against my desk, buzzing loudly in the quiet squad room. It's a text from Cross, letting me know he's headed back to HQ.

We'll go over everything when Cross gets here, I Send, *see what we can put together. If this guy has been trying to contact me, we're going to have to figure out if he did the same with the other victims. It doesn't make any sense that he'd only reach out to me.*

It seems pretty obvious that he tried to contact Emma, Priya says, floating toward my desk. *Her diary certainly points to it.*

And Moore knew someone was coming for him. No reason for the tattoos otherwise.

Casey had the knife and the book, Priya says, *but I don't remember seeing anything else.*

Her notes at the museum seemed to point toward her being obsessed with it. She certainly fixated on it during her analysis of the items in the collection. Maybe that's how he was able to contact her, through the knife itself?

I can feel excitement welling, something in my gut telling me we're onto something.

Hewitt was already partway to finding everyone involved in the binding ceremony, Priya continues. *We've assumed that he knew who was involved because of something he found in his research. But what if Baker's descendant was feeding him that information? It would explain why he had full names for everyone* but *Baker.*

It would have given him too much to work from, I Send. I can feel pieces falling into place, bits of disparate information suddenly making coherent sense.

Baker's a common last name, but being a Passenger isn't. A first name and that Affinity in the hands of a trained historian? Hewitt would've found something.

So, this guy is contacting each of his victims before he kills them, Priya says. *But why?*

Let's see what Cross thinks. I need to get some of this written down, and we're going to have to head down to the morgue later, check out Danny's body to see if we can figure out how he died.

There's a painful pause, then Priya settles near me.

I'm sorry, Kim. I know you cared for him.

It's been years since we last talked, I say as if that will somehow ease the ache in my chest. *I'll be okay.*

I start looking up contact information for Danny. His folks have their Facebook pages locked down to people outside of their friends, so I can't get phone numbers from there. They're also unlisted in the online White Pages. Instead, I pull the number for the police department in their town, then request their contact information. The secretary tells me it will be an hour or so to get it to me, but they'll fax them as soon as they find the numbers. I thank her and hang up just as Cross walks in.

"Hey," he says, falling gracelessly into his chair. "Abramo's got the body scheduled for an autopsy first thing tomorrow. From what he could tell, there weren't any defensive wounds, no signs of injury at all, actually. Just a healthy twenty-something-looking guy, dead in a dumpster."

He pauses, then flushes. "Sorry, I forgot for a second that he was your…"

"It's all right," I say, shrugging it off and pushing aside a twinge of grief. "I'll head down tomorrow morning, talk to Abramo."

"Okay, if you're sure."

"You don't need to handle me with kid gloves," I say, my mouth quirking up into a half smile. "I can still do my job."

"Fair enough," Cross says. "What's our next step?"

"Priya and I were talking, and we think this guy may have been reaching out to his victims before killing them."

"Yeah? Catch me up, partner."

I fill him in, running over the various pieces of evidence that point to the killer trying to contact his victims. Cross looks stunned but nods along.

"But why would he do that?" he asks, brow furrowed

in confusion. "Wouldn't it just give you a better opportunity to protect yourself?"

"I think some of them did," I say. "Moore had the warding tattoos, and Murphy tried to put up a binding of some kind before he got to her. And once I figured out that I might be a target, I warded the hell out of my apartment and myself. But Hewitt and Casey didn't have anything in place that would've prevented an attack."

"They didn't know that there was a murderer on the loose," Cross says thoughtfully. "If he changed his approach, made himself less threatening, they might not have known to put their guard up."

"So he's learning, adjusting. *And* escalating his timeframe."

"That still doesn't answer the question of why he's contacting his victims."

It's so they know what's going on, Priya says suddenly. *If we hadn't become involved in the case, we'd never have known about your grandmother's connection. And if you're right about his motive, that it's about revenge for Baker, he'd want to make sure that his victims knew what happened with the binding.*

Damn, I Send. *That makes a hell of a lot of sense.*

"He's making sure we know why he's targeting us," I say, shaking my head. "None of us knew about what happened until the killer led us that way. He's making sure we know why we're being punished."

"Has he contacted you?"

"I think so. I've been having dreams, more like nightmares, and then there have been a few incidents while we've been investigating the case that could be him."

"The attack with the knife and Moore's corpse talking to you," Cross says, looking thoughtful. "Has he said anything specific, tried to tell you about the binding?"

"No, not yet, but with the wards I put up, he might not be able to get to me anymore."

"So, he contacts his victims, lets them know what happened to Baker, and kills them as soon as they realize what's going on."

"If I haven't already given away that I know what's going on," I say, thinking, "I might be able to stall him. He probably won't want to kill me until after I understand why he's targeting me."

"It's a possibility. In the meantime," he says, pushing back from his desk, "it's getting late, and we should be heading out. There's not much more we can do today."

"I've got to make a few calls before I can leave. I'll see you tomorrow?"

Cross looks puzzled. "I thought I'd made it pretty clear earlier. I'm not leaving you on your own until this is settled."

"What are you implying?" I ask, tone suspicious.

"I'll hang around until you're ready to leave, but then I'm following you back to your place and crashing on your couch."

"The hell you are," I scoff.

"Phillips, this guy is out for blood. If I'm with you, I can at least restrain you if he takes control."

I don't like it, but he has a point.

"I don't have a futon, and the place is a mess."

"That's fine," he says, smiling. "I'll make do."

I call Danny's folks after their numbers arrive. It's heartbreaking, and I find myself stumbling through conversations I've had time and time again with other victims' families. Cross watches me quietly, eyes assessing and kind. I finish up a little paperwork and get ready to go. He grabs his things, follows me out to the parking lot, and falls behind me as I pull onto the street. The drive home is slow and steady, Cross staying close behind me through the winding turns of Chicago.

Walking up the five flights of stairs to my apartment leaves me slightly winded, Cross just a few steps behind me the whole time, and I refuse to accept that it might be anything besides exhaustion taking my breath away. I swear I can feel the warmth of his body as I go to open the door but shrug it off as I push my way inside.

Cross makes himself comfortable in the living room, side-eyeing the clutter that has accumulated around the room. I catch him straightening one of the pictures on the wall and grin.

Can't say I didn't warn him.

CHAPTER TWENTY-FOUR

C ross and I are getting ready to go to the morgue in the morning when we're told that Danny's car has been found. It's in a parking lot near the Thirty-First Street Harbor on the edge of Lake Michigan, reported by a meter maid to be towed. When they ran the plates, his name was flagged for the suspicious death investigation, and we were called.

It's a quick drive to the harbor, and though it takes us a few minutes wandering through the parking lot, we find Danny's car. It's an older-model Honda, the back bumper faded and cracked. There are a handful of parking tickets hanging from beneath the windshield wipers. They whip around in the wind, tiny scraps of orange paper barely staying in place. I grab a couple and pass them to Cross.

"Looks like someone has been keeping track of his car, at least. Judging by the dates on these, it's been here for nearly a week."

Cross takes the tickets, then pulls a pad of paper and a pencil from his pocket.

"I'll follow up with the meter maid who left these, see if they've seen anyone hanging around. The thing I don't get is how he moved from here to the dumpster. It's at least five miles from where we found his body."

"There's always public transit or Uber," I say, checking the driver's side door. It's locked. I sigh, then look to Cross. He's making notes about the tickets, shifting through the pile and organizing it. Impatient to get into the car, I close my eyes and *reach*, looking through the door until I find the lever leading up to the door lock. Sweat beads on my forehead. The metal arm on the lock refuses to give at first, but with a strong tug, it slips up. I hear the lock click, and when I try the door again, it pops open. Cross looks at me, eyebrow raised.

"It was open," I say. I snap on a pair of gloves as I lean in and start looking around. There's nothing too unique about the car. Empty soda cans are piled up in the backseat and receipts are stuffed into the center console. I find the registration in the glove box, and pass it to Cross.

"It's definitely Danny's car. He was always a bit of a pack rat, could never manage to keep his car clean."

"No wonder you guys got along," Cross says, eying the interior suspiciously. "You see anything interesting in there?"

I start digging through the receipts. They're a mix of McDonald's and Starbucks, time stamps ranging from last week to three months ago. I find a business card for a local mechanic and an empty package of gum. There's a forgotten birthday card in there, too, the edges stained and bent.

"No." I stand back up, coming out of the car. "Nothing. Just junk."

I bang my hands against the doorframe and cuss.

"None of this makes sense." I glance up at Cross, who's frowning.

"Hey, we're not getting anything from this right now, and we still have to make it to the morgue. Let's have the car taken to processing, see if they can get anything, and we'll go from there."

"Yeah, you're right," I sigh and step back from the car, slamming the door shut. "It just doesn't make any sense. Why was he here in the first place? He lives in fucking *New York*. And why'd he leave his car here?"

"We'll figure it out," Cross says, tone serious. "Let's get to the morgue, all right? Abramo's expecting us."

"Can you give me a minute?" I ask, pulling off my gloves angrily before running my fingers through my hair. "I don't know, I just need to try to clear my head before…"

"Yeah, all right. I'll get someone down here to tow the car. I won't be far."

"And I won't be long, just need a few minutes."

"Just make sure you stay in sight," he says with a frown.

I ignore the comment and head from the parking lot to a pathway leading to the lake. Storm clouds still clog the horizon, and the wind comes in quick and cold. A few trees are scattered along the path, their empty branches reaching toward the sky, and my feet crunch in the bright leaves that litter the cement. There's a wide concrete platform overlooking the choppy waves. I wander down the shallow steps, looking over the lake, trying to figure out what is going on.

Why was he here? I ask Priya, shaking my head slowly.

I don't know.

We stand quietly, looking out over the water as the sun winks in and out from behind clouds. The light glances off the rough water of the lake in flashes of gold, then disappears to deep, dark blue.

I walk closer to the edge and shiver, my hair whipping around my face in the wind. Something about the lake pulls me closer, and I find myself up against the edge of the concrete platform. Below me, waves crash loudly, the spray whipping up in the wind to sting my face. I feel a tug in my chest, and I'm about to take another step forward, into empty air, before I stop myself. I close my eyes, fall into Second-Sight, and cast about. I find a faint line heading west, away from the lake. It suddenly pulses with bright light, and as the light washes over me, I fight the urge to move forward again.

Priya, we have a problem.

She hovers around me, her hands tracing up and down my skin in quick shivers. When her hands pass over where the line is connected to my body, I feel nauseous.

I can see that, she says. *Where is it going?*

I don't know, I say, falling deep enough into Second-Sight that the living world disappears in a dark hum around me. *But we need to get rid of it, or I'm going to end up in the lake.*

Give me a moment, she says, flaring with blue-white light as she pulls power. I trace around my body, then press my fingers hard against where the line enters my chest. Priya rests her hand on the top of mine, and I can feel her energy flow into me. With a gut-wrenching push of power, I force our combined energy down the line. It shatters into bright shards as the pulse of energy races away to the west, leaving a glittering trail behind.

You think that was the Passenger?

I don't know who else it would be, I say as I drop out of Second-Sight to stare after where the trail disappeared. *He's getting more subtle.*

We've at least got a direction now, Priya says, resting near me. We're both a little drained, and I can feel power slowly trickling back into my reserves.

I look out over the lake again, ready to get on with the rest of the day. Hopefully, Abramo will be able to shed some more light on how Danny died, and maybe his body will give us some clues to follow to find his murderer. The filament of power is a literal string we can follow, and I feel better knowing that the killer may have misstepped and given away his location.

I'm going to find you, I think, watching the waves. *We're getting closer, and then you're mine.*

My phone buzzes and I pull it from my pocket. Looking down at a text from Cross, I'm about to turn back to the car, when I catch someone rushing toward me from the corner of my eye. I veer to the side, watching as a hulk of a man comes hurtling out of the darkness.

He spins around, teeth bared in a feral but familiar grin. His dirty hair is tangled around his face, whipping about in the wind.

"What are you doing here, Richardson?" I ask tentatively, shifting my weight so my feet are braced, one in front of the other, ready to move. "You're supposed to be in custody."

He laughs, the sound coughing out of his throat.

"He let me go," he says, leaning forward. "He told me to get you."

He shifts and rushes me again. I dive out of the way, landing hard on the concrete. My phone goes sliding across the concrete as Richardson tackles me. He's on top of me before I can get up, his heavy weight pushing the air from my lungs. My gun bites into my side and I struggle to get free. I gasp for breath, pulling in the smell of unwashed skin and alcohol, and then his hands are around my throat, fingers pressing so hard into my neck I can hear the bones and muscles creak. I claw at his hands, leaving deep scratches next to partially healed scabs.

Priya! I scream. She shoves him away with a sudden blast of energy. I feel her collapse beside me, but it gives me just enough time to get to my feet and draw my gun. My hands are unsteady and I can't help coughing, but I keep it pointed at him. At this range, a .40 cal doesn't need to be accurate, it just needs to hit.

"Back off, Jerry," I say, staggering backward. "I don't want to shoot you."

"Are you sure about that, Kim?" he asks, his mouth still twisted in a rictus of pleasure and pain. I shudder. There's something wrong about his voice, like an echo, and his eyes begin to roll back in his head, showing white. I quickly drop into Second-Sight. A thin cord leads from his chest, bright blue and pulsating, like the one that I just released, heading west. He's got a Passenger Riding him.

My Passenger.

Priya, can you follow the tie? I tighten my hands on my gun. Richardson keeps stalking closer, weaving back and forth, pushing me closer and closer to the edge of the platform.

I'll try. She shoots off in the direction the cord is coming from, quickly stretching our bond to the limit. *It's heading west, but I can't go any farther, not without leaving you. It feels the same as the other one.*

"What do you want?" I ask. My feet crunch on fallen leaves, and he starts to laugh.

"I want what anyone wants, *Kim*." He rolls my name around on his tongue as he moves closer. I feel my foot slide out from underneath me, and I drop to a knee. Adrenaline rushes through my veins, my heart pounding, but he doesn't take advantage of my slip. He just keeps coming toward me with the same slow saunter, eyes white and rolled back in his head, teeth bared in a skull-like grin.

"Educate me," I say, getting back to my feet. He keeps coming closer, pushing me farther and farther from the parking lot and closer to the lake.

"I want the air on my face. I want the warmth of the sun on my skin. I want to go where I want, when I want. I want *power*." He keeps coming toward me, hands twisted and reaching.

"I want what everyone wants, Kim. What you want."

I stumble again, my feet slipping on the leaves.

"I want to be *free!*" He charges, and my feet slide as I try to get out of the way. I'm not fast enough, and I fire a shot. I smell blood, feel it hot against my stomach when he lifts me. I scream and see Cross raising his weapon from the sidewalk, and then the breath in my lungs disappears in a cold rush.

He's pushed us into Lake Michigan, and even though the water is deep and churning, he doesn't slow. I feel him push off the sea wall, and my head goes under for a paralyzing second.

I struggle, hitting him on the temple with the butt of my gun, but his grip doesn't loosen. The water is ice cold and soaks my clothes. My jeans feel like lead weights as I try to kick my way free. I start to shiver, but he seems unaffected. When the water washes over his head, spilling into his mouth, he keeps swimming. We go under completely, and the world disappears in a wash of darkness and rushing silence. I hold my breath, but I can feel him breathe in the water where his chest is pressed against mine. Whoever's controlling him doesn't want either me or this guy to make it out of the lake.

My lungs burn, and I fight to hold my breath longer. He squeezes tighter around my chest. I feel my ribs groan under the pressure, and I clench my teeth, forcing my mouth to stay shut. I hit him again and again with my gun, but each blow is weaker than the last, my vision starting to go gray around the edges. It's inky dark, and even in Second-Sight, everything is dim. I push the muzzle of the gun against his temple. The trigger refuses to pull back, though my finger aches from how hard I'm pulling. A couple of bubbles of air escape from my mouth and cold, bitter water forces its way in. I see stars and struggle with a last burst of adrenaline. It doesn't help, and my lungs start screaming. I gag, and the water comes rushing in, forcing out my last breath. Everything starts to go dark, and I cast out for Priya.

There's a splash, gentle, familiar arms around me, lifting me, then cold air against my face. I start coughing, vomiting up lake water. Priya is nearly corporeal around me, bright white and casting light throughout the water surrounding us. Her eyes blaze and her hair is spread out around her head in a dark, glowing halo. Energy pours off her in huge waves. We keep rising into the air, the surface of the lake now ten feet below me, tinted with the light spilling off Priya. I don't see any sign of Richardson.

Stop! I shout. She stares at me blankly, then starts to drift upward, her arms losing their grip around me. I fall back into the water. It stings like cement against my skin, and my head slips under for one heart-stopping moment. I feel the Bond between us start to stretch. I keep fighting toward the wall, all the while calling to her.

Priya! You have to stop!

Slowly, she turns in my direction.

Kim. There's a beat, and then the light vanishes. The pull on our bond disappears just as quickly, and I hear her voice, faint and tired.

I'm sorry, I couldn't—

Then she's gone.

I grab onto the rocks that make up the sea wall, shaking and sobbing. Cross leans over the edge of the platform, reaching down.

"Grab my hand!"

I throw my arm up and our fingers meet for a second. I can't get a grip on him, my vision blurred by tears and lake water, my hands numb and slick. I fall back into the water, sobbing. He leans over farther, teeth clenched, and shouts again. I dig deep, teeth bared on a primal scream, and reach up again with a last burst of energy. His solid fingers wrap around my hand, the pressure of his grip a sharp pain, and he starts dragging me onto the stage. I'm still shaking and crying when he pulls me, a soaking wet pile of raw emotion, onto solid ground.

"Hey, you're all right, it's okay." He pulls me into a warm hug. I press my face into his chest and scream, clawing at his jacket. I feel like I'm about to have a panic attack, and I start coughing, unable to control my body as it slips into shock. He holds me tighter, murmuring quiet reassurances into my hair. I keep reaching out for Priya, trying to find her, like an amputee trying to grab something with a missing hand. The silence that echoes back is deafening.

"She's gone." It comes out broken and lost. "She's gone, Cross. I can't feel her."

"C'mon, it's gonna be okay. We'll get this figured out, but we've gotta get you warmed up first, all right?" He squeezes me tightly again, then starts ushering me back to the parking lot. I stumble toward the car. If it weren't for him supporting me, I'd have fallen. I'm not sure I'd have been able to get back up. The whole time, I feel the gaping hole where Priya was. I can't stop shaking, and Cross almost pours me into the car, cranking the heater as he clambers into the driver's side. I hear him calling dispatch, and I fight to muffle my sobs, curling over into my lap in a tight ball.

Priya, where are you? Where are you?

There's no response.

CHAPTER TWENTY-FIVE

W e wait for the crime scene unit and detectives from the second district to arrive. There's no sign of Richardson. Cross gives me his jacket, which I wrap around myself with shaking hands. I'm soaked to the bone and shivering, even with the heat maxed out in the car. He rubs gentle circles on my back until I stop crying, my eyes red rimmed and burning.

"Do you want me to call an ambulance? We can get you to a hospital, have a doctor check you out, make sure you're okay."

"No, I just… I want to go home." I fight back a sob and lean my head back against the seat.

"They're gonna need your statement about what happened tonight. You think you can handle it?"

"Yeah," I say, numb and aching. "I can handle it."

I keep reaching out for Priya, but all I find is an echoing void. Ten years with her by my side, and suddenly nothing. I struggle to keep myself calm. I rock back and forth in the passenger seat of Cross's car, fighting down the panic. I'm close to losing it again when he opens the driver's side door to step out. He leans back in quickly. In the faint glow of a streetlight, I see a familiar officer standing behind Cross, shifting awkwardly.

"You know Officer Williams," Cross says. "He's going to ask you to go over everything with as much detail as you can provide, and then I can take you home. Be as specific as you can, Phillips. In the long run, it'll make it easier. You won't have to do this over and over again."

"I know," I say, starting to get angry. "I've done this before, Cross. Just… Let him in."

He steps aside. Williams slides into the car.

"I'll do my best to make this quick. You've had a hell of a night, Detective. Start at the beginning and we'll go from there."

I tell him about the drive out here, about Daniel's car, about Richardson.

I stop when I get to what happened to Priya. I shake my head, my eyes tearing.

"I can't. Just. Cross can tell you, he saw it."

He pauses. "I'll talk to him," Williams finally says. He reaches out to rest a hand on my shoulder, rubbing slightly. His hand is warm through the weight of Cross's jacket, and I nod slightly, thanking him for the offered comfort.

"Is there anything else you can remember? Anything else you think we need to know?"

"I dropped my gun," I say, voice and body numb. "If you could get it back…"

"We'll do what we can," he says. "Let Detective Cross take you home, go get some rest. We're gonna need you back on your feet soon. Oh, and we found your phone."

He hands it to me. I tuck it into the coat's pocket as I wait for him to get out of the car. He's talking to Cross, their voices muffled through the glass. I think I hear my name, Cross's voice raised in anger, then it fades. The door clicks open, and Cross spills in.

I fumble for my seat belt and force my hands open. Between the cold and how hard I've been clenching them, they're stiff and sore. Cross's shoulders slump when he sees me struggling with the clasp, and he reaches over, his hands gentle when they pull mine away to buckle it for me.

"Thanks," I say, feeling uncomfortable with the tender gesture. I pull his jacket tighter around me. He doesn't say anything as he shifts into reverse and drives out of the parking lot.

The lights lining the street shine into the car, the sky dark and roiling with storm clouds. They whip past, casting the car in broken stripes of dark and light. After a few minutes, a heavy rain starts. It cracks against the glass, the drops streaming past. I slowly relax to the steady sound of the wipers, my grief and adrenaline finally giving way to exhaustion. I don't keep track of where we turn or how many lights or stop signs we pass. The ride is silent except for the rain. At some point, I must fall asleep because I wake to Cross shaking my shoulder softly. We're outside his place.

"I don't live here," I say, shaking my head, trying to clear the sleep from my mind. I sound tired even to myself. He huffs out a laugh, then turns off the car.

"Yeah, I know. It was closer than your place. C'mon, let's get you inside."

I unbuckle and fumble for the door handle, popping it open before I'm prepared, and lurch out of the car. The rain slaps into me, Cross's coat barely holding it back. It soaks through my already drenched hair and clothes, and I start shivering again.

He comes around to my side and grabs my arm gently, helping me toward the steps. I take a moment to steady myself but pull away.

"I've got it," I say. I take a careful step and make my way up to the front door. At first, Cross trails behind me but steps forward to open the door. I lean against the wall as he pulls it open with a shriek. I stumble on the steps, and he quickly slides his shoulder under my arm, helping me keep my feet.

The walk up to his apartment is long and arduous. My legs feel like lead, and each step takes more energy from me than I think I have. Somehow, I keep moving forward, Cross's body warm and solid where it rests against mine.

He lets my arm slide free when we stop in front of his door. I lean against the wall and watch as a puddle slowly forms on the carpet beneath my feet. Cross shoves the door open, and I shuffle inside, his coat still wrapped tightly around my shoulders.

"Just wait here a moment, okay?" he says, stepping close and carefully brushing wet hair from my forehead. "I'm gonna go grab you some towels and a change of clothes."

I nod and wonder where I'm going to go. All of his furniture is white, and I'm covered in lake water and mud. I bend down and start fumbling with my boot laces. The knot refuses to give at first, my fingers still numb and clumsy, the laces swollen with water. Eventually, it gives, and I turn to the other boot. It slowly comes loose, and I slide my drenched shoes off with a watery squelch. My socks are next, landing with soft splashes on the front mat. Barefoot, I walk into the apartment, wet footprints trailing behind me.

When I was here before, I hadn't gotten past the front room. Now, as I wander farther into the apartment, I start catching more signs of the man who lives here. Photos hang on the walls of the hallway Cross disappeared down, and I lean closer, squinting in the half-light the storm lets in through the windows.

They're all Cross with other people. He's wearing graduation robes in one, his arms thrown over the shoulders of two other guys who look his age. They're all smiling and cocksure, their mortarboards at angles, the graduation tassels dangling in front of their eyes. In another, he's standing in his police dress uniform, looking serious, with an older man and woman. He has Cross's hair, and she has his eyes, and there's something about the shape of their faces that hints at his square jaw and high cheekbones.

I reach out and run my finger over Cross's face, tracing the lines of his frown, when he comes down the hall, arms full with a fluffy dark towel and a pile of police academy sweats.

"Oh, Jesus. You startled me," he says, taking a step back. He looks down, then frowns. "You're tracking water on the floor."

It's so mundane and poorly timed, I can't help but laugh. "Really? *Really*?"

He at least has the good grace to blush before he gestures his head farther down the hallway.

"Bathroom's this way. The super replaced the hot water heater last year, so the shower should warm up pretty quick."

I follow him down the hall and step into his bathroom. He sets the pile of clothes and the towel on the sink counter before stepping back into the hallway. He runs his hand through his hair quickly, shedding a few raindrops that stubbornly refuse to fall, and shifts his weight.

"I'll be right out here if you need anything, okay? Just holler."

I give him a small smile and close the door on his concern. Any further response to it is more than I can handle right now.

The water hisses on, and the bathroom fills with steam as I struggle out of my wet clothes. My jeans cling to my legs like clawing hands, and my shirt peels from my skin in a cold caress. I leave both in a wet pile on the floor.

There are bruises blooming on my ribs, and I run my fingers over them slowly, testing the skin. I hiss when I press too hard, but I can tell that they'll fade within a few days, no broken bones hidden beneath. I step into the shower and groan. The water is hot, the pressure heavy and solid against my skin. I let it beat down on my back, leaning my head against the cold tile, breathing slow and deep. I keep my eyes shut and close off my Second-Sight. It's dark and quiet. All I can hear is my heartbeat and the sound of falling water on hard tile. I stand there for a long time, listening.

The water starts to go cold before I feel ready to leave. The mirror is fogged, and when I wipe away the steam, I see a broken version of myself. My eyes are red and there are dark circles under them. I towel off and slide Cross's borrowed sweats over my clean skin.

He's sitting on the couch with a book, a pair of reading glasses perched on his nose. He looks up, startled when I walk out.

"C'mon." He stands. "I'll get you some shoes and take you home."

I shake my head and flop onto the couch, snuggling into the armrest.

"I just want to sleep," I say, trying to tuck my toes into the space between the couch cushions. Cross eases back down next to me and pulls my feet into his hands, rubbing them and warming my toes. I relax into his grip and sink deeper into the cushions.

I fall asleep again and wake up as Cross is setting me on his bed, the blankets pulled back. He sits down next to me on the mattress and flashes me a soft smile when I look up at him groggily. His touch is gentle as he brushes my hair back from my eyes.

"Get some rest, okay? I'll be right outside."

I grab his arm before he can stand up. "Stay."

"Are you sure?" he asks, his hand still resting against my hair. He moves it slightly, lightly cupping my face. "There's plenty of space on the couch."

"I don't want to be alone," I say, curling deeper into the bed. "I haven't been alone in a decade, and I can't…"

He nods, then pulls his hand away. I close my eyes and hear him moving around.

It's dark in the bedroom, and he doesn't turn on a light. There's the quiet sound of buttons clearing holes. The clink of a belt, the heavy sound of pants hitting the floor. Dresser drawer, clothes shuffling.

By the time he moves to the bed, the mattress dipping behind me, I'm wide awake. My muscles are tight, all the good the shower did gone in the time it took for him to undress. The bed shifts, creaking softly, and I curl tighter in on myself.

"Phillips," Cross says, voice quiet, "Kim. If you're uncomfortable, I can…"

"No," I say, turning to face him. He's sitting on top of the blankets, wearing a white undershirt and boxers. His hair is slightly mussed, his eyes unreadable in the darkness.

"I just don't know what to do," I whisper. "She's gone, and the Passenger is still out there. I don't know how I'll be able to face him without Priya."

"We'll figure it out." He places his hand over my clenched fist, his palm warm and rough against my skin. "And you won't be going after this guy by yourself. I've got your back, no matter what."

Slowly, I let my hand relax, and his fingers fall into mine. He runs his thumb soothingly over the back of my hand and weaves his fingers tight with mine. Slowly, inexorably, I settle into the softness of his bed, his thumb continuing its slow, steady movement over my knuckles.

My nose is pressed into the pillow, a hint of Cross's cologne worn into the pillowcase. I slowly relax and drift off with the warmth of his bed, his quiet breath filling the emptiness of the room, his presence keeping away the darkness and fear, at least for now.

CHAPTER TWENTY-SIX

I open my eyes to the abandoned building. The sigils and runes that cover the walls are a dark, bloody red, shedding a low light into the hallway. I'm barefoot, still wearing the academy sweats Cross loaned me. The whole building is silent, and when I take a tentative step forward, the sound echoes. Broken linoleum bites into my foot. I hiss out a breath and bend down to feel at the cut. It's wide but not deep, and I stand, carefully putting my weight on the foot. Runes flare, then subside, bleeding red light. I shudder and wrap my arms tightly around myself, the malevolence of the place overwhelming. When I take another step, I leave a bloody footprint behind.

I make my way down the hallway, walking carefully. Whenever I step on a rune or sigil, it flares into white-hot light, blinding me in brief, sporadic flashes, my blood powering the marks. I see shifting forms behind me each time the light blazes, and I pick up my pace, moving as fast as my injured foot lets me. They keep creeping closer as I make my way down the hall, their undulating forms tinted red by the arcane marks on the walls and floor.

Something brushes against my mind, and I instinctively pull back, shielding quickly. Whatever it is presses harder, and I grab my head, temples suddenly pounding. I gasp at the pain, then feel my shield drop. There's a familiar warmth, tinged with panic, and a voice.

Kim, thank God, I—

And then it's gone, Priya's voice echoing in my mind.

Priya? I Send, then feel a weak, answering touch. There's a stronger response from closer by, and when I turn around, I see glowing eyes in a formless blackness, and I start to run, foot forgotten.

I keep casting about for Priya, turning whenever I feel her touch on my mind. Slowly, the connection gets stronger. The black creatures keep moving closer, flashing into terrifying detail as my blood triggers runes and sigils. I reach the end of a hallway, crashing into a door that refuses to give.

"Priya!" I shout, pressing my hands against the safety glass windows set into the door. I jiggle the handle, but it refuses to move. Furious, I smack my hands against the glass and yell. I can hear the creatures behind me getting closer.

He's got me trapped, Kim.

Priya appears on the other side of the glass, her figure faded and indistinct. All I can see are the burning lights of her eyes and the ghostly halo of her hair. She presses her hand against the glass, and I match my hand up with hers, desperate.

It's all him, everything that we've been doing. He's the one behind it all.

Who is? Baker's descendant? I'm going to get you out of here, and then you can tell me everything.

I step away, then kneel to look at what's jamming the door. There's no lock on the door, just a blank space where the knob should be.

You've got to find the lock, I say, standing back up. *I can't get the door open, but maybe there's something on your side I can move or that you can manipulate to get it to open.*

Listen to me, Kim, she says. Her face flickers into clarity, her expression serious. *You have to get out of here. He's going to find you, and there's nothing I can do to keep you safe, not now. He's in Elgin, near the mental health center. You have to be careful.*

I'm not leaving without you, I say, wrenching on the door again.

I hear the creatures behind me, their movements loud on the broken ground. There's a final flash of light; then everything falls into darkness.

Kim, you have to go! You have to go now, Priya says, pressing both hands against the glass. *I'll be fine, but you have to go. Tell Cross, he'll help.*

I step back, startled by her vehemence. I turn to run, and all I can see is a wall of writhing black. Eyes like burning coals stare at me, and the whole thing moves closer, mouths opening into lava-bright depths. I take a step back, falling against the door. The blood pooling under my foot is slick, and I fall, crashing to the floor. There's a soundless roar, the creatures reaching for me, mouths wide to swallow—

I wake up, tangled in the sheets and blankets, the bed next to me empty. I look around the room, frantic, and see Cross's slumped figure in a small armchair in the corner of the room. He lets out a deep, even breath, then snores softly on the inhale. He must've moved after I fell asleep, and I feel something warm settle in my chest. It's painful, and I struggle to name the emotion welling up. I take a shuddering breath and slide out of the bed. I stare at Cross for a long moment—the careless fall of hair across his forehead, the awkward shape his body makes in the too-small chair—and then I leave the bedroom, shutting the door behind me with a quiet click.

Chapter Twenty-Seven

I eventually find my clothes in Cross's dryer, the machine tucked inside a hall closet. The fabric is still warm when I slide it on, and I leave his sweats in a folded pile on the washer. My jacket was lost in the lake, so I take Cross's again. I find his keys on the coffee table and grab them. I look back toward the bedroom when they jangle loudly, but the door stays shut, the apartment silent. I lock up when I leave, that indistinct feeling in my chest warping to something jagged and uneven.

Inside Cross's car, I reach out with my senses, trying to find Priya. There's nothing for the longest time, seconds slowly ticking to minutes, and my heart clenches, the grief flooding back in a sudden rush. Then, faintly, I feel something. I focus, falling as deep into Second-Sight as I can until everything around me disappears beneath blue-white lines of power. There's a thin line, nearly lost in the tangle of power swirling around me. I stretch out an astral hand and touch it, and I can suddenly feel her. It's muted and distorted, but it's Priya. I laugh and sob at the same time, and I open my eyes to turn on the car and peel out of Cross's parking lot.

I don't turn on the radio, just sit in silence as I speed west. I split my focus between what little traffic there is and the thin tendril connecting me to Priya. Like a compass drawn north, I realign myself to her. Turning down unfamiliar streets, flying down unknown roads, I slowly creep closer, the bond strengthening with each passing mile.

I'm broken from my half trance by my phone. Its ringer is brash and loud in the silence, and I jerk the wheel slightly, veering into the empty lane next to me. I fumble it out of the pocket of Cross's jacket, and the caller ID shows his number. I consider not answering for a second. Guilt prompts me to pick up the phone and put it on speaker.

"Hi," I say, awkward and uncertain.

"Where are you?" he asks, his voice deceptively calm.

"In your car," I answer. I can feel my heart rate start to pick up, and I take a deep breath.

"In my car," Cross says, tone still calm and collected, "which is not in the parking lot where I left it. So, follow-up question, where is my car?"

"Look," I say, speaking quickly. "I found Priya. I don't know how or why, but she's trapped near Elgin, and I have to get to her."

"So, you're heading somewhere, with no backup, no gun, on a *hunch*, all while there's someone out there looking to kill you," he says, calm demeanor gone. "Are you a fucking idiot? What the hell do you think you're doing?"

I don't know how to answer, and in the long pause, Cross starts speaking again.

"I told you I had your back, that we were going to face

this together. And you leave me behind while you go on some reckless mission to try to figure this out all on your own. I'm your goddamn *partner*." His voice breaks on the word, and I feel shame wash over me in a dizzying wave.

"I know," I say, voice quiet. "I know. But she needs me, and I can't just leave her."

"I think *you* need *her*," Cross shoots back. "And I don't think you need me."

"Cross, I—"

"You're lucky the car's fucking LoJacked," he says, cutting me off. "I'll have backup to you whenever you stop. And so help me, Phillips, if I get there before they do, you're going to be in such deep shit—"

I hang up. His voice, filled with anger and betrayal, still echoes around the car. I take a slow, uneven breath, then turn my phone on silent and stuff it into the passenger seat. I close my eyes for a moment and refocus on the strengthening connection between Priya and myself. It pulses softly, a tug at the core of my body that tells me to head a little farther south, a little farther west. I look for an off-ramp and follow the pull while my phone, the sound muffled by the seat, vibrates next to me.

When I reach the exit for Route 31, my skin is on fire, humming as the connection tries to reform. It crackles and stings, but I can feel Priya again, at least a little, and there's some comfort in the pain. There's a dissonance, too, the bond trying to repair itself and failing again and again. I rub at my chest, then take the exit. There's something, probably some*one*, blocking the connection, but I feel it getting stronger the closer I get to wherever Priya's being held.

Part of me wants to ignore what my gut is telling me. That Baker's descendant must be what's blocking me from Priya, that I'm driving closer and closer to wherever he's waiting. Now that I've had time to stop and think about it, the whole situation feels like a trap. He's taken part of my power, pulled me out of familiar territory, and he's done it without my fighting it at all. I look down at my phone, think about Cross, and feel guilt and fear twist in my stomach.

I should've brought him, I think, looking back up at the road as I near Elgin.

Suddenly, I feel like my body is struck with lightning. I jerk out of my seat, and my eyes roll back in my head. I think I hear a voice call out, but then I'm whisked from my body.

I'm in a dark space, a somehow familiar man in a wheelchair waiting at the end.

"You came," he sighs, grinning widely. "I didn't think you would. I mean, I hoped, but I didn't know." He rolls closer, the wheels of the chair moving without him touching them.

"Through the back, now, by the sports complex. They won't let you in through the front. Find me."

I'm thrust from the darkness before I can say anything, snapping back into my body with a rush of nausea. My arms and legs are filled with pins and needles, and I gasp, writhing against the taut line of the seat belt across my chest. I jerk the wheel as I come back to myself, horns blaring as I pull out of oncoming traffic and back into my lane. I bounce onto the shoulder too fast and come to a jarring halt.

"He took me," I say, voice shaking, fighting a rolling wave of nausea down. I don't know why, but I find some comfort in the sound of my own voice. "He *took me* out of my *body*, and he brought me to him. *Fuck*, that hurt."

I pant, hands clenched on the steering wheel. Resting my forehead against it, I breathe deeply and fight down panic. I'm unprepared. Unarmed. I reach for my phone and dial Cross's number. It rings, but there's no answer. His voicemail clicks on and I hang up.

The only choice left is to move forward, so I edge back onto the road and follow the pull toward Priya.

I head down State Street, fighting through shivers as I pull up outside the Elgin Mental Health Center. The parking lot is empty and pitch black apart from a few halos of light from lamps. A small line of trees separates me from the main part of the health center. There are empty tennis courts in the distance, a basketball goal peeking out from over the fence line. It's all cast in darkness, and there's something ominous about the quiet, empty space.

I can feel the pull toward Priya tugging me south, toward the health center. I unbuckle my seat belt, grab my phone, and open my door, stumbling out into the dark. I slam the door, then break into a run, following the pull into the darkness.

CHAPTER TWENTY-EIGHT

I make it through the tree line and reach a fence blocking the sports complex from the mental health center's cemetery. The top of the fence is covered in rusted and bent barbed wire. It's cold outside, the air still wet and heavy from the rain, and I shiver as I slide out of Cross's jacket. It catches on the barbed wire as I throw it over the top of the fence, and I start climbing. I reach the top, then take a deep breath before throwing my leg over, letting the coat protect me from the jagged metal. I jump down and give a tug on the jacket's sleeve, but it's stuck solidly on the fence. I sigh and leave it, feeling another twinge of guilt.

Ghosts float around aimlessly in the darkness, softly lit outlines of people in old, tattered clothes. As I walk through the cemetery, I brush past the specters that surround me. Their hands move through my body, sending shivers up my spine.

Later, I think. *I'll take care of them later.*

I see a building in the distance, and the pull on my bond with Priya strengthens. I speed up, hitting a low jog, then a run, then a full-out sprint. My legs burn and my blood thunders through my ears.

Priya! I scream down our connection, praying to get a response. I feel something like a call back, and I nearly sob in relief.

The front doors are locked, but I grab a quick surge of power and break the lock with sheer will. I burst inside, the doors echoing loudly in the entryway as they slam open. I look around, frantic, and freeze.

There's a desk in the front with papers strewn across the top. Plastic chairs are scattered around the room and wide double doors lead farther into the building. The air has a familiar, musty scent and a quiet sense of malevolence that sends a shiver dancing across my skin.

"Oh shit," I say, my breath stolen from my throat.

I know this room. I've seen it time and time again in my dreams, in the nightmares that have been haunting me since I Burnt Murphy. I take a step back, then turn and retreat to the front doors. My hands slam into empty air first, and the rest of my body comes crashing into the invisible shield. I fall back, my palms stinging.

"Oh shit. *Shit.*" I throw my body against the barrier again, only to bounce back.

I start pacing, then pull my phone from my pocket. I've got one bar of signal, and I dial Cross's number, cursing. It rings, and Cross picks up with a click.

"What?"

"I fucked up, I fucked up bad. You need to get here, or backup needs to get here, and it needs to have happened five minutes ago. Those dreams I've been having?" I say, still pacing, running my free hand through my hair. "They weren't dreams, they were fucking *visions.* I'm here, I mean

I'm there. Where I was in those dreams. And that's not good."

"I called Elgin PD, and they're headed your way now. I'm still twenty minutes out, but I'm coming. In the meantime, you've got to get out of there," he says, voice shaking with a sliver of fear and a lot of anger.

"I'd love to, but I can't. There's some sort of shield around the building, and I can't break it. I think there must be warding on the exterior of the building, something that I can't get to from inside. When you get here or the Elgin cops get here, I need someone to look for it, see if it can be broken."

"What are we going to be looking for?" Cross asks.

"Sigils and runes," I say, "like what we saw at Casey's crime scene. Anything carved into the building or into the bricks."

I try to think of how to describe the right symbols to a complete novice and fail.

"There'll be a lot of them. Just start scratching them out. I don't know what you'll need to do to break the warding, not without seeing them, and I don't know that I haven't tripped something by coming in here. In the dreams, I only have a few minutes before bad shit starts to go down."

"I'll do what I can. Just stay where you are. I'll call you back once I get there."

"Okay. Just promise me you won't come inside," I say, turning to face the desk. "I don't know if you'll be trapped in here, too."

"Got it," Cross says. "Just stay put, we're on our way."

"And Cross? I'm sorry, I shouldn't have—"

The phone disconnects, and I stare at it for a long moment before cursing and shoving it back into my pocket. I'm still trapped, but there's a slight comfort knowing that help is on its way, even if it's understandably pissed off. I walk toward the desk and pick up some of the papers. Unlike in my dreams, I can read them clearly. Elgin State Hospital is written in block letters across the top with a date from the early 1930s. It's basic paperwork, commitment and release forms for people long since dead. There's a pay stub stuffed into one of the desk drawers, but otherwise, the paperwork doesn't shed any light on why this building was closed and left to fall into disrepair. The double doors gape open, the hallway beyond them dark and beckoning. I take a deep breath, then drop into Second-Sight.

Everything around me erupts into blue light. The walls are covered with pulsating sigils and runes. Most of them are for binding and warding, but there are flashes of symbols I don't recognize, ancient marks that are filled with arcing bands of power. I can see down the hall, too, but there are no signs of anyone being here in a long time, just the marks slowly flaring, then dimming as I breathe.

The double doors call to me, and I take a few tentative steps before pausing and feeling the faint connection that runs between Priya and myself. I take another step and feel the connection tug in the opposite direction. Eyes still closed, trusting my other senses, I follow the pull down a side hallway, the door rotten and hanging from its hinges. I step over it, moving deeper into the building.

There are rooms lining the hallway. Most of them appear to be storage closets or small offices, but there's a room at the end. The door has a pane of glass in the upper half, and Priya is waiting on the other side.

Oh, thank God. I Send, running to the door and pressing my hands against it.

Kim, Priya says, and it's faint, fainter than I've ever heard from a ghost in my life. *You shouldn't be here. You need to go.*

She wrings her hands, then presses them against the door. I sense her struggling against whatever is binding her there, and I start looking on my side of the door for anything that would keep her confined. I don't see anything in Second-Sight, but as I run my hands over the doorframe, I can feel slivers of wood missing where sigils have been crudely carved. I pull on the power coiled in my veins, feel it pool in my chest and stomach, and let it out slowly into the symbols. They fill and light, blue and pulsing. In Second-Sight, it's clear what they're for. There are symbols for binding, for hiding. And for alarm.

"Shit."

I pull my silver knife from the top of my boot and dig it into the soft, rotten wood. It gives way easily, pieces falling to the floor. I dig out a couple of the more important symbols, the ones that tie everything together. The light around the door flickers. As I pry the last symbol free, it flares, then dies.

My connection to Priya twists and turns as it reforms, snapping into place with a solid thunk that I can feel to the soles of my feet. My body covered in pins and needles, I shakily put my knife back into its sheath and stand, unsteady but feeling stronger with every breath. Priya floats on the other side of the door for a moment, and then she's flowing through my body, wrapping her arms around me and sending a great wave of love and relief through the bond. I close my eyes, fighting sudden tears, as I send an answering wave of emotion back. The bond is strong and shimmering between us and I laugh.

We need to get out of here, she says, pulling away to blow past me. *He's coming.*

We can't leave, I say, following her at a quick run. She's blazing ahead, fleeing to the front room. *There's a barrier around this place and I can't break it.*

You have to try.

Priya slams into the invisible wall keeping us inside. I grit my teeth and join her, pushing forcefully against it. After a few moments, I stop, panting.

"This isn't going to work," I say. I turn toward the beckoning double doors and start walking forward.

What're you doing? Priya asks, flowing in front of me. *You can't go after him.*

"What do you want me to do? Just wait for him to come find us?"

He's twisted, Kim. There's something wrong with him, something I don't understand. She's shaking, wringing her hands together in an echo of life. *He's evil.*

What do you mean? I ask, suddenly confused.

I don't know how to describe it, but something at the core of him is broken. It's dark, *Kim. Like Turning, but worse.*

We're going to have to face him, I say, turning back toward the hallway and the gaping, taunting darkness.

We need to wait for help, Priya says. She's still scared, uncertain.

Priya, I say, reaching for her through our bond. I feel her through it, the connection visceral and necessary. *I know you're scared. I'm scared, too. But this guy has killed five people. Five Mediums. We can't let him get away.*

There's a long pause. She reaches back for me through the bond, and I let her take comfort from the contact. There's a shudder, like something settling into place, and when I meet her eyes, they're resolute rather than afraid.

We won't have much time, she says. I nod and walk through the double doors.

The hallway is familiar, though darker than it was in my dreams. The lockers are more rusted, more broken down. I switch to Second-Sight to help me see, and symbols start to appear on the walls. Unlike in my dreams, where the sigils and runes shifted and turned into different shapes, or the main entry room, which was covered in a variety of sigils and runes, there's only one symbol here. It's repeated over and over again, covering almost every inch of the walls and floors. A circle, bisected by a cross, with one arm longer than the other. The symbol from my grandmother's book.

That's not ominous at all, I say, shaking my head.

I told you, he's twisted, Priya says, floating closer to the walls and brushing her hand over the symbols. They stay still and dull beneath her fingers, but flare to life as I step closer.

What does it mean? I wonder.

Priya doesn't answer and starts heading farther down the hall. I jog after her, watching the floor. There aren't any gaping holes, but I still tense every time the floor creaks beneath my feet. All the while, that same rune bursts into bright life whenever I step closer, leaving a fading trail behind us as we head deeper into the building.

There's no sign of anyone else here. I consider calling out but decide against it. Whoever's trapped us here knows that we're stuck. There's no need to let him know exactly where we are.

There's another set of double doors at the end of the hallway. These, unlike the ones from the lobby, are still solid in their frame. In Second-Sight, I'm able to see sigils and runes of preservation, of strength, of binding, intermixed with the same symbol from the hallway. There's no dirt or rust on the doors, and there's a heavy set of chains wrapped around the handles, closed with a solid steel padlock. The unknown symbol is carved into the back of the lock in jagged gouges, the metal deeply scarred.

I pull on the lock and the chains rattle, but it's solid. I look at the lock in my hand, considering.

What do you think? Do we break in or leave it alone?

Priya lays her hand on the door and shudders.

I don't know. I think he might be inside, but there's something else that's been trapped in here. Something that shouldn't be released.

Can we bind it again, if we need to?

Yes, probably, Priya says, hesitant. *But it may leave us weak against the Medium behind all of this.*

I wave in acknowledgment and fall into Second-Sight. The lock is slightly rusted inside, and the tumblers refuse to give way under my questing touch. After a long, tense moment and a sudden push with power, they grate into place, and the lock opens. It slides apart with a quiet click that echoes down the hallway, and the chains fall away with a crash. I pant heavily for a moment and wipe sweat from my brow.

He's going to know we're here now, I say. *Get ready.*

Priya nods, power skittering across her skin like lightning. Her eyes are gray and wide, poised and ready. I take a deep breath, steady myself, and pull power from the world around me until I can hardly contain it. I push the door open, my hands sparking where they touch the metal.

The door opens easily, revealing an operating theater. A large central area and a raised series of deep steps lead up and back with metal railings on each level. The place has fallen into disrepair, the seating overhead broken and filled with rubble, some parts of the metal banister hanging down toward the main floor. There are a few discarded chairs tilted on their sides or rotted through. Ivy snakes its way into the interior of the building, weaving between the broken cracks in the ceiling. Moonlight sneaks its way in, too, though it's intermittent, broken up by the clouds still rolling in from the earlier storms.

The center of the room is empty except for a wheelchair. Unlike everything else in the room, it appears brand new, the metal gleaming and bright. The padded leather seat and seat back are bright blue, well-oiled, and shining in the broken light. Heavy iron chains wrap in and around the wheels, though they're rusting and look close to falling apart. In Second-Sight, their surface is a roiling mass of symbols, all of binding. I shiver and take a step forward.

As I walk farther into the room, the chains start to rise, climbing up the wheelchair like slowly moving serpents. They grate and clank, the noise echoing in the theater. Slowly, a figure starts to appear in the chair. The white hair and dark, wrinkled skin are familiar.

"Kim," he says, his voice scratchy and dark. "You've finally come."

"Who are you?" I ask, my body on edge, power struggling to be unleashed.

"You know my name already," he says condescendingly, at last raising his head to look at me.

Comprehension washes over me in a sudden, dizzying wave. "*Baker?*"

He laughs. "I'm surprised it took you this long to figure it out. You seem so… bright."

"You can't be him," I say, voice shaking. "He's been dead for forty years."

"Yes, though I have been Bound for longer. Soon, that will change."

Priya, get ready, I Send, steadying my stance as he shifts to face us fully. *He's old and he's dangerous.*

Understood, she Sends back, her body glowing with power.

Baker's eyes are black and sunken, but there's a hint of red fire in their depths. His whole body is emaciated, skeletal, but there's a certain confidence to his movements that hints at hidden strength. He starts to smile and his mouth pulls too far back at the corners.

"I'm surprised you came alone."

I shake my head and start walking around the edge of the room. I can feel Priya tense behind me, focused on Baker.

What is he? she asks.

I don't know.

Oh, you do know, Baker Sends, mouth still wide and grinning. *You've been dealing with my kind for years.*

"You're dead, a ghost. How can you talk?" I ask, freezing in place as he turns his head to look at me, neck twisted past the point of possibility.

"I'm not just some specter trapped between worlds, waiting to cross over. I know things, Kim."

His body slowly twists, undulating unnaturally as it moves, the wheelchair's wheels sliding smoothly against the floor untouched until he's facing me entirely.

"Your powers were Bound. You shouldn't be able to do anything," I say, continuing to move around the perimeter of the room.

He tips his head back and starts laughing, his long, thin body shaking with the motion.

"You are such a smart thing," he says. "Just like your grandmother. But just like her, you underestimate me."

He flicks his fingers and a bolt of power shoots out

from them. It races toward me and I'm unable to dodge it. It slices into my cheek, leaving a trail of fire that has me gasping. I raise a hand to my face and pull away fingers stained with blood.

"She Bound you," I bit out, wiping my hand on my jeans.

"She *betrayed* me," he roars, suddenly rushing toward me. I hastily back up, fighting to keep distance between us. He stops just as suddenly, the chains around his chair clanking, the sound echoing around the room.

"Phillips and her friends. Abbot, Moore, Brennan, Bell, Barrett."

I stop, frozen in place, a sudden lance of fear like ice skating down my back.

"I had no children, no family," he says, voice filled with scorn. "Just my fellow Mediums. And they Bound me, tied me to this world. Left me to rot."

"So you've been seeking revenge," I say, continuing to slowly circle Baker as he sits in the center of the room.

He turns my way, eyes calculating, waiting. The wheels of his chair whisper over the floor, moving without being touched.

"Yes and no," he says, moving closer in a quick rush. I jump to the side, using power to push myself into an unnatural leap. He cackles from the other side of the room as I get back to my feet.

"Then why?" I ask, anger and fear hot in my blood.

"Because, dear child," he says, continuing to move closer, "their binding is tied to their blood and their power.

And when their blood and their power end, so too does the binding." He seems disappointed and shakes his head sadly. "I would think you'd have figured this all out before you came here."

"You know why I came here now. Why don't you just get it over with?" I ask, body bowstring taut as I wait for his next move. Priya is circling the room, but I can tell that she's at as much of a loss as I am for our next move.

We've got to take him out, I Send, keeping the thought focused and tight. Baker doesn't respond, so I assume that Priya's the only one who's heard it. She nods slightly, hair flaring into a massive halo, eyes bright and flaming white.

"Oh, I will, my dear child. But first, you need to understand the mistake that your dear grandmother made. You see, I was looking into those things that are forbidden to our kind. Not because they're dangerous, oh no, but because they make us too *powerful*."

He keeps coming toward me, and I trip over something, falling back only slightly before the backs of my legs hit the low wall that separates the seats for the operating theater from the central area.

"It's ignorance and fear that stops us from truly embracing our powers. We tie ourselves to a single Affinity, limit our powers to that which we are most attuned. But we can meld and shape the world around us, to reach past death itself and *control* it. Your grandmother and her friends, the whole community, they all failed to understand that. And so they Bound me, stripped me of my powers, and left me to rot in the prison of my own body."

I slide around the edge of the room, making my way back toward the doors.

"What do you mean, we tie ourselves to a single Affinity?"

He smiles indulgently. "Have you ever wondered what twist of fate makes you a Burner and me a Passenger, why Mediums have Affinities at all? Or if, maybe, all Mediums possess the same powers, the same Affinities, if they are just willing to reach past their own limitations to embrace the entirety of their abilities, their being?"

"You're crazy," I say, the words slipping from my mouth more out of fear than conscious choice.

He laughs, eyes burning red. "I spent my whole *life* training to become a Medium. I worked until I thought I could go no further, and then I pushed myself past that exhaustion. I shed blood and tears and sweat, and when I found something more, something extraordinary? They *stole* it from me!"

He screams the last part, and there's a wave of power within the sound. It pushes me back, my feet sliding on the ground, my hair whipping around my face.

"What happened to you?" I ask, getting my feet solid and steady beneath me.

"I spent the rest of my life looking to undo what they had done. At first, I tried killing them, but they knew I would come for them and were prepared. I was locked away, confined. They said I had lost my mind, and I suspect part of that was true. You felt a piece of it when you lost your partner. Only there was no relief for me, just emptiness. They put me in here, then waited for me to die.

And once I did, I found a new power. New friends. New partners."

I see something dark start to move in the corner of the room and with growing horror slowly recognize one of the black creatures from my dreams. It's smaller, but it's growing, its body covered in glowing runes. It creeps next to Baker, curling through his legs like a dog. He reaches out and pets the creature, its body flowing over and around his hand like smoke before coalescing.

"They've kept me company these long years," Baker says, voice fond. Another creature starts to grow out of the other, then another. Soon, a pack of them are circling his chair in a writhing mass of smoke and fire-lit eyes while he smiles down at them, his expression a mix of affection and all-powerful control.

One by one, the creatures slow and settle by Baker's feet. He smiles down at them again and coos quietly. They begin to sink into his body. He grows, his physical shape warping as the creatures meld with him. His hair is darkening, his emaciated and skeletal frame filling in uneven bulges that slowly turn to the curved form of muscles.

Priya, get ready. This is going to get bad fast.

I feel her at my back, waiting.

"You're all that's left," he says. He raises his head, and his eyes are bright red and flaming. Shadows shift and swirl within him, darkening his skin and licking out in small wisps of smoke.

"They didn't know you were coming," I say, readying myself. "I do."

He grins, body now young and powerful. The chains wrapped around his chest creak and groan. I see a link start to split, and I start pulling power from the world around me, holding as much of it as I can, my belly burning.

"I've always loved a challenge," he says as the iron gives way with a scream.

CHAPTER TWENTY-NINE

The room's suddenly filled with a raging wind. I throw my arm over my eyes and raise a shield to stop the debris that's filling the air from striking me. When I move my arm, Baker's gone.

Quick, Priya! Help me find him!

I cast around the room, keeping the shield tight around me as dirt and wood slam into it. Baker's dark spirits circle the room, invisible against the inky blackness of night except for their glowing red eyes. When I drop into Second-Sight, they are just masses of teeth and burning light, red and fiery against the blue light that makes up the world.

I can't find him, Kim, Priya shouts, flickering in behind my shield. *I don't know where he went.*

"Kim," he says, his voice echoing from behind me. I whirl around, the shield moving with me as I stumble back. There's no one behind me, just more darkness and raging wind. I curse, casting around frantically.

"Do you really think you can stop me?" he asks, and there's rancid breath against my cheek. I feel something slice into my arm, and I throw out a half-formed ball of power behind me, the action instinctive and wild. It crackles off into the distance, striking one of the writhing shadows. It leaves a gaping wound in its side, a blue and burning gash that fades as the creature falls shrieking, then dissipates in a steaming cloud.

"You know what kind of power there is in the dark."

There's another flash, and I feel something cut into the side of my neck. I press my hand to the wound, only pulling it away when the blood trickles slowly over my fingers.

Where the fuck is he?

I'm looking, I'm looking. Just keep the shield up. I don't think he can really get through it, though his attacks might.

Very reassuring, Priya.

I spin around again and dive into Second-Sight deeper than I've ever gone before. I can see Priya like a spotlight, burning brightly in the dark. Behind her is the twisted figure of a man, body bent and broken, fingers like claws rising over her shoulder, mouth too wide and gaping open.

Behind you! I scream, throwing power out in a white sheet, the binding a habit from a decade of Burnings. Priya twists and the bright sheet hits Baker in the chest, sending white fingers of flame throughout his skeletal body. His mouth opens in a grimace, the inside burning red behind jagged teeth, and he screams. The white light dances over his skin, cutting in and breaking through the wretched remains of his soul.

Yes, I think, readying another sheet. I channel all my reserves into it, and the power flows out of me in a great wave of light. It slams into Baker, whose mouth opens again on a soundless scream. I watch as Priya wraps her arms around him, adding to the glow shrouding his body, holding him in place.

I struggle forward, an unseen force pushing out from Baker, the smoke creatures stalking and snapping at my shield with every step. I feel their teeth skitter across the surface of it, a rasping, jittering sensation that leaves me shaking as I try to keep my defense up. He struggles against my grip, and I can feel the power crackling as he tries to break through. I grit my teeth and keep moving forward until I'm standing in front of Baker, his arms pinned by Priya and the light, eyes wild.

I lean down, panting, and pull my knife from its sheath. The blade is vibrating in my hand, singing in concert with the waves of power pulsing from my body. I press the tip to my thumb, cutting through the skin, and I watch as blood beads in a bright red drop on my fingertip.

Burning without a circle is dangerous, but something compels me to do it now. I press my thumb against his forehead, and his skin starts to smoke.

You think you can defeat me? he Sends, eyes flaming, the red glow flickering out in licking tendrils. I can feel the heat of it against my hand, my skin screaming as it starts to burn, and I keep pressing my thumb into his bubbling skin.

"I think you need to shut the fuck up," I say through gritted teeth, and then I close my eyes. With a ragged scream, I reach into the core of myself, into the very essence of what makes me a Medium, a Burner, and I release *something* with a wrenching pain low in my gut. Whatever I've unleashed rolls up through my body and out through my thumb in a stinging rush. There's a flash of light, then a soundless explosion, and I'm tossed back and into the air, the room suddenly dark.

There's a long heartbeat, a moment that fills the space between my pulse before it all comes crashing down. I'm thrown to the ground, body sliding until I slam into the low wall around the theater. My head is ringing, my back scraped and bleeding from where the broken concrete has torn through my shirt. I roll to my side, coughing, my breath knocked out of me.

Priya? I Send, struggling to push myself upright. I feel an answering pulse through our bond, and I sigh, falling back to the ground.

Is he gone? she asks, slowly materializing near me.

I think so. I can't feel him, and those creatures are gone.

I blink exhaustion from my eyes and look around the room. It's empty, though there's debris littering the floor from the fight. The wheelchair lies broken in the middle of the room, the previously pristine leather and metal a twisted, torn mess. As I watch, rust climbs up the metal, engulfs everything, and the remains fall to the floor as dust.

That's fucked up, I think, and Priya laughs. I laugh with her, relief tripping through my veins. I lay my head on the floor and allow the emotion to roll over me, to sweep me up in a wave of dizzying exhilaration. The emotion courses through the reformed bond between Priya and myself, and I can feel her own joy and relief echoing back.

There's a creak from the doorway, and I lift my head to face this new threat.

"You can't visit a place without destroying it, can you?"

Cross stands in the doorway to the theater, surveying the place with familiar disdain.

"Holy shit," I say, forcing myself to stand with a pained groan. "Perfect timing. You missed a hell of a show." I brush myself off, knocking dust and rocks from my clothing. With a sigh, I face him, feeling uncertain. "Cross, I'm so sorry. I should've woken you up."

He shrugs his shoulders, his body turned away from me as he looks around the theater.

"Seems like you were able to handle things on your own." His voice is tight, uncompromising.

"That doesn't matter," I say, walking toward him. "You're right, you're my partner and I should've trusted you. I'm sorry."

"Nothing to be sorry about, Phillips. Case solved, right? Everything tied up with a neat bow."

His shoulders are tight, his back to me like a wall.

"I'm sorry," I say. "I fucked up."

He shakes his head. "It's too late for that, Phillips. You made it perfectly clear what you think of this *partnership*. When we get back to Chicago, I'm requesting a new partner. I can't work with you, not if you don't trust me."

I reach for him, hand shaking, and place my hand on his shoulder.

"Cross," I say, voice and throat tight. "I do trust you, more than I ever thought I would. I just, last night…"

I pull on his shoulder and force him to turn. When his eyes finally meet mine, I see that they're red and burning, and his face twists into a familiar, terrifying grin.

White light bursts out of his body, smashing into me, sending me flying. I cough when I land, my body protesting the pain and shock. I stare at him, uncomprehending.

"Do you really think you're going to walk out of here alive?" Cross asks, his tone pitying as he slinks forward. He raises a hand and another bolt of power shoots out of him. It slams into me, pushing me back up against the wall. The pressure grows and forces the breath out of my lungs. I try to inhale, but all I can do is choke on nothing. Cross laughs, eyes red and glinting in the darkness, and the pressure lessens. I gasp in a breath, then throw a bolt of power at him. He laughs and sidesteps it.

"Careful, Kim," he says, voice taunting. "You might hurt the boy."

"Baker," I say, disbelieving.

I ready my power again, pulling it back, ready to unleash it when I feel something like iron bands wrap around my body, pinning my arms.

"I must thank you for breaking that binding," Cross/Baker says, looking toward the remains of the chair. "It was a little morbid of them to tie me to that, don't you think? It's much more comfortable being free of the thing."

I keep struggling, then watch as Priya throws herself at Baker. She wraps around him, blazing with light. His face spasms, twisting in anger, and he sweeps his arm out, throwing Priya from him with a wash of power.

"Pest," he spits, turning to face her. He reaches out and

grabs her, his hand somehow tangling in her intangible body. I see her face go pale, feel fear course down the bond as she struggles in his grasp. "I should've sent you beyond earlier."

He throws her away from him, and she disappears with a scream. I feel the bond wrench and I grab tightly to it, teeth clenched. I'm not going to lose her again, not after I just got her back. I feel the bond tighten, feel it want to give, but I pull harder against it. The stretch slows, then stops, and I feel it solidify. It's safe, at least for now. On the other end, though, Priya is exhausted, her power drained.

Meanwhile, the thing wearing Cross's face has walked closer to me. He bends down where I'm lying on the floor, grabs me by the collar, and pulls me to my feet.

"Thank you for bringing this vessel along with you, too," he says. He lets go of my shirt, and I fight to stay on my feet. "He's very strong, you know. Should keep me nice and safe for years to come."

"Let him go," I say through gritted teeth, trying to pull power into my body, still fighting against the invisible bonds keeping my arms pinned.

"None of that now," he says, and the bands tighten. I feel the power leech from my skin and watch as it trips and crackles from my arms into his body. He twists his hand, letting the power dance over his fingers in small jumps of light. He grins, and it's painful to see something so familiar as Cross's smile with someone else behind his eyes.

"You know, you look a lot like her," he says, stepping closer and pulling me into his arms. "Just like Sadie when I first met her."

He smells like rot and sulfur, and when he traces a hand over my face, it's like burned leather against my skin.

"Do tell her I said hello when you see her. I do miss her, sometimes."

He leans in and his lips part. There's a moment where he exhales against my face, the smell of decay and death so strong that I gag. Then he breathes in, and something tugs at the core of me. What little power I have in reserve sparks, then disappears, leeching up through my arms and out of my mouth into Cross/Baker's. It goes from a slow trickle to a rushing torrent, tearing from my body in painful waves. The light pouring from my mouth is blinding and I close my eyes against it. The cut on my thumb starts bleeding again, and the blood leaves my body along with whatever power Cross/Baker is stripping from me.

I think I hear Priya screaming. I see her rushing toward us, but something holds her back. Cross/Baker pulls me closer, brushes hair from my face.

It's such a shame, he Sends, staring into my eyes, Cross's familiar green swirling with burning red. My fingers twitch, vision going black. I watch him, his fingers digging into my skin.

"Cross," I whisper, and I think I see something flash in those green-red eyes, something I recognize. "Riley."

I struggle to raise my hand to his chest, the bands around me loosened just enough for me to move my arm. My palm lays against his shirt, and I can feel his heart beating. Blood from my thumb leaves a dark streak on his

T-shirt, and I slowly move it, tracing a shape on the fabric.

"Forgive me."

I make a circle, bisected by a cross, with one arm longer than the other. I send a whispered prayer to anyone willing to listen, and with the last of my power, the remaining sliver that Baker has yet to steal, I force it into the mark on his shirt.

Everything erupts into white light, Baker screaming as the sudden aura overtakes him, and I shut my eyes, blinded.

When I open them again, I'm in a dimly lit room. The walls are rough wood, the floor dirt. There are candles around the edges, shedding enough light for me to see five other figures. They're all speaking, but it's muffled. There are words coming from my mouth, but I can't hear them. I can't stop speaking, even though I try.

In the center of the room is Baker. He's young and strong and weeping. His hands are bound behind him, and he screams, trying to drown out the chanting that fills the room. A chalk circle surrounds him, and at the feet of each of the figures is a symbol. I recognize them from the book, from all of the books.

A crescent moon that overlaps the edges of the circle. A curved line with a straight one cutting down the center. An eye within an eye. A V, with one arm longer than the other, cutting the circle in two. A circle in a circle. A circle with a square touching all the edges.

And finally, at my feet, a circle bisected by a cross, with one arm longer than the other.

Baker keeps screaming, keeps crying, and the words

continue to flow.

"Why are you doing this?" he shouts, jerking against the ropes that bind his hands. He's shirtless, his body covered in sweat. He looks at me, pleading. "Sadie, please. You know me, I'd never do anything to hurt anyone."

"Quiet," a voice says, and I turn. One of the hooded figures steps forward and pulls back the dark cowl covering its head. It's an older woman, her face patrician and implacable. Wrinkles tug at the corners of her mouth and her white hair is pulled up in a tight bun.

"You know why this has to happen, Joseph," she says, voice cold and furious. "You cannot be trusted with this power."

"You don't understand," he says, groaning. "You're limiting yourselves, limiting all of us. There's so much more that you don't understand—"

"I said, *quiet*," she says, cutting him off with a quick motion of her hand. A rune flies from her grasp to slap across his mouth. Suddenly, his voice is muffled, his words unclear.

"Caroline, are you sure?" I ask, unable to tear my eyes from Baker's.

"Complete the ritual," she says, pulling her hood back up around her face with a jerk. I hesitate, then nod and resume my place in the circle.

As we chant, the light in the room grows, slowly filling every corner, lighting up the faces across from me. They're all familiar. I've been studying them and their deaths for the last week and a half. We're all speaking in unison, and as our hands reach out, a gleaming dagger in each, my own body moves. I don't feel the blade when it cuts into my skin. I don't feel the blood as it drips down my fingers. All I can see are the bright eyes of the others in the room, staring at me, mouths moving like mine, as Baker screams and screams and screams, his eyes filled with tears and despair.

CHAPTER THIRTY

I wake up to a quiet beeping. Something's tickling my nose, and my arm feels cold and sore. I blink my eyes, clearing the grit that seems to be filling them. After a long moment, the room clears.

I'm in a hospital, and Cross is passed out in a chair next to the bed. There's an IV in my right arm and a nasal cannula pumping oxygen through my nose. I reach my leg out from underneath the thin blanket that's covering me and kick Cross. He rocks back for a second, then sits forward, gasping.

"Hey." My voice sounds weak and raspy. "Who let you in here?"

"Oh, Jesus. Phillips." He stands up and rushes over to the bed, wrapping his arms around me tightly. It pulls on my IV, but I hug him back anyway. I start to shake, and he lays me back down.

"How long have I been out?" I ask, making note of the thick stubble that covers his face and the rumpled state of his clothes.

"About two days." He rubs a hand over his face.

"What happened?"

"I'm not sure. I was still trying to find a way to take

down the barrier when there was an explosion. Then I don't remember anything. I came to inside that operating theater with you passed out next to me." He shakes his head. "You were bleeding out of your ears and eyes. And I had this on my chest."

He pulls the collar of his shirt down, and I can see a familiar raised mark on his skin.

"Fuck," I whisper, eyes wide. The mark is burned into his skin, the wound red and puffy. "I didn't know, I just…"

"What happened?" Cross asks, letting his shirt fall back into place.

"It was Baker," I say, closing my eyes for a moment. "He was behind it all, not his descendant. When they Bound him, he went looking for power." I laugh mirthlessly and shake my head. "Boy, did he find it."

"So it was revenge."

"And freedom," I say, looking away from him, from the wound on his chest. "If he'd killed me, he would've been free. And then… I don't know what would've happened after that."

He frowns at me but doesn't say anything.

"And then he possessed you," I say, the words still not making any sense to me. "I don't know how, but he took over your body. I thought he was going to kill the both of us at the end. That's when I…" I look back at him and wave at his chest. "I'm sorry about that, about everything."

"What's next?" he asks, looking away, mouth tight.

"I don't know," I say honestly. "Baker's gone. I don't

know how, but I Burnt him. There's going to be a hell of a lot of paperwork." My mouth quirks into a painful grin. "And the Lieutenant is going to have my ass."

"You're going to be on desk duty for a while," Cross says. "Walker's been furious since they got you stabilized."

"You going to be stuck there with me?" I ask, my heart pounding. He keeps staring into the distance, not looking at me.

"I don't know," he finally says, glancing at me with a frown. "I haven't decided."

"Okay. Whatever you choose," I say, throat tight. "You're a good partner. I'm sorry I didn't realize that sooner."

He doesn't say anything, just looks at me, his green eyes bright and unreadable. He slowly stands and stuffs his hands in his pockets, rocking back on his heels.

"I'm going to head out, let you get some more rest. I'll see you around the office?"

"Yeah." I fight back unexpected tears. "I'll see you around."

He looks at me again and nods. He slowly turns and walks out of the hospital room, and I roll onto my side, the IV pulling on my skin painfully.

It's okay, Priya Sends, a soft touch in my mind. *I'm here.*

She settles next to me and starts running her fingers through my hair, not saying anything further. I close my eyes, allowing her to comfort me, and drift into dreamless sleep.

I end up spending another three days in the hospital, partly for observation, partly because I barely have the strength to walk to the small bathroom connected to my room. When I finally get home, I do what I can to piece together what I know of Baker. The last vision I had in Elgin, that room filled with chanting bodies, is familiar. My notes from Reading Casey's knife confirm it. She somehow saw Baker's binding before he'd killed her. She was the closest to finding out what was happening, besides myself.

Researching him goes slowly, but I finally manage to find a crumpled obituary that someone scanned onto a website.

Joseph Baker, sixty-five, died of natural causes on Monday, June 13, 1977. He leaves no family. Memorial on June 23 at the Baptist Church of Evanston. Donations should be sent to the Field Museum.

That's it. I'm unable to find anything else, no details of his life or his death. Nothing more than a wrinkled, faded newspaper clipping to try to explain why he was Bound or why he died. It's frustrating, but with the trail cold, I'm only left to speculate.

I do visit his grave. It's snowing, the ground covered in a thick layer of white, the top of his simple tombstone encased by white powder. His name is carved in fading letters, wind and rain dulling the hard-cut edges. His birthday is indistinct, same with the day of his death, but the epitaph is still clear.

A light shines in the darkness, and the darkness has not overcome it.

I shiver, pulling my coat tightly around my shoulders. I reach out and touch the tombstone, struggling to understand. Slowly, I step away and head back to the car, Priya floating closely behind me.

I take the time to read through all of my grandmother's diaries. She talks about Baker often, now that I know what to look for. She'd been half in love with him before my grandfather swept her off her feet, but every time she mentions him, it's touched with a twinge of sadness, of regret. I wonder what she'd think of the twisted creature he became, which she helped create, and I have to put the books away, sick to my stomach. I also read *On the Summoning and Capturing of Spirits through the Use of Inscribed Circles* again. It doesn't help, but I idly trace the symbol imprinted on the back cover, the symbol that somehow Burnt Baker by itself. It scares and fascinates me, and when I go to sleep, it haunts me, flashing up from the dark corners of my dreams.

I study the other Binders. Cross brings me Hewitt's research after much cajoling, and what I find worries me. They're all tied to upheavals in the Medium community, even my grandmother, everyone angling for more power. Those early days, there were a lot of shake-ups, and, of all the names, Caroline Moore's shows up the most, always at the center of the controversy. I find some of her speeches and they're isolationist, antagonistic, and dangerous. I wonder at the woman and her motivations, wonder why she would have noted Baker as a threat that needed such a strong response. I don't like my conclusions, remembering the power that he wielded as easily as breathing and his screaming sobs as he was Bound.

Slowly, everything relating to the case wraps up. There's little we can do in terms of prosecution. Richardson's body was found shortly after Cross and I left the lakeshore. His DNA matched the samples found under Murphy's nails, and the case was closed. The rest of the cases are all marked as suicides or natural causes. The newspapers get wind of the whole thing, and there are some strongly worded editorials about Dr. Abramo and the Cook County Medical Examiner's office, but otherwise, it all dies down long before I'm back to work.

Through it all—the convalescence at home, the continued icy silence from Cross, the innumerable questions surrounding Baker and his binding—I find myself struggling for control over my powers. They leap to respond at the slightest touch and I have to fight them back almost constantly. Priya helps me leash them, taking the strain, but something about my interaction with Baker has changed my connection with the afterlife. Something about that final, desperate moment, where he'd pulled my spirit and power from my body, opened a door I'm afraid shouldn't have been opened. I feel death more strongly, see things more clearly in Second-Sight than when using my normal sight. I can hear spirits calling for me, whispers of my name that wake me from deep, troubled sleep. I force myself to meditate, to try to wrangle the snapping power that fights my every move. Sometimes, I can get it to fall back into familiar shapes, make it respond to my command. More often than not, though, it leaps from my control, sparking up and down my arms in painful arcs.

Snow is falling outside, and I stand by the window in my kitchen, staring out at the gray and faded city that stretches out before me. A cup of coffee steams in my hands, and I take a sip, wondering about what's next. Even though the case is over and the killer's been taken care of, there's still a feeling of expectation, of suspension that puts me on edge. Baker may be gone, but something is on the horizon. Something I cannot define, yet it leaves me waking up from nightmares, sweating and panting in fear. I can feel it in my blood, in the power that fights me with every breath, in the spirits that fill the world around me.

Something is coming, and as the snow falls and the city breathes around me, I force myself to wait.

GLOSSARY OF TERMS

Medium — A person possessing the ability to interact and communicate with the afterlife and spirits of deceased people. Mediums make up about 0.2 percent of the population, depending on the area. They Bond with ghosts who have yet to Turn as the final step of their training, which increases their power and stops the ghost from Turning.

Turning — When a ghost loses their sense of reality and becomes dangerous to living people. After Turning, ghosts may cause damage to property, as well as people.

Affinity — The specialized skill set a Medium possesses. The seven Affinities, from most common to least, are Burner, Reader, Healer, Speaker, Shaker, Seer, Passenger.

Burner — This is the most common type of Medium. They can speak with and exorcise ghosts and usually work in criminal justice or as independent contractors.

Reader — Gains memories and emotions from physical objects. Clarity of images and depth of information is dependent on their power and how long they're in contact with the item. The longer they spend trying to find out information from something, the better it is, but there is a limit to what they can discover. Most items will not trigger anything when a Reader is in contact with them, but some items that have a strong psychic aura will cause them to fall into a vision without warning. Second most common type of Medium.

Healer — Possesses healing abilities and can view internal structures. They are regarded with extreme respect and sought out regularly by hospitals and convalescent homes. They tend to be very caring individuals, who form significant emotional bonds with the people they trust and love. The strength of the Medium determines how severe of an injury or illness they can heal. Third most common type.

Speaker — Can communicate telepathically with other Mediums and people who have a predisposition for the supernatural. Work with Burners and Readers regularly. Also tend to work in special forces or the military due to their ability to Speak to people. The strength of the Medium determines how far and how many people they can Speak with at a time. Fourth most common type.

Shaker — Can move things and people without physically touching them. The weight of the item or person they can move is determined by the Medium's power. They tend to work in dangerous construction jobs, like underwater drilling and high-rise construction and repair. They are also commonly found working in disaster areas, especially earthquakes, as support teams. Fifth most common type

Seer — Can see into the future or past. The length of time into the future or past and the clarity of what they See is based on their inherent power. Generally work in the financial, military, or political sector. Sixth most common type.

Passenger — Can possess people for brief moments. Very little is known about this Affinity as it is so uncommon. They have been steadily declining in numbers since the early 1800s. Almost no Mediums of this type are alive currently. Seventh most common type.

Second-Sight — The specialized vision that Mediums use to view and interact with elements of the afterlife. Said to appear as a brightly lit outline of the living world.

Sending — When a Medium or ghost shares a memory or thought with another Medium or ghost. Used as a form of communication for Mediums and their partner ghosts, as well as Speakers when communicating with other Mediums.

Circle — A circle written in chalk used by Mediums to do various things, such as Burning a ghost or Seeing something that happened previously in a location. The function is determined by the sigils and runes used to construct the circle. Powered by the blood of a Medium, otherwise inactive. Will completely disappear after being used.

Runes — Arcane marks that describe the nature of things. Used in circles to describe what the circle is supposed to effect.

Sigils — Arcane marks that link runes together and focus arcane energy in circles. Directs and channels energy in circles.

Wards — Sets of sigils and runes used outside of a circle to protect an area from entry or exit. Generally used on Mediums' homes to stop malevolent or unknown ghosts from entering. Can also be used to stop a ghost from leaving an area.

ACKNOWLEDGEMENTS

There are so many people that I need to thank for their help with this novel. First, my husband, who has been my rock during this long and sometimes tedious project. Second, to the rest of my family. You have all cheered me on since I first started writing *Burner*. Having your support helped me through the difficult times, when I thought giving up was the best choice, and your excitement as we neared publication lifted me through those last, excruciating steps. Thank you so much for your love and support. Big thanks to my best friend, Babbs, for putting up with me rambling about my plot line and uncooperative characters for literally years. You are a saint.

I also want to thank all of the artists who have contributed work to this novel. Megan Bradbury (busy-matches.tumblr.com) for her amazing portraits of Kim, Priya, Cross, and Baker. Megan Tupper (caffeinescribbles.tumblr.com) for the amazing background art in use on the website and, in part, here, as well as the gorgeous cover. MJ Erickson (kreugan.com) for the first character sketches of Kim, Priya, and Emma Murphy, which helped direct the other character art, and the amazing illustration of one of my favorite scenes in the novel. Izzy Rae Brown for her phenomenal animation that you can find on the Affinity Series Facebook page (https://www.facebook.com/affinityseries/). Sarah Cloutier for her beautiful illustration in the first chapter, where Kim and Priya are facing off against Emma's angry ghost. You were all amazing to work with, and I am so thankful for the beautiful art that goes hand-in-hand with this story.

I also want to thank my writing group partners, Jennifer Peine and Michael Kolozsvari, whose in-depth and thorough analysis of *Burner* has helped me immeasurably. Thank you guys for putting up with my endless ramblings about ghost magic and whether or not "toward" or "towards" sounds better. In the same vein, I want to thank my early readers: Donya Abramo, Barbara McLemore, Karen Rought, Danielle Zimmerman, Courtney Guy, Patrick Cunningham, and—as always—my husband, Shawn. You guys bolstered my confidence as I was writing, giving me proof that I had something worthwhile here.

Big thanks to my editor, Nikki Busch. I'm sure you were tired of removing commas by the end of this project, but *Burner* would not be nearly as polished as it is without your significant contribution.

Thank you, also, to Officer Nick Gallico from the Indianapolis Metropolitan Police Department for his help with the technical questions relating to criminal investigations. Expect more random middle-of-the-day questions about response times and policies in the future.

And, finally, I want to thank all of you: my readers. Thank you for taking a risk on an indie publication. Thank you for making it all the way through! And I sincerely hope that you have enjoyed Kim's story. There's much, MUCH more to come in the next six books of the *Affinity Series*. I hope you'll stick around to see how it all ends.

If you'd like to stay up-to-date on what's happening with the *Affinity Series*, you can sign up for our mailing list at:

AFFINITYSERIES.NET/LIST

We'll be releasing early previews of *Reader*, along with art and other behind-the-scenes exclusives, only to members of the mailing list. You can also stay up-to-date with what I'm doing by following my personal and writing blog at:

JSLENORE.COM

Thank you, again, for taking the time to read *Burner*.

Please enjoy this advanced preview of the first chapter of Reader, *the next book in* The Affinity Series. *Please note, the final version of this story and first chapter may change between now and the final release date, expected end of 2017.*

BOOK TWO OF THE AFFINTY SERIES

CHAPTER ONE

The door to the apartment opens with a quiet groan. I reach inside, flipping the light switch next to the door. The dim interior of the room doesn't change, and I sigh.

"Welcoming place you've got here, Bobby," I say to the previous tenant, then step inside. The door clicks shut behind me, and I look around the place, trying to get my bearings.

There's a large central room, the floors a dark and slightly scratched hardwood of some kind. There are a few windows to the right, but they're shrouded in heavy drapes. I walk over to the closest window, and pull one of thick curtains to the side, kicking up a few motes of dust. It's cloudy outside, and the thin ray of gray light that comes into the apartment does little to help brighten the room. I watch as a car drives past slowly, kicking up slush and snow onto the sidewalk. *Winter in Chicago*, I think. *Charming as ever.*

Priya, what do you see? I Send, looking back into the apartment. She slowly appears in the center of the room, spinning in a lazy circle to take in the outdated kitchen and the dark hallway leading toward the rest of the apartment.

This is probably the best spot, she Sends. She's frowning, though, and floats close to the floor, holding an ethereal hand close to the wood. *There's energy here, but it's old. Probably from when the wood was originally harvested. I'm surprised it's still available, honestly.*

I bend down and lay my palm to the floor. It takes a moment, my brow furrowed as I try to feel the thrum of power beneath my hand. It's there, faint and weak, but present.

I'll start scribing, I say, pulling chalk from my pocket. The circle sketches out in familiar forms in front of me, the runes and sigils flowing from my hand and onto the floor almost without thought. As I reach the end of the diagram, I pause. I've drawn Burning circles for a decade, but something makes me add a now-familiar symbol in the center of the pattern: a circle, quartered by a cross with one arm longer than the others. Priya pauses in her investigation of the apartment, looking down at the circle with a blank expression.

Kim, she starts, but I shake my head, cutting her off.

It worked on Baker. It'll work on this guy, too.

She sighs, but doesn't press the issue.

You think Bobby's hanging around? I Send as I walk around the edges of the circle, checking for any flaws.

Possibly, Priya responds. *The landlord seemed fairly certain that he would manifest around now. Something about getting the paper?*

I love creatures of habit, I Send. The circle is good, so I nod to myself, then head into the kitchen. There's a pile of one-sheets on the apartment neatly stacked on the counter, and I pick one up.

Twelve-hundred square feet? Damn, this place is huge, I say, looking around with new interest. *Maybe we should put in an offer.*

Priya scoffs. *Like you'd give up your grandmother's apartment. Plus, you'd have to start paying rent again.*

True, I laugh, then look back down at the informational sheet. *But it's still tempting.*

Priya and I are here to find and Burn the ghost of Robert Fredrikson. He'd been the original tenant here, had lived in the apartment for over thirty years, and he'd died here a couple of weeks ago. His family had cleared the place out, taking his stuff and leaving behind his ghost.

Literally.

The landlord had been struggling to get new renters,

even with the massive square footage. The previous resident still hanging around and creating indoor snowstorms was making it a little hard to find new tenants. When Bobby had chased a couple of prospective tenants into the street, leaving them scared, cold, and a little bloody, the landlord had called the police, and as usual, they'd called me.

I put the paper down and head back into the main room. Standing before the circle, I close my eyes and start pulling power. It's a familiar sensation, but just like the circle, something feels off. I take a deep breath and try to center myself before pulling again. At first, the power refuses to budge, a stubborn beast unwilling to be woken. But slowly, as I continue pressing, it starts to flow. It's in fits and starts at first, but then it smooths out, the energy coming into my body at an unhurried pace. As the power slowly builds, so does my impatience. I can feel the two fighting, and then the influx of power sputters and stops. It creates an unpleasant feeling beneath my skin, like a limb that's fallen asleep and is just starting to wake up. I shake my hands out, then crack my knuckles quickly.

Where is this g—

I stop. My skin is assaulted by a wash of cold air, goosebumps rising on my skin so quickly, it hurts. My breath frosts in the air, something it hadn't been doing before. I lick my lips and feel the warm saliva cool almost immediately.

What are you doing here? an unfamiliar voice asks in my mind. It's old and creaking, thick with a Chicago accent. When I turn around, power stretched out to find the spirit,

I'm greeted by an old man. He's wearing a threadbare bathrobe that's loosely belted, showing off hints of a stained undershirt and boxers. His thin and spider-veined legs travel down to loose, thick socks and a pair of plaid slippers. His face is heavily wrinkled but somehow gaunt, his cheekbones sharp ridges on his face. There's a thin sweep of white hair covering the liver-spotted top of his head in a combover that probably didn't fool anyone except himself during life. His eyes, set deep into his face, glow a cool gray as he watches me, expression stern and distrusting.

Are you Bobby? I ask. I brace my feet, then start pulling power into my hands for a binding.

It's Robert, he says, voice clipped. *I don't know you. Why are you here?*

I'm here to help, I say, taking a hesitant step forward. Power flares from him in a wave, and the room drops another couple of degrees.

Help? he scoffs, shaking his head. *I don't need help.*

Bob— Robert. My name is Kim Phillips. I'm a Medium, a Burner.

A Burner? I don't need a Burner. His tone is hard, tense. *There aren't __any__ ghosts here. Never have been.*

I've got some bad news— I start, but he cuts me off with another blast of energy. I gasp, the cold air cutting into my lungs in pinpricks of pain.

Get out.

I sigh. *Robert, if you'd just calm down...*

His eyes snap from gray to black in an instant. The

room fills with a wind, whipping my hair into my face. The darkness spreads across his face like cracks in ice, fracturing his skin with black, jagged lines. He grins, then disappears with a sharp crack.

Shit, I say, pouring more energy into the binding in my hands. It sputters, dimming for a second, but I grit my teeth and force more power into it. *You see him anywhere?*

No, Priya says, appearing next to me. She's pulling in power, too, her hair whipping up around her face, her eyes starting to spark white. *I can't feel him at all.*

Where the fuck did he go? I ask, throat tight. I can feel the binding in my hands start to unravel, and panic builds like a hard knot in my stomach.

Kim, behind you! Priya's voice breaks my concentration, and I turn frantically, looking over my shoulder at the spirit racing toward me. Robert's eyes are a deep black from Turning, and the air around him swirls with snow. He reaches for me as I spin around, his hands gnarled and twisted, fingertips black and covered in frost.

Get out of my home! he screams in my mind. He whips through me. It doesn't hurt, but it's nauseating and sucks the heat from my body. Power flickers in my hands, sparking painfully against my palms. Body shaking with cold, I re-center myself unsteadily, looking around the apartment for him again.

Hasn't been your home for a couple of weeks, buddy, I Send, trying to draw him out of hiding. A cold wave of power washes over me, and I shiver and reach for more of the energy that swirls around me. It's a struggle to wrangle it, the blue-white light dancing away from me as I try to pull it closer. I fall deeper into Second-Sight, casting around the apartment for any sign of the spirit. I catch Robert in the corner of my eye and throw the binding at him.

The sheet of energy flies out of my hands, bright white and blinding, but it starts to fray at the edges. Power bleeds from it in sparks. By the time it reaches the ghost, there are large gaps forming in the center. I can see his black eyes through the binding before it crashes into and wraps around him. It holds him for a heartbeat, and then it shatters like ice, the binding falling in sharp shards that disappear into the floor. I can feel the power vanish in a rush that leaves my body sagging.

Priya, where are you? I Send, looking for her in the dimly lit room. She flashes into being, then speeds toward the ghost. He grimaces as she approaches, mouth twisting into a snarl. With a soundless crash, they meet in a flash of light. Priya's eyes glow white as she lets her power go in a flash. Lightning dances from her hands, spearing the other ghost. He pulls her closer, refusing to let go, and unleashes another freezing wave of energy into the room. Priya's eyes dim, frost spreading across her skin where it touches the other ghost. She visibly steels herself and starts pulling in more energy. It swirls around her, blue-white lines surrounding her body in crackling light. It seeps into her skin, the frost melting away, and then fills her eyes with white light. With a shout, power sparking from her open mouth, she throws the other ghost from her. As he tries to recover from the push, an unfocused blast leaves Priya's hands. The other ghost darts to the side, avoiding Priya's attack.

You're leaving, one way or another, the ghost Sends. Priya's no longer between us, and he speeds toward me again. The blackness from his eyes seeps into his skin, pooling in the sockets like bruises. The temperature in the apartment drops further. Snow thickens around him, twisting in spirals and vortexes on the wooden floor. Another wave of energy sweeps through me, wicking all of the heat from my skin. I grit my teeth, breath frosting in the air, and *pull*. Energy comes stuttering into my body, but it quickly becomes a torrent of power that licks through my veins like fire. Breath shuddering out of me in relief, I fall to the ground. My knife is cold and familiar in my hand, and I stab its sharp tip into the flesh of my thumb. Blood quickly coats my skin, and I smear it onto the chalk lines spread around my feet.

The ghost's eyes widen, his mouth stretched open on a scream, and then he's washed away in a blaze of blue-white light. Once the swirling flecks of light fade from my vision and I'm sure he's gone, I drop my head, panting. The snow scattered on the floor melts from the warmth of my breath, leaving only small droplets of water behind.

Dammit, Kim. A soft breeze kicks up as Priya quickly crosses the room to hover near me. *He was barely Turned.*

I sigh, then lift my eyes. Her hair is whipping around her face in an unseen wind, eyes still crackling white.

He's also barely dead, I Send. *He shouldn't have Turned at all.* I stagger to my feet and brush my hair back.

Priya frowns. *This is what, the fourth Turned ghost we've Burnt since December?*

I don't know, I Send, thinking. *He might be the fifth. And most of them recent deaths, rather than old ones. But all Turned...*

I resettle my jacket on my shoulders with a quick shrug and look around the room. The floors are now clear of chalk and snow, but covered in damp one-sheets. Besides the scattered pages, though, there's no damage.

And fewer old ghosts, too, Priya says, tone thoughtful. *Just new ones.*

They're Turning too quickly. We need to talk to Taka about this. I rub at my eyes and unwillingly drop out of Second-Sight.

I curse, close my eyes again, and focus. Sweat breaks out on my forehead as I struggle to get back into Second-Sight. There's a trick to it, like looking at one of those patterned images that turn into three-dimensional pictures. I can't get it, though, the room flickering briefly with blue-white light, but dropping back into mid-day dimness. I take another deep breath, frustration clogging my throat, and push. My head starts to throb as I force my body to settle. When I open my eyes, wincing slightly, the lines of power that outline the world are back. They shift from dim to bright as I move, my control shaky and uncertain, but they stay.

You lose it again? Priya asks, her eyes dimming as she frowns.

Yeah. It takes effort to get the message to her, and I fight against the sudden, overwhelming urge to punch something.

I'll be fine, I Send to Priya before heading toward the front door. *We've got to get to district HQ. Lieutenant Walker's got to be wondering where I am by now.*

Kim, Priya starts, but I shake my head, cutting her off.

We've got dinner with Taka this week. It can wait until then. In the meantime, we've got work to do.

She doesn't say anything, just brushes against me. It's part warning, part comfort, and I feel a twinge of guilt.

I'll be careful. I promise, I Send, hoping she can hear me.

Priya fades from view, either because she's chosen to no longer manifest a form or because I've fallen out of Second-Sight again. I hate that I can't tell which it is.

———

Continue Kim's story in *Reader,* expected in late 2017. For updates and exclusive content, sign up for the Affinity Series's mailing list at:

AFFINITYSERIES.NET/LIST

ABOUT THE AUTHOR

J. S. Lenore was born and raised in the suburbs of Chicago. She attended Elgin High School, graduating within the top ten of her class. She studied Japanese Studies at Earlham College and graduated with honors before getting her Masters in Teaching, also from Earlham College. She started creative writing at a young age, mainly writing fanfiction, but did not find much success until after graduation. In 2013, writing under the handle p1013, J. S. Lenore posted her first fanfiction for MTV's *Teen Wolf.* This story, titled *The Full Moon Like Blood,* and others gained a moderate following. In the same year, she decided to branch out into original fiction, writing the rough draft of *Burner* during National Novel Writing Month. Three and a half years later, she is still writing original fiction, and is currently working on the sequel to *Burner, Reader,* which is expected to be published late 2017.

J. S. Lenore currently lives in Indianapolis with her husband, daughter, three cats, and zero ghosts.

Made in the USA
Lexington, KY
31 March 2017